perfect Shot

OTHER BOOKS AND AUDIO BOOKS
BY SONIA O'BRIEN:

The Raging Sea

perfect shot

a novel

sonia o'brien

Covenant Communications, Inc.

Covenant

Cover images: camera lens © Stockbyte/Getty Images, Inc.; street scene by John A. Rizzo ©
Photodisc/Getty Images, Inc.

Cover design copyrighted 2006 by Covenant Communications, Inc.

Published by Covenant Communications, Inc.
American Fork, Utah

Printed in Canada
First Printing: March 2006

12 11 10 09 08 07 06   10 9 8 7 6 5 4 3 2 1

ISBN 1-59811-073-X

To my husband Eric, I love you!

acknowledgements

There were several people whose help was invaluable in bringing this novel to fruition. Without their support, talent, and insight, I would still be staring blurry-eyed at the computer screen. I express my gratitude to Angela Eschler, Shauna Humphreys, and the entire Covenant publishing team. To my readers' group (who also just happen to be members of my family): Buffie and Jesse Poff, Vickie Larsen, and Kyler O'Brien. Thanks for reading, rereading, and then reading again. Your comments and suggestions were extremely helpful—your support immeasurable. Finally, I express my gratitude to my Heavenly Father for giving me the opportunity as well as the ability to do what I love—write.

prologue

Jonathan Schmitt pulled a second roll of film from his camera case, quickly reloaded, then pointed his lens toward an old building that sat against a twilight sky of burnt orange and hot pink. He clicked off several shots, then tilted his camera to take the building from another angle. He smiled with satisfaction. These pictures were going to make the perfect addition to his up-and-coming photo exhibit, *Cities Across America*. Off in the distance, Jonathan spotted a run-down apartment building with clean clothes hung out to dry over a fire escape. The moon had climbed into the sky just to the left of it, giving the shot a romantically melancholy feel.

"Perfect," he said aloud.

Pointing his camera toward the building and adjusting the focus as he walked, he made his way down the dark alleyway that led toward the old apartment building. He was so engrossed in getting the perfect shot that he didn't pay attention to the voices that floated across the narrow alleyway until he was merely feet from them. More out of instinct than intent, Jonathan followed the voices with his camera, snapping off several shots of the alley before fully realizing what he was seeing. Jonathan's breath caught, his eyes riveted on the scene before him. Two men had pushed a third against a brick wall. Though Jonathan couldn't hear exactly what they were saying, their threatening tone was undeniable. Another man stood just back from them, calmly leaning against a black car with dark, tinted windows. Jonathan could feel an icy shiver crawl up his spine as both men released their prey, then stepped to the side. The man against the wall was now trembling with terror. Before Jonathan could do anything, the guy next to the car raised his gun and fired at the victim. Jonathan gasped, then fell back a step. His hands tightened around his camera out of reflex, causing him to snap off a shot. All three men jerked around, straining their eyes and pointing their guns in his direction. Jonathan stood there numbly, praying to be hidden by the shadow of the building next to him. He could barely breathe, though the breaths he did take seemed amplified. His instincts screamed for him to run, but his legs were unwilling. He stared in horror as one man started toward him, his gun cocked and raised. Though the darkness protected him at the moment, Jonathan knew that it was just a matter of seconds before he was discovered. At that moment he heard the insistent whine of a siren some-where near. The man who was quickly approaching heard it too. He stopped, glanced briefly in the direction of the persis-tent sound, then returned his eyes to the darkened alley. He hesitated as if weighing his chances, but before he could take another step, one of the other men had grabbed his arm and was pulling him back to the car.

Jonathan stood motionless as the black car screeched back-ward, smashing into a large metal dumpster before it raced recklessly down the narrow alleyway. As the sound of the siren grew increasingly louder, Jonathan's eyes went from the car to the lifeless body left crumpled in the shadows. With his heart still thundering in his chest, he raised his camera toward the fleeing car's license plate and took the shot.

Chapter 1

The wind came like a tyrant; it was ruthless and cruel, caring nothing for those left in its wake. Reegan buried her hands deep in the pockets of her coat, then looked up at the sky. The night was clear, and the stars were out in full force, but with no cloud cover to blanket the sky, the air had a frigid bite. Reegan quickened her pace as she lowered her head to avoid the wind's constant assault. Once she reached the end of the neat row of streetlights that lined her neighborhood, she stopped and looked behind her. The street seemed to be completely empty. Piles of snow that had been plowed a few days before sat in heaping mounds along the side of the street. The chilly night air had crystallized the top layer of the snow so that it sparkled like the Christmas lights adorning the surrounding houses.

Reegan could hear Christmas music coming from a home two doors down. She could see several people through the living room window. They were laughing and singing, thoroughly enjoying the evening with family and friends. It looked warm and inviting, everything that this time of year should be. Reegan looked farther down the street to her own house. It was dark and empty. There was no music or laughter or loved ones gathered within to celebrate.

As she turned and slowly began walking away from her neighborhood, she listened to the snow crunch beneath her feet, and her mind instantly flooded with one of her most valued memories—a time when she was little and her father had taken her sledding. The snow had been crisp and slick, just like tonight. She could remember sliding down a gentle slope and giggling when her father fell off the sled. She had been very small, so the memory was vague, but the feelings it evoked were vivid and real. That was one of the few memories she had of her father. He'd died when she was six—or so she'd always been told. Reegan could feel her face instantly flame hot with anger. Eight months ago, while searching in the attic for a box of summer clothes placed there the previous fall, Reegan had come across a small tin box tucked away in a dusty corner. Allowing curiosity to get the better of her, she'd opened the box, revealing a well-worn Book of Mormon. After she picked up the book, a letter postmarked June 3, 1994 had slipped from within the pages. By the time she had finished the letter, she was numb. Reegan swallowed hard, mentally rereading the haunting words that were now branded into her memory.

Dear Elizabeth,

I know at the time it didn't seem like it, but I do understand your reasons for leaving. With everything that has happened since you left, I now see that it was for the best. Because of the situation, I won't try to contact you again, but I do want you to know that I will always love you and Reegan.

With all my love,
Jonathan

In a split second Reegan had learned that her father was still alive, and that her mother, whom she had always completely trusted, had lied to her.

A car making its way down the slick road immediately pulled Reegan from her thoughts. She lowered her head, partially covered her face with the oversized hood connected to her coat, then quickly made sure that her dark hair was safely tucked inside it. Her long, silky hair had, on more than one occasion, drawn attention, but tonight she did not want to be recognized. The driver hesitated for just a moment as the car neared her, but then drove on. Reegan let out a sigh of relief, then turned and watched as the car made its way down the street. The car belonged to Reegan's next-door neighbors, Mr. and Mrs. Whiley. Lucinda Whiley was president or vice-president of just about every civic and social organization in town. She also just happened to be the biggest busybody in the whole county. Reegan's stomach began to churn. What if Mrs. Whiley had recognized her? Reegan let her breath out in a long, white puff. There was no sense in worrying about it now. If she had recognized her, Reegan would know it first thing in the morning. Invariably, Mrs. Whiley would pay Reegan's mom an unexpected visit to drop off a plate of homemade cookies. Her claim that they were homemade was almost as far-fetched as her colorful stories. Then she would touch Reegan's mom's arm, cluck her tongue, shake her head, and say something like, "You *poor* dear. I don't know how you do it with Reegan getting into so much trouble lately."

Reegan rolled her eyes, then glanced down at her watch. It was a quarter after ten and, according to Mrs. Whiley and all the other fuddy-duddies in Maplecove, long past the time that any respectable girl should be out on the streets alone. Not that there was any real threat of danger. Reegan had lived in

Maplecove, North Dakota, for three years now. It was a thriving metropolis if you were from the neighboring town of Pinewood. Pinewood consisted of a run-down gas station, a small drugstore/photomat, which also served as the Friday-night hangout for the local teens, and a bar. All the children in Pinewood were bussed to Maplecove, but even with that, the graduating class was two kids short of one hundred. Not very impressive according to city standards, and not at all accept-able in Reegan's mind. But there wasn't a whole lot that she could do about it. Her mom was dead set on staying. So for now, like it or not, she was stuck in this dinky town.

Reegan kicked at a small chunk of snow and ice that had been dropped by a passing car. She might be stuck here now, but in five months when she graduated from high school, nothing and no one would stop her from leaving. She would get on the first bus headed out of town, and she'd never look back. Reegan felt a small twinge of guilt. She quickly pushed the feeling aside, not wanting to think about her mom, Maplecove, or the empty house that waited behind her.

After walking another five minutes, Reegan came to the business section of town. She quickly looked around to determine if anyone could see her. When she couldn't find anyone, she made her way toward a dark alley between the barbershop and Mike's Grocery. Across the street a stray dog growled and flashed his sharp teeth. She tried to ignore his low, hungry snarling as she peered into the alley, straining her eyes to see anything in the shadows.

"Pssst. Reegan," came a voice from the darkness.

Reegan jumped, then took a step back, her heart instantly thumping in her chest.

Three figures slowly appeared from the dark cover of the alleyway. Reegan recognized them immediately. Tera Lanning had long blond hair and impressive green eyes, combined with a big, cheerleader smile and dimples to match. The guy next to her was Reegan's next-door neighbor, Seth Whiley—Tera's latest catch. He was the star quarterback of their high school football team and the heart-throb of almost every girl in the senior class, Reegan being one of the few exceptions. The bulky guy next to him was Wayne Durby, one of Seth's cocky teammates. Wayne was nice-looking in a rough kind of way, maybe six foot, and broad through the shoulders. He had sandy hair and a boyish face. He'd hounded Reegan relentlessly for several months to go out with him, though she had resisted up until a couple of weeks ago.

"We weren't sure if you would come or not," Tera said with an approving smile.

Seth draped an arm across Tera's shoulders. There was a half-empty bottle of beer in his hand, but from the smell of him, Reegan guessed that it was not his first bottle of the night, nor would it be his last.

"Hi, Reegan," he said, as he openly appraised her attractive form.

Reegan fought the urge to roll her eyes, though from Seth's immediate scowl she was assured that her distaste was written across her face. With prestigious colleges all over the country sending scouts his way, and the whole town singing his praises, Reegan's obvious disinterest seemed to prick his overgrown ego.

"You better not let your mom catch you drinking," Reegan said sarcastically.

Seth laughed, then took a few steps back to lean against the hood of his black sports car. "She's too focused on what everybody else's kids are doin'."

Reegan nodded her head in irritation, knowing firsthand just how true that was.

"It's not his mom he needs to worry about anyway," Wayne began as he moved in next to Reegan. "If Coach Richards or the college scouts find out what's floating around in his bloodstream—"

Seth shot an icy glare at Wayne that instantly froze Wayne's mouth. "You just worry about tonight," he said tightly. "And leave the scouts and Coach Richards to me." Then he turned to Reegan, the edge to his features slowly easing as his lips lifted into one of his charismatic smiles. "Besides, there's nothin' in my blood but the makings of a nasty hangover."

Reegan lifted a brow but didn't comment. "What's happening tonight?" she finally asked. "And why did you want me to meet you here? It's freezing."

"We're going to break into Mike's Grocery and get us a little spending cash," Seth said bluntly.

Reegan laughed out loud. "Yeah, right!" But when no one else laughed, her smile slowly faded. "Are you serious?" she asked, the pumping of her heart suddenly accelerating.

Seth started laughing. "It's perfect. No one would ever suspect us."

Reegan's eyes raced across the small group. Tera squirmed uncomfortably, then looked away, but Wayne met her gaze head on, his expression causing her stomach to knot into a tight ball. Finally, in desperation, she turned back to Seth.

"This is all a joke—*right?*"

"It's just a couple of bucks," he said, playing it down. "Besides, I just want to see if we can do it."

"You'll go to prison."

"Only if we get caught," Seth shot back smugly as he eyed her.

Reegan felt sick. Though she didn't want to admit it, he was right. No one in town *would* suspect him, his surface charm and good looks being his most effective weapons. Reegan slowly began to shake her head, but before she could speak, Seth burst out laughing.

"*What?*" Reegan asked skeptically.

"You should have seen your face," Seth blurted, turning to Wayne and slapping him on the shoulder. "Did you see her face?"

Wayne hesitated, his eyes searching Seth's features before his own face lit into a grin.

"You're *not* robbing the store?" Reegan asked in confusion.

Seth shook his head. "You're more gullible than I thought. We're just hanging out—having a couple beers." He pulled a bottle from a paper sack and extended it to Reegan. When she didn't take it, he smiled. "Don't worry. I didn't steal it."

Reegan took the bottle, her eyes sweeping across Seth's face before slowly letting the air escape from her lungs in a surge of relief.

* * *

"Where were you last night?"

Reegan slowly opened her eyes to look up into her mother's face. She blinked her eyes to try to get them to focus, but they seemed to be darting around in their sockets like a couple of loose Ping-Pong balls.

"Reegan, I want an answer."

"Mrs. *Snitch* was quicker getting over here than I expected," Reegan mumbled as she lifted her hand to her throbbing head.

Elizabeth Richards arched her eyebrows sternly at her daughter. "Don't be smart. Mrs. Whiley has nothing to do with this."

"Oh, really," Reegan began sarcastically. "Then who says I wasn't home last night? It sure wouldn't be you, because you're never home to know what I'm doing."

Her mother looked like she'd just been slapped. Reegan felt a stab of guilt and for a moment wished that she could take her words back. But it was too late—the damage had already been done.

"I called last night to apologize for working late this close to Christmas, but you weren't home."

Reegan lowered her eyes, unable to meet her mother's gaze. Deep down she knew that her actions last night, along with the rest of her behavior over the past year, were way out of line. The guilt of it all seemed to be souring in her stomach this morning along with the alcohol she'd consumed the night before.

"I'm out trying to make enough money to pay the bills, and you're running the streets."

"I was with some friends."

Elizabeth was pacing back and forth in the room now. Her light blue eyes had deepened in color, reminding Reegan of the sea just before a storm.

"Look, I'm sorry," Reegan said weakly.

"Sorry isn't enough, Reegan." Her mother's eyes were flashing, her voice rising in intensity. "I have to know where you are and who you're with at all times. Can't you understand that?"

Reegan could feel her own defenses rising.

"I'm almost nineteen, and you're still treating me like a baby! Anytime I leave the house, you go bananas. When we lived in the city I could understand you getting worried. But out here? Mom, we're three stones from nowhere."

"You don't have any idea how much danger you could have been in."

Reegan shook her head despite her pounding headache. "Boredom isn't exactly fatal."

Elizabeth pointed a shaking finger at her daughter. "You're grounded! Do you hear me? You're not to leave this house for a month."

"So my punishment is pretty much to live the way I've always lived."

Elizabeth stared at her daughter in open shock, the disappointment in her eyes cutting through Reegan more deeply than any words. Reegan wanted to turn away, but something in her wouldn't allow it. Instead she met her mother's disapproval with outright defiance.

"It's *my* life anyway."

"And *this* is what you choose to do with it? You're not living the Word of Wisdom, you're hanging out with kids who are clearly nothing but trouble, and I don't even want to think about what else you might be doing."

Reegan could feel her face flush, knowing full well what her mother was insinuating. "The Word of Wisdom?" she began tightly, concentrating on her mother's first accusation rather than the latter. "We haven't set foot in church since I was a little girl."

"Then there's your grades," Elizabeth continued, ignoring her daughter's verbal jab. "You used to be a straight-A student. Now I'm getting calls from your school weekly. If you don't pull your grades up in your AP classes, you probably won't be able to pass the tests this spring." Elizabeth stopped, her eyes suddenly showing more fatigue than anger. "Your father would be sick to know how—"

Something in Reegan snapped. She was on her feet, her face hot with anger and her eyes flashing.

"My father? *What father?*" Reegan gestured her arms around the room. "I don't see him. *Do you?*" she continued, not waiting for a response. "No! Because he's not here. You left him, remember? But even if you hadn't, he probably would have left anyway because you would have suffocated him just like you're suffocating me."

If Reegan had wanted to hurt her mom, she'd succeeded. The pain was written all over her face. For several seconds the two of them just stood there staring at each other. Reegan could feel her heart thundering in her chest as she glared at her mother. Finally Elizabeth slowly walked to the door. As she reached for the handle, she turned back around to face Reegan. Her eyes were red and glistening. She paused as if she might say something, but then shook her head and walked out the door.

Reegan plopped down on her bed and buried her face in her pillow. Her eyes burned, though she stubbornly fought to hold back her brimming tears. Instead, she sat up and flicked on her stereo, cranking up the sound several notches louder than usual. Despite her effort, she could feel the warm tears that pushed at the corners of her eyes begin to spill over. She pushed at them angrily with the back of her hand, then looked over at the jewelry box on her nightstand. She swiftly lifted the lid and removed a tattered picture that she had hidden there. It was a picture of her, as a little girl, with her father. She had salvaged it, as well as a few others, from a pile of pictures that had been placed in a throw-out box a couple of years after her father had supposedly died. At the time she'd assumed that they were in the box by accident, but since her mother wouldn't talk about her dad, she'd silently hidden them all these years, pulling them out on rare occasions just to wonder how different her life would have been if he were around.

Reegan touched the picture gently with her fingers as she looked down at it. Her father had a smile on his face that was almost as big as the one on her little face. He was holding her above his head as if he had just tossed her up into the air and then caught her. Reegan brushed at a warm tear that was making its way down her cheek. Then she turned her head to glare over at her closed bedroom door. Her head was still pounding and her stomach churning, but all of that seemed to be numbed by the resentment seething through her. She quickly stuck the picture back into the box and shut the lid.

Ten minutes later Reegan slowly opened her bedroom door and slid out into the hallway, her backpack draped over one shoulder. She quickly glanced at her mother's bedroom door. Finding it shut, she crept down the hall, being careful to avoid the creaking spots on their old hardwood floors. Once she'd reached the living room she noticed a pine tree in the corner of the room. Her mom must have brought the tree home last night to surprise her. A few colored bulbs hung from its scrawny limbs, along with a handful of hastily placed tinsel. Reegan again felt those familiar pangs of guilt that had pestered her the last few months, but this time it only seemed to stoke the fire that was building within her. Reegan reached for the doorknob. She wasn't going to allow her mother to control her life any longer. Stepping onto the front porch, she slowly closed the door behind her. Then, without a backward glance, she ran across the newly fallen snow.

Chapter 2

Once Reegan reached the outskirts of town, she turned down a dirt road that led to the old Graham farm. Reegan had never known the Grahams. Mr. Graham died long before Reegan and her mother moved to Maplecove. After his death, Mrs. Graham had put the farm up for sale and moved back east with her son. When the run-down farm didn't sell, the locals, headed by Mrs. Whiley, had the place condemned, then planted a thick wall of pine trees around the eyesore. Now the little house was completely hidden from view.

Reegan slowed her steps as she made her way through the tangle of brush and low-hanging branches. Once she made it into the clearing, she wiped at the soft powder that had fallen from the trees onto her shoulders. Then she glanced at the small, framed wooden house before her. The paint had peeled in several places, exposing raw, cedar planks, and the wooden shutters next to each window creaked and moaned as the wind touched them. To gain access, vandals had ripped off the plywood that had been nailed over each window and door, then left their mark here and there with multicolored spray paint.

As Reegan reached the house, she carefully placed her foot on the rotted steps that led to the front door. The old boards squeaked, scaring a little brown squirrel out from under the stairs. Reegan instantly jumped, startled by the small animal. She turned and watched as the squirrel scampered toward the woods. Once he got a safe distance away, he stopped, sat up on his hind legs, and looked back at Reegan. She stood in the doorway shaking her head, chiding herself for being so easily scared. After watching the frightened animal disappear into the woods, she quickly turned back to face the house. Though it was still early in the day, the surrounding trees cast their long shadows over the little home. Reegan knew that it was silly, but it was more than just the squirrel that had her feeling so jumpy. Pushing her fears aside, she reached for the doorknob. The door was heavy, but to Reegan's surprise it opened without much effort, leaving her to wonder how recently someone had been inside. She slowly edged forward to peer inside. A few streams of light that somehow made it through the dirty window panes allowed Reegan to see a rock fireplace made up most of the far wall, with an old rocking chair positioned in front of it. One look was all it took to see why the rickety thing had been left behind. Next to the rocking chair the rock wall opened up to a small kitchen. Reegan brushed at a few cobwebs that draped across the doorway, then slowly made her way inside. After lowering her backpack to the floor, she immediately turned and closed the door behind her. The brisk air was quickly chilling the tiny room. With the door shut, Reegan turned to survey her find. On the mantel over the fireplace there were several half-used candles in tarnished candleholders. A small trail of wax had dripped from the candles onto the mantel.

Reegan looked from the fireplace over to an old trunk that sat below one of the two windows that lit the room. A thick layer of dust covered the top of the trunk. When she lifted the lid, the dust flew up into the stream of light coming in through the window. The tiny particles danced in the air, then slowly descended to the already dusty floor. Reegan bent down to inspect the contents of the trunk, but found it empty. If something had been left behind, vandals had long since stolen it.

After a quick look around the front room, Reegan made her way into the kitchen. It consisted of a small porcelain sink with a hand pump instead of a faucet, and an old wooden cupboard. A worn spot on the hardwood floor, and a boarded-up hole in the wall behind it, showed where a wood-burning stove had probably sat. Other than a few cobwebs, that was the extent of the kitchen. A tiny room off the kitchen caught Reegan's attention next, though once she found that it was empty, she made her way back to the front room. She rubbed her hands together for warmth, deciding that if she were to spend the night here, she would definitely need to gather firewood. She figured that no one would see the smoke at night. The house provided shelter, but without a fire, the thin walls would be little defense against a winter night in North Dakota.

After trudging back into the cold for an armful of wet wood, then searching fruitlessly for matches, Reegan sat down heavily in the old rocking chair. The chair creaked and moaned but still managed to hold her. As Reegan's stomach began to growl, her thoughts quickly changed from warmth to food. After the confrontation with her mom this morning, she had slipped out without thought of food or money. If she were serious about getting on a bus tomorrow morning and leaving this sinkhole behind, she would need to sneak back home tonight. Reegan shook her head with a labored sigh. The trick would be getting in and out undetected.

* * *

The sun had been down for at least an hour now, and the
bite of the wind was becoming increasingly sharp. For a
fleeting moment Reegan wished that she were in her bed
with the covers pulled up to her nose and reading a good
book. Instead, she slowly made her way down her street,
being careful to avoid the glow of the streetlights. As she
neared her house, she could see that her mother's car was not
in the driveway. Slipping quickly into the shadows of the
neighbor's snow-covered bushes, she sat in silence, watching
for any movement. The small lamp in the front room—one
her mom usually left on for her—was turned off. A brisk
breeze flurried the top layer of snow on the overgrown
shrubs in front of their wraparound porch, but other than
that, there was no movement at all. Reegan stayed crouched
down for several minutes, but everything appeared to be
normal—as if she'd never left. Reegan felt surprisingly disappointed. Where were the police cars? Or in Maplecove's case,
she mused sarcastically, the one beat-up Jeep with a strobe
light duct-taped to the roof that served as the county's one
and only police car? Where were the concerned neighbors
who should be frantically searching the area? More importantly, where was her mother?

When Reegan was sure that no one was home, she crept
out from her hiding spot and made her way over to the front
porch. She bent down to get the spare key that her mother
kept hidden under the mat, but the key was gone.

"We need to talk."

Reegan swung around to face the far end of the porch.
"Mom!"

Elizabeth was sitting in the dark, concealed from the
front view of the house by the snow-covered bushes. For a

moment Reegan thought about running. But then, as if her mother could read her mind, she interrupted Reegan's thoughts.

"You could turn and run. I may or may not be able to stop you this time, but if you really want to leave, sooner or later you will." There was an unexpected calmness in her mother's voice, which instantly caused Reegan's temper to flare and set her mind on their last argument, as if no time had passed.

"How could you let me think all these years that he was dead?"

Elizabeth lifted her head to expose a tear-streaked face. "Fourteen years ago your father witnessed a horrible crime."

"*What?*" Reegan exploded, pent-up anger welling inside her like molten lava. "Mom, I read the note. You *left* him."

"I know what the note said," Elizabeth said gently, then tilted her head, her eyes pleading. "Reegan, just hear me out."

"So you can tell me another *lie* to keep me here?"

"I lied to protect you!"

"*Oh*, to *protect* me," Reegan mocked sardonically.

"To protect us all," her mother countered, her tone and the intensity in her eyes instantly silencing Reegan. She took a deep breath, obviously trying to subdue the frustration and fear that was written on her face. "The people who committed the crime found out that your father had turned them in. When your father went to the police, they said that the only way they could protect him was to put him into hiding." She took another deep breath, only this time her expression was disheartened. "At first we went with him, but we were constantly on the run, living in fear. With the stress of it all, your father and I started fighting. I knew it was irrational to blame him since he hadn't done anything wrong, but I did. Then we had a few close calls. The men who were after your father just wouldn't let up. The agency relocated us each time, but after a while I just couldn't take it. Neither of us wanted you raised like that. So I left. Sad thing is, in the end, we ended up being on the run anyway. That's why we move so much. That's why I waited an extra year before I dared enroll you in school."

Reegan felt as if she were in a daze. Though the words coming out of her mother's mouth were almost surreal, something in the pit of her stomach told her they were true. She slowly sat down on the porch, her legs no longer able to hold her. For a few minutes neither of them spoke. Reegan was trying desperately to digest everything.

"Why didn't you just tell me?" she finally asked in frustration.

Elizabeth let out a long sigh. "The first few years you were too young to understand. Then, when you were old enough, I—I was scared. I justified that the fewer people who knew, the safer you'd be. Plus, I knew what it was like to live in fear, and I didn't want you to go through that." Elizabeth shook her head—remorse, guilt, and frustration etched on her features. "There was just no right answer. I knew it was a horrible thing to do to you, telling you that he had died, then not telling you the whole truth when you found the note." Elizabeth wiped at her cheek. "The whole thing has just been so awful."

"Is he still alive?" Reegan whispered, bracing herself for the answer.

"I don't know," Elizabeth admitted as she reached over and touched Reegan's hand.

Reegan immediately withdrew her hand, not yet willing or able to surrender her anger. "I need some time to think." Her mind was racing a mile a minute, yet at the same time it was as though she couldn't think at all.

"I'm sorry," Elizabeth began gently. "I never meant to hurt you. You're all I have left. If something happened to you—if I lost you too—" Elizabeth stopped and shook her head as if the very thought of that was too much to bear. She waited for Reegan to respond. When Reegan didn't, she slowly stood. "I'll leave the light on."

* * *

Reegan poured a bowl of cereal, then looked across the table to where her mother was busily sorting through a stack of paperwork before heading to the office. Though Reegan had always considered her mother to be an attractive woman, the stress of the last two weeks—since she had revealed the truth about Reegan's father—was written across her features, the dark circles under her eyes confirming that she, too, was having a hard time sleeping. Reegan watched as her mother yawned, then threaded her fingers through her short blond hair, her arms propped on the table and her eyes still scanning her paperwork. Reegan lowered her own eyes, her conscience momentarily pricked. Since the night her mother had revealed their involvement with the Witness Protection Program, Reegan had gone through a gamut of emotions—a year's worth of anger and frustration was not easily extinguished. The first week had been an emotional roller coaster of arguing and crying, which was replaced the second week by an uncomfortable silence that had proven almost worse than the fighting. Reegan had wanted desperately to ask her mother questions about her father, but each time she considered it, she quickly abandoned the idea. Her mother had lied to her, smothered her with rules and boundaries that were extreme, almost ludicrous . . . and yet, each time she contemplated it rationally, it came down to one question—why had her mother done all of it? The answer was obvious. She'd done it all, forsaking everything, to protect her daughter.

As if on cue, her mother looked up, her eyes filled with a combination of hope and pain. Reegan immediately lowered her head, pretending to read the back of the cereal box. She held her breath, feeling her mother's eyes on her, hoping that her mom would be the one to make the first move. Yet, because of the situation, she knew her mother would wait on her. After a moment, her mother began to gather her papers together, then stood to leave.

"What was he like?" Reegan asked, the broken silence surprising her as much as it did her mother.

Relief quickly replaced the surprise on her mother's face. She slowly placed her stack of papers back on the table and sat down, her expression suddenly reflective.

"He was smart and funny, always the center of attention no matter where we went. Once," she continued, her eyes lighting up with delight as she remembered a particular incident, "we were at one of his art exhibits—"

"He was an artist?"

A hint of pain flashed across her mother's face. "A photographer. Actually, that's how he ended up witnessing the murder. He was working on material for a new exhibit—*Cities Across America*. He wanted to capture the heart of each city—its beginnings—which usually meant the run-down side of town. He was taking some shots of Jersey City at dusk when he saw some men in a dark alley. They had a man pushed up against a wall—" She shook her head, then took a deep breath. When she began to speak, her voice was strained with emotion. "Before your father knew what was happening, it was over. Not long after that, our life together was also over."

Reegan suddenly wanted to change the subject, hoping that the pain in her mother's face would vanish and that the knot in her own stomach would do the same.

"Tell me about the exhibit you two were at," she pressed.

It took several seconds for the words to finally come and several more for the melancholy in her mother's face to begin to lift. "At the exhibit, in all the mingling, we somehow got separated. After several minutes I found your father in the center of a large group of people. He was telling them how we'd met, and the group was roaring with laughter."

"How *did* you meet?" Reegan asked, her curiosity piqued.

"Your dad was working as a waiter in a restaurant in Jersey City."

"Dad lived in New Jersey?"

"We both did."

Reegan's mouth dropped open. "I thought you were raised in Nebraska."

A sad shadow crossed Elizabeth's face. "Over the years, I've had to tell you a lot of things that weren't true to protect you. Nebraska was the first place we moved to after your dad was relocated. We only lived there for about six months before we had to move again, but since I was vaguely familiar with the area, it was easy to say I'd grown up there."

Reegan nodded slowly, realizing for the first time that it wasn't just her life that was affected by all of this.

"Anyway," her mother began again, continuing on with her story, "one night a guy that I had been dating for quite a while took me to the restaurant that your dad worked at. I found out months later that Charley had planned to propose to me that night."

"Were you in love?"

"I wanted to be, but—there was just something missing. I realized that when I met your father." She smiled at the memory. "He just happened to be our waiter that night. He handed us our menus, then disappeared. He came back a couple of minutes later to tell Charley he'd left his car lights on. After Charley left, your dad made his move. He sat down in the chair next to me, and before Charley made it back, he had me—hook, line, and sinker. Of course, I found out later that Charley gave up his job as a cop in Jersey City and now owns an extremely lucrative consulting firm, drives expensive foreign cars, and travels the world in his down-time, which is about six months out of the year."

"Are you sorry you married Dad?"

Elizabeth shook her head emphatically. "I wouldn't have traded all the money in Charley Madison's overseas bank accounts for the years I got to spend with your dad. Reegan, I loved your father. We had some tough times together while we were on the run, but I loved him. I still do. Besides, if I had married Charley, I never would have had you."

Reegan could feel a hard lump forming in her throat. "I didn't realize you were only trying to . . . protect me."

"Every stranger that moved into town, every time the phone rang and nobody was on the line . . ." Elizabeth closed her eyes and shook her head. "I knew I was holding you too tight, but I also knew that if they found us, they would use us to bring your father out of hiding. These men wouldn't think twice about hurting a young girl to get what they wanted."

"I'm sorry," Reegan choked out, tears now falling unrestrained down her cheeks.

Elizabeth stood and walked to her daughter, wrapping her within her arms. "It's okay," she soothed as she stroked Reegan's hair. "Now that we've got this all out in the open, maybe we can start over."

Reegan nodded, lingering in the security of her mother's embrace. "I'd like that."

Chapter 3

Jonathan Schmitt slipped into the sterile hospital room that had housed his mother for the past month. The room had a medicated smell that immediately reminded him of death. He paused in the doorway to look over at his mother. She lay motionless on her side with her face toward the window. Her usually impeccably kept hair was ruffled from her nap, and the natural gray that she had successfully concealed through the years was beginning to peek through at the roots.

"Hello, Jonny," she whispered, though she remained still.

Jonathan smiled. He was always amazed at how his mother seemed to sense his presence. "How are you feeling?"

Helen slowly turned and smiled over at her son. "I'm fine."

Jonathan lifted an eyebrow at her blatant lie, but Helen dismissed his look with a wave of her hand. "I see you're posing as a medical student today instead of a doctor."

Jonathan looked down at the nametag that was clipped to the white medical jacket he was wearing.

"This way I won't be stopped in the hall to help out with some poor guy's bypass surgery like last time."

She smiled. "Come over here and sit by me."

As Jonathan quickly made his way over to her side, Helen reached out and took her son's hand in her own.

Jonathan was shocked to feel just how cold and frail it was. It was painful to see how fast this disease was stealing the life from this once strong and vibrant woman. As Helen gently squeezed his hand, Jonathan smiled, trying to keep the concern that he was feeling from showing on his face.

"It's okay. I'm not afraid to die," Helen began candidly, taking Jonathan by surprise and causing an instant lump to form in his throat. Jonathan opened his mouth to speak, to fervently deny the obvious, but she wouldn't allow it. "I've done everything that I set out to do," she insisted, her eyes adamant yet tender. "I married a man who loved me despite all of my faults, and I have a son who is tenacious, selfless and—"

Jonathan began to shake head, instantly looking away.

"And strong," Helen persisted firmly. She squeezed his hand, then smiled tenderly as he turned back to face her. "Jonny, I'm ready to see your father again. I miss him."

"I know," Jonathan whispered, understanding her loss on a deeply empathetic level.

Helen touched his cheek knowingly, her eyes filled with compassion. "We've both had to spend a lot of years without the people we love, haven't we?"

Jonathan dropped his eyes, not wanting her to see the emotion that was quickly surfacing.

Helen slowly reached over and picked up an object that was on the nightstand next to her bed. When she looked at Jonathan again, her expression was one of regret. She opened her hand to expose a beautiful antique key.

"This and the box that it opens should have been hers," she admitted, glancing back down at the key.

Jonathan swallowed hard, instantly reminded as he thought of the handcrafted wooden box that he was not the only one who ached with missing her.

"It's been in our family for generations, given to me by my grandmother and to her by hers."

Helen began to cough, her frail body hunching over in pain. Jonathan immediately began to pat her back, then squeezed her hand, helpless to do anything else but watch her struggle until the coughing subsided.

"I'll never see her again. I know that now," she admitted weakly, still trying to catch her breath.

Jonathan put his finger to her lips. "Shhh, Mother, you need to rest."

"I just wish that I could have given her this one last gift," Helen persisted, the regret and anguish in her eyes almost more than Jonathan could bear. "It's all I have to give."

Jonathan's gaze went from her to the tarnished key in her wrinkled hand, then back to her face, his insides feeling as though they were being ripped in two—not just for her loss, though that was overpowering, but for his own as well.

"I'll take it to her," he blurted out impulsively, instantly reaching out and taking the key from her hand.

Helen began to shake her head, her eyes wide. "*No.* Jonny, it's too dangerous."

Jonathan shook his head, aware of the risks involved, but tired of the constant running. "I'll be careful. I promise!"

"Jonny. They haven't forgotten."

Jonathan let out a long sigh, realizing the truthfulness of his next words even as he said them. "This decision has been a long time in coming." He gestured to the key. "This is just the excuse I needed to act on it." He bent in close to her, needing her to understand. "I have to go. I have to see them again."

Helen searched her son's eyes for several seconds, the lines across her brow gradually softening. She nodded her head slowly, her eyes welling up. "I know," she whispered.

Jonathan bent and kissed her cheek.

"*Please* be careful," she warned.

He nodded, then opened his mouth, but it was almost impossible to speak because of the sudden tightness in his throat. "Mother, I—"

"I know," she said, touching his wet cheek. "I know."

* * *

Jonathan slipped back into the hallway, keeping his head lowered as if concentrating on something on his clipboard. But as he stood there, his eyes scanned the corridor, searching for any face that didn't belong. Two nurses sat manning the nurses' station. Jonathan could make out bits and pieces of their conversation as it floated across the hall. Somewhere farther down the hall a man slipped some loose change into a candy machine. When the candy didn't drop, the man thumped the front of the machine angrily with the palm of his hand, then walked away grumbling under his breath. Jonathan followed him with his eyes until the man disappeared into a nearby room. At the very end of the hall, a man in a waist-length, black leather jacket was sitting with one leg crossed over the other and holding a newspaper propped up in front of his face. Jonathan scrutinized him quickly. Paranoia and extreme precaution were almost second nature to him now, but tonight those senses were so keen they prickled down his back.

Lifting his eyes to the bold, green exit sign that marked the staircase, he resisted the urge to rush to the door. Instead he took a deep breath and tried to remain as inconspicuous as possible. He could feel his heart pounding ruthlessly against his chest. He glanced back over his shoulder at the closed door he'd just walked through. The woman inside lay weak and dying. He wanted to take her in his arms and whisk her away from these white unfeeling walls, but just coming to see her had put her and those he loved in danger.

A doctor passed him going in the opposite direction, but Jonathan didn't raise his eyes. He was within inches of the door now. He again glanced forward to the man with the newspaper at the end of the hall. The man had the paper lowered now and seemed to be looking right at Jonathan. Jonathan could feel the hair on the back of his neck raise. His mind was racing almost as fast as the blood that was pulsating through his veins. Jonathan's legs began to move faster even though his mind screamed for him to remain calm. Out of the corner of his eye, Jonathan watched the man with the newspaper. He'd gotten up and was walking quickly down the hall toward the nurses' desk. The newspaper he had been reading was rolled up and tucked under his arm. Just as Jonathan reached to grab the door handle, a hand reached out and took him by the shoulder. Jonathan whirled around, his hand searching for the .45-caliber pistol that bulged slightly beneath his starched medical coat.

"Sorry, I didn't mean to startle you."

Jonathan stared blankly at the man before him as his hand gripped the metal handle of the pistol still concealed beneath his coat.

"You look like you just saw a ghost."

Jonathan gulped down hard as he stared at the man before him. The man was stout with short, wheat-colored hair and dark-rimmed glasses that seemed to sit just a little cockeyed on his beaklike nose.

"It's my first day of rotations. I guess I'm a little nervous," Jonathan said, forcing a smile.

The man shrugged, then grabbed ahold of the stethoscope that was draped across his shoulders. "Believe me, I remember those days. No sleep, endless studying, no money, and—did I mention no sleep?"

Jonathan laughed, but it came out dry and tense. He glanced nervously back over at the man with the newspaper, who had just reached the nurse's station.

"The name's Bailey," the doctor said as he extended his hand.

"A pleasure, Dr. Bailey," Jonathan said, trying desperately to control the fluctuation in his voice as he put out his hand.

"Can I offer you a little advice?" Dr. Bailey asked with a smile.

"Certainly," Jonathan said, trying to sound genuine.

"Relax. Take a deep breath. It will all come in time."

The doctor reached into his pocket, pulled out a pack of gum, and began to unwrap a piece. Then he tossed the pack of gum to Jonathan. Jonathan quickly took a piece, then tried to hand the pack back to the doctor, but Dr. Bailey held up his hand. "Keep it, and try to remember—*relax!*"

Jonathan nodded, though relaxing was the last thing on his mind right now.

Dr. Bailey slapped him on the shoulder. "I'll be seeing you around." The doctor turned, then, as an afterthought, glanced back at Jonathan. "By the way, you might think about cutting that ponytail. It's not very professional."

Jonathan flashed a forced smile as he watched the doctor go. When he turned back to the hall, the man with the newspaper was gone. The only trace that the man had even been there was the rolled-up newspaper on the counter at the nurse's station. With a surge of relief, Jonathan let out all the air that had been building in his lungs, then pushed open the door to the stairs.

* * *

Jonathan blended into the shadows of the night. The full moon above him provided just enough light to see while still blanketing him in the darkness. As much as he hated being on the run, it was now as much a part of him as breathing. Every couple of minutes he shot a quick glance over his shoulder to see if anyone was following. The stench of garbage and human waste assaulted his nostrils as he slid through the dark alleyways of Jersey City. Damp steam shot out from vents and lifted as clouds of mist into the night sky. The back door to one of the businesses opened, and a man appeared. He hefted a bulging bag of garbage into an already heaping metal dumpster. Immediately a cat screeched and jumped from the dumpster. The man cursed, then fell back a step, frightened by the furry black intruder. A little farther up the alley a homeless man huddled in the meager warmth of a ragged blanket. Jonathan could feel the chill of the night air seeping easily through his own thin black overcoat and was grateful that he had left the medical jacket on underneath for extra warmth.

Small white flakes danced in the sky around a light pole on the other side of the street. Just past the light pole was the opening to another alleyway. It was there that Jonathan had parked his car. He turned and looked back into the darkness of the alley behind him. After looking at the light pole, it took a moment for his eyes to readjust to the dim light. For a fleeting moment he thought that he saw movement back by the dumpster, but as he strained his eyes on the dark shape, there was nothing. *It's probably just the cat searching through the new bag of trash.* Jonathan shook his head, then watched as his breath dissipated into the night. He took one more glance at the open street and the sporadic night traffic.

Most people avoided this area of town after sunset, so that left only the locals who had no choice at being there, and the slime that slithered in after dark.

Jonathan flipped the collar up on his dark trench coat, partially for warmth, but mostly to conceal his face as he crossed the street. Then he plunged headlong into the darkness of the next alley. His car was right where he had left it, hidden in the shadows. He stopped several feet from it and peered at the area around him. Everything was still and quiet. The distant sound of traffic several blocks away seemed to blare in his ears in contrast to the stillness around him. Jonathan could feel his stomach knot. It was almost too silent. His eyes strained in the dim light, searching the narrow alley. His senses had played a major role in keeping him alive over the years, and they were now screaming that something wasn't right. Jonathan slipped his hand into his overcoat, resting his hand on his gun. He folded his fingers over the handle, though he didn't pull it out. Instead he walked swiftly to his car, opened the door with his free hand, and quickly slipped inside. As he drove down the narrow street, the violent beating of his heart showing no signs of abating, a man slowly stepped from the shadows of the alley and pulled a cell phone from his inside coat pocket. "We've got him," the man said confidently, then clicked his phone off and placed it back in his pocket. He smiled menacingly as he watched Jonathan's car disappear, then began to whistle, his breath and the eerie tune lifting into the chilly night air as he slowly strolled off into the darkness.

Chapter 4

Clifford Craddick sat with his fingers interlocked and his elbows propped on the slightly worn arm of his expensive leather chair. He sat there silently surveying the young man before him. The individual wasn't much more than a punk kid, maybe twenty-three if that, the same age that Craddick had been when he got into the business. Allowing a moment of self-indulgence, Craddick's eyes swept the room. If the kid before him reminded him of where he had started, the office he was now in was evidence of how far he had come. He was in a position of respect. If the don of the family, Antonio Sabatini, or the underboss had a problem, Craddick saw to it that the problem was solved—permanently, with the evidence usually somewhere at the bottom of the Hudson Bay.

Craddick turned his eyes back to the kid, a little taken aback by the uncanny family resemblance. Craddick would have easily picked him out in a crowd. He had the same shocking black hair, prominent cheekbones, and tanned skin, which contrasted sharply against the white T-shirt exposed beneath his black leather jacket.

"Your old man and I go way back," Craddick finally offered.

Blaine Sabatini nodded his head but remained silent.

"We did two years in lockdown together." A slow grin spread across Craddick's face. "Course, we were innocent, you know."

"What was he in for?"

"Taking care of business," Craddick said in a matter-of-fact tone. Then he reached into his suit coat pocket and brought out a cigar. "I hear your old lady wouldn't let you have anything to do with him."

"I'm my own man."

"And your old lady's dead now. How convenient."

Blaine came straight out of his seat, but Craddick only laughed. "Sit down, boy. No disrespect intended." He bit off the tip of his cigar, spit it in the ashtray, and then lit it. "So, what are you doin' here?"

"I want to know my old man," Blaine said tightly.

"Too late for that. He died of a heart attack five years ago on death row."

"Two weeks before he was scheduled to get the needle," Blaine said, arching his brows dubiously. "How convenient." His mother had left Antonio when Blaine was just a child, leaving him with very few memories of his father, especially since Antonio wasn't around much before that. Once they left, his mother had seldom talked about him—and what she *had* said was not complimentary. One thing she was vehemently adamant about was that Antonio *The Snake* Sabatini was still alive.

Craddick shrugged.

"You and I both know that warden was dirty," Blaine began. "His face was on every newspaper in the country two years ago for accepting money from a known Mafia kingpin."

"He was investigated, not convicted," Craddick pointed out before taking a pull on his cigar.

Blaine leaned forward. "Do you want to know what I think? I think my old man worked a deal with the warden to help him fake his death, then slipped out of the country free and clear."

Craddick looked at the boy long and hard, then laughed. "It sounds like you've got a pretty vivid imagination." He got up from his chair and crossed to the front of the desk, placing his cigar in an ashtray. "You've got spunk, kid, just like your old man. I like that." He hesitated while giving Blaine one more appraising glance. "Tell you what. I'll talk to the boys. If you check out, maybe we can find something for you to do." Then his eyes narrowed to two thin slits. "Until then, I wouldn't be spreading a bunch of stories. Your old man is dead, *understand?*"

"Whatever you say," Blaine mumbled sarcastically.

Craddick raised an eyebrow. This boy would have to be taught his place, but at the same time, there was a fire in him that might prove useful.

"Don't look for any information under Blaine Sabatini. You won't find anything. I've spent most my life as Nicolas Pierce."

Craddick nodded, then motioned over to the two men that stood with their arms folded on either side of the door.

"Show Mr. Sabatini out."

Blaine slowly stood, his eyes every bit as rock-hard and challenging as Craddick's. "I'll be back to meet my old man and to claim my rightful place."

Craddick's eyes blazed, but he held his temper. "Loyalty is thicker than blood. You want a place in this business, you earn it."

"Oh, I'll earn my place—and your loyalty," Blaine said smugly, twisting Craddick's words. Then he turned to sum up the two gladiators that stood by the door. Even though they towered over him like granite statues, Blaine didn't blink at his assessment. He turned back to Craddick. "You tell my old man I want to see him." Then, without another word, Blaine sauntered out the door.

As soon as the door was shut, Craddick picked up the phone on his desk, then popped a couple of sunflower seeds into his mouth.

"You'll never guess who just walked through my door," Craddick began, tilting his chair back and plopping his feet up on his desk. "Sabatini's kid."

"*Blaine?*" the voice on the other end asked.

"He was fired up and looking for his old man. He made it quite clear he wants in. He could provide an interesting twist on this job."

There was a long pause on the other side of the phone. "Maybe."

Craddick cracked a seed open with his front teeth. "Revenge is a powerful tool."

"As long as it doesn't become a reckless one," the man said dubiously.

"What do you want me to do with him?"

"I'm putting him in your hands, Craddick. This could make or break you. Do you understand?"

Craddick almost choked on the seeds in his mouth. He sat straight up in his chair.

"What are you talking about—make or break me?" Craddick snapped.

"Put word out on the street that we want Schmitt and we're willing to pay. Make it tempting enough to attract someone from the inside. This job should have been finished a long time ago. You take care of it once and for all or—well, you just take care of it."

Craddick spit a shell into the ashtray on his desk. "Consider it done," he said, forcing his voice to sound cool and collected despite the sudden tightness in his throat.

* * *

Jonathan looked out across the old cemetery to the small group of people assembled around a freshly dug grave. The woman who had given him life was now being laid to rest, and he had to hide at the edge of the cemetery to avoid being spotted. He felt as though his heart were being ripped in two. He wanted to stand next to her grave and pay her the respect that she had rightfully earned instead of cowering like a scared rabbit from the wolves that might be lurking.

He looked down at the key clutched in his hand. He had carried it around with him for the past two weeks. Though he had driven past his mother's high security apartment complex more times than he could count, he still had not retrieved the old box. He didn't fear for his own life anymore. His life and happiness had been snatched away in an alleyway years ago, but he didn't want to lead anyone to his family.

He looked back over at his mother's headstone, knowing, though he couldn't see it from this distance, that his mother's name was now etched next to his father's. When Jonathan and his family had first gone into hiding, his mother, a recent widow, had come with them. But when they had to continue relocating, his mother had graciously suggested that they might be able to blend in better without her. Jonathan had quickly agreed, thinking of her safety and health. Though Sabatini continued to pursue Jonathan, his mother was able to spend the next eleven years safely tucked away in Arizona under an assumed name. It wasn't until she got sick that she finally came home, stubbornly insisting that she was dying anyway and would be of little use to Sabatini, especially since she truly didn't know where Jonathan was.

Jonathan took a deep breath, finding solace in the fact that his mother was finally where she wanted to be—home. He shoved the key deep into his pocket, his thoughts immediately turning to his own little family. His heart yearned to hold Elizabeth in his arms and to see his little girl. He shook his head. She wouldn't be little anymore. Reegan would turn nineteen in a week. Jonathan tried to fight the anger that was brooding inside him.

The regret of not being able to watch her grow up was like bile in the back of his throat, but there was no sense in drudging up the what-ifs. He had already made those decisions. There was no going back. Jonathan looked out across the cemetery, then glanced up at the gray sky above him. Thick dark clouds had completely blocked the rays of the sun. The forecast for the next two days promised to be no better. Tonight would be the night. He would slip into his mother's apartment by the cover of night and retrieve the wooden box that now belonged to his daughter. He took one last look at the grave, then turned and cautiously made his way across the lonely cemetery.

* * *

Clifford Craddick leaned down to peer into the open, tinted window of the limousine that had just pulled up next to him. A dark-haired man with dark sunglasses sat in the seat next to the window. Craddick recognized him immediately, but he was not familiar with the man that sat next to him. He was smaller than the first man, with sandy-blond hair and a receding hairline.

"Welcome back, Antonio. What can I do for you?" Craddick asked.

Antonio Sabatini reached into his pocket and pulled out a piece of paper with an address on it. Then his eyes locked on Craddick. "You can finish what you started."

Craddick reached out and took the piece of paper, trying not to let the effect of Sabatini's threatening tone show on his face. Antonio Sabatini was a man used to getting what he wanted, when he wanted it; patience was not one of his strong points. Craddick was fully aware that if he let Schmitt slip through his fingers this time, there would be no chance for redemption.

"I saw Schmitt myself at his mother's funeral," Sabatini offered, the hate in his voice impossible to miss.

"Well, it won't be the last funeral he attends this week," Craddick said, a wicked smile slowly lifting his lips.

Sabatini patted the back of the seat in front of him, and the chauffeur immediately rolled up the window and pulled away. Craddick looked down at the address in his hand. It wasn't more than five blocks from where he now stood. He had scoured four continents looking for Jonathan Schmitt, and now here he was almost within arm's length. Craddick wadded up the paper in his hand, then strode purposefully to his black BMW.

* * *

Jonathan tossed the last of his few possessions into the unzipped duffel bag that he had placed on his lumpy hotel bed. Then he took a quick glance around the room. He had been in more hotels, high-rise penthouses, and run-down apartments in his life than he cared to think about. He had traveled the world under assumed names and changed jobs and lifestyles like they were clothes—different day, different life. The prominent dimple on his left cheek had proven to be the most challenging aspect of his disguise. Whenever he grinned, which was becoming less and less frequent, the dimple deepened. What he wanted now, more than anything, was to put his name on a mailbox and spend the rest of his life making up for lost time with his family. He let that thought pass with a disheartened sigh. That was never going to happen and he knew it.

Jonathan glanced over at the beautiful wooden box that he had placed on the dresser. It was no bigger than a small shoebox and not much heavier. He had retrieved it from his mother's apartment late the previous night, taking a great chance in getting it. He had taken several risks in the past month that he'd usually never dream of taking. But a little over three weeks ago, Garret Woodard, the agent assigned to his case, had told him that Helen was dying. Two days later, Jonathan slipped out from under the cover of the Witness Protection Program and headed for home. He couldn't let his mother die without seeing her. He thought back to the day he had showed up for the first time in her room. He'd been dressed as a doctor and had dyed his hair blond, but his mother had recognized him immediately. It was as if she had known he would come all along and had just been waiting for him to get there. He wondered if his family would react the same way.

With a sigh Jonathan ran his fingers through his hair. He had dyed it back to its normal color, which was only a couple of shades lighter than the jet-black hair of his youth, but it was still much longer than he usually wore it. Through the years he had sported many different looks and a variety of styles to accommodate each alias. Now, with his black leather jacket and neat ponytail, he looked like he would be right at home joining a motorcycle gang. Jonathan quickly zipped his duffel bag and tossed it over his shoulder. Once he found his family, he would find the time for a quick haircut and a nice shave, but for now, he hoped the rough street look might help keep him alive.

Curious as to what little treasures his mother was now passing on to his daughter, Jonathan walked over and ran his fingers across the top of the old wooden box. He had been tempted to open it himself, but had refrained. He would save the secrets of the box solely for the eyes of his only child. A surge of excitement shot through him. If all went well, in a few days he would be reunited with his family. A creaking of one of the floorboards outside the motel room brought Jonathan instantly out of his thoughts. His eyes shot to the door, then back to the bed where he had placed his gun. He stood there motionless, his mind leaping from one scenario to another before his feet could catch up. Before he could make a move, the doorknob began to turn. Jonathan didn't have time to reach the gun. Instead he grabbed a lamp on the dresser. He yanked the plug from the wall and leaped toward the door just as a tall man appeared in the doorway.

"*No!* Jonathan, it's me!"

Jonathan came to a dead stop within inches of the man before him.

"*Garret?*"

Garret Woodard quickly stepped inside the room and shut the door behind him.

Jonathan shook his head slowly as he stared in disbelief. "How did you find me?"

Garret locked the door. "It wasn't hard," he offered, his voice heavy with sarcasm. He crossed the room to take a quick peek out the window. "Get your things. I'll give you your new destination when you're in the air."

"I'm not going."

"What are you talking about?"

"You heard me. I'm going to see my family."

Garret let out a sigh of exasperation. "We don't have time for this, Jon. Your life's in danger."

"What life?" Jonathan snapped.

Garret walked over and grabbed Jonathan by the shoulder. "I've risked my life countless times to protect your life, so don't ask *what life*. Now let's go."

Jonathan jerked his arm away. "Garret, I've got to see my family. Now you can either tell me where they are, because I know you've tracked them all these years, or I'll break into your files and find out myself."

Garret reached out to grab ahold of him again, but Jonathan sidestepped him.

"I mean it, Garret. Help me or stay out of my way."

"You're talking crazy!" Garret exclaimed.

Jonathan looked at the man before him. Garret had been assigned to his case for most of the fourteen years that Jonathan had been in hiding. Even though it had been frowned upon by the agency, somewhere along the way a deep friendship had formed between the two.

"I need your help, Garret. I just want to see them, then I'll go back under."

Garret crossed back over to the window and peered outside. He stood there for several seconds before speaking. "You're asking me to go against everything that I've been trained to do. I could lose my job," he protested stubbornly.

Jonathan's jaw tightened. "I've lost everything."

Garret shook his head, then turned back to face him, mumbling something incoherent under his breath.

"You know I'll go one way or another," Jonathan continued. "With or without your help."

Garret's eyes locked with his, as if to challenge his resolve, but Jonathan's face was like chiseled stone. Garret's expression softened. Finally he lifted his pointer finger. "One day! Do you hear me, Jon? I'll give you one day with them, that's all."

"That's all I'm asking," he replied with a huge smile. "Just one day."

* * *

Clifford Craddick picked up his cell phone and dialed as he watched the man that he'd been hunting—for more years than he cared to admit—climb into a car not fifty feet from him.

"I've got him!" Craddick stated. "Garret's with him too."

"Just follow them. I want to see him myself."

"Maybe we should get the kid involved," Craddick suggested.

There was silence on the other end for a moment. "Bring him in, but keep him low-key for now."

"Whatever you say." Craddick hung up the phone, then quickly dialed again.

"Kid, this is your lucky day," Craddick said as soon as Blaine picked up the receiver.

"Who is this?"

"Just shut up and listen. I want you to get in your car and drive exactly where I tell you. Do you understand?"

"And if I do?"

"There better be no *if* about it, boy."

chapter 5

Reegan stared out the window blankly, barely able to keep her eyes open. She and her mother had stayed up late every night for the past two and a half weeks. It was as if her life up to that point had been a giant puzzle with half of the pieces missing. Every time she tried to put it together, the picture was impossible to make out. Now it was almost a complete picture, with only one piece still missing—her father. She yawned, then interlocked her fingers and stretched them out in front of her.

"I'm sorry, Reegan. Are we keeping you up?" Mrs. Finegan asked, the question a subtle reprove.

Reegan immediately lifted her eyes to Mrs. Finegan. "What?"

"Christmas break is over," she said, shaking her head disapprovingly. Then the woman glanced over at Tera with the same expression, as if Tera was the source of this former honor student's slipping from grace.

Reegan wanted to jump up and explain everything. So much had changed in the past three weeks, but she knew that she couldn't talk about any of it. Instead she slumped down in her seat and watched as Mrs. Finegan turned back to the chalkboard. Tera immediately looked over at Reegan and rolled her eyes, then took out a sheet of paper and quickly wrote something on it. Reegan watched as the note passed from one hand to another until it finally made its way over to her. She retrieved it just as Mrs. Finegan turned back around to face the class. Unable to determine the cause of the whispers, she gave Reegan one more glance, then turned back to the board to work out the algebra problem.

Reegan slowly opened the note: *Reegan, Wayne wants to see you again. Meet us at the same place Friday night.* Reegan shoved the note into her backpack, but diverted her eyes, evading Tera's questioning gaze. Instead she picked up her own pencil and began to work on the problem.

* * *

To avoid having to see Tera after school, Reegan decided to go to the old Graham farm. She had gone there several times in the last week, taking different items like matches, food, blankets, and cleaning supplies to help make the old place more useable. She had also taken her jewelry box over there, placing it on the mantel, so she could look at the picture of her father whenever she thought of him, which was often.

Since her mother was going to be home early tonight, after a few hours of algebra and biology homework, Reegan slung her backpack over her shoulder and headed for home. She found herself whistling as she walked down the dirt road. The sun was low in the sky, sending splashes of orange and red across the horizon. She stared at the sky in wonder. It looked as though an artist had used the sky as a canvas, hand-painting the whole scene in intricate detail. Reegan was so caught up in the view that she jumped when a small twig snapped somewhere off in the bushes. She jerked around and stared apprehensively in the direction from which the noise had come. With it being January, dusk had come quickly.

The trees were already casting long shadows across the road. For a moment Reegan stood motionless, staring into the brush, her heart beginning to race. Then, out from under a thick entanglement of shrubs, a white ball of fluff suddenly emerged. Reegan jumped as the rabbit darted straight for her before quickly changing directions and zigzagging off into the distance. Reegan shook her head as she watched him go. He looked almost as startled to see her—out here in the middle of nowhere—as she was to see him.

Reegan breathed a quick sigh of relief, then turned back toward town. She glanced up at the sky again, but the brilliant colors of the sunset had already begun to melt into the grayish tones of nightfall. Within minutes the sun would sneak beyond the horizon leaving only a partially exposed moon to light her way. Reegan quickened her step, knowing she had stayed too long at the farm. As she rounded a bend, an image in the center of the narrow dirt road brought her to a dead stop. Not twenty feet from her was the silhouette of a man. Reegan could feel the hair on the back of her neck stand on end. The dark form stood motionless in the middle of the road. For a moment Reegan was too petrified to move. The last sliver of the sun was directly behind the man so she couldn't see who it was, not that she had any intentions of sticking around to find out. She was just about to turn around when she heard someone begin to laugh. At first Reegan thought that it was the man, but the sound wasn't coming from in front of her. Reegan turned to look off into the woods.

"Tera? Is that you?" she asked breathlessly, suddenly recognizing the laugh.

Tera and Seth emerged from behind an old elm tree. Seth had a smile on his face that reminded her of a cat that had just pounced on a fat mouse. Reegan would have given him a piece of her mind had she not been so utterly relieved.

"What are you doing out here?" she snapped as she fought to control the quiver in her voice.

"Just walkin' home," Seth said, gesturing up the road toward Pinewood.

"*You?* Walking?" she asked, her tone more sarcastic than she had intended. "Where's your car?"

"He's having some fancy detail work done on it."

Reegan turned toward Wayne, the dark shape in the middle of the road heading straight toward her.

"I've missed you," he said as he reached her, immediately bending to kiss her.

Reegan quickly turned so that all he got was a cold cheek, literally.

"What's the matter?" Wayne asked, his tone a combination of rejection and irritation.

"Nothing. I just need to get home," Reegan offered, overwhelmingly relieved that she had maintained her virtue despite all of his previous advances.

"What are *you* doing way out here?" Tera asked.

Reegan shrugged. "I just decided to take a walk."

Reegan brushed past Wayne and started back toward town, but the three of them just followed suit.

"You didn't answer my note," Tera stated accusingly.

Reegan didn't even turn to look at her. "I already have plans for Friday night."

"Oh, you do?" Wayne broke in, his tone instantly sharp. "With who?"

"My mom," Reegan offered, shooting a quick glance at Wayne. "Maybe some other time," she said, though she knew it was a lie.

Reegan tried to walk faster, but they continued to stay right with her.

"We made a score at Mike's Grocery," Seth bragged.

"*What?*" Reegan exclaimed, stopping midstride. "I thought—"

"Not from the till, just a six-pack and some cigarettes. Mike won't even know the difference."

Reegan shook her head in disgust, but if Seth saw it, he gave no indication; instead he and Wayne spent the next few minutes bragging about all their petty theft in the last few months. They had shoplifted several hundred dollar's worth of merchandise from different convenience stores and gas stations in the region. Reegan couldn't help but wonder how long it would take for their misdemeanors to turn into felonies. Finally when they got bored of reliving their conquests, or when she didn't supply the affirmation they were seeking, Wayne turned back to her.

"Forget your mom and come with us Friday night."

"I can't."

"You can't—or you *won't?* You got another guy on the side?" Seth asked, glancing quickly at Wayne with a hint of a smile.

"Hey, shut up!" Wayne snapped, taking a step toward Seth.

Seth lifted a brow in warning, his jaw rippling with tension, which immediately silenced his friend. Hanging out with Seth Whiley, the pinnacle of the *in* crowd, had its upside, but as anyone who got in his way was painfully aware, it also had a costly downside. More than one reputation had been tarnished, or outright destroyed, by a couple of loosely dropped fabrications, many of which Reegan was sure he fed to the town through his own mother.

"Come on, Seth," Tera began, hoping to alleviate the strain between the two. "Let's go. It's getting cold."

Seth gave Wayne one more sharp look, then reluctantly started down the road ahead of them with Tera clinging to his side. A part of Reegan wanted to call Tera back so that she wouldn't have to be alone with Wayne, but a bigger part of her was relieved that Seth was gone. She glanced over and took a good look at Wayne. He was tall and broad with a distinctive square jaw. His nose curved slightly to the right near the bridge, from a football injury, but it was only vaguely notice-able. Just to look at him, he was rather handsome, but once he opened his mouth, especially around Seth . . . Reegan shook her head.

"Why do you hang around with him?"

At first Wayne looked surprised by her question, then he let out a burst of exasperation and shook his head. "I don't know. So, are you hanging with us Friday night or not?" he asked, changing the subject.

"I can't," Reegan said gently.

Reegan could see the rejection in his eyes, but he shrugged it off as if it were no big deal. "Whatever."

Reegan knew that she should tell him how she felt, but the truth was, she was just a little scared of what his reaction would be.

Chapter 6

"We're being followed," Garret stated evenly. "That BMW has been following us most of the night."

"*What?*" Jonathan exclaimed, nearly injuring his neck to look over his shoulder.

"Just turn around."

"Great!" Jonathan mumbled, smacking the steering wheel with the palm of his hand. "He'll be able to drive circles around this heap."

"If he planned to catch us, he would have already done it."

Jonathan glanced over at his traveling companion. He was amazed at how calmly Garret did his job. He seemed to have a natural instinct when it came to things like this.

"Why do you do this?" Jonathan asked with a shake of his head.

"What? You mean protect people like you?"

Jonathan smiled. It was his first real smile in several days. "Yeah."

Garret looked back out the window. "When I first got into undercover work fifteen years ago, I wasn't married. I figured it was better that I was the one in danger rather than someone who had a family to go home to. As you know, things have changed since then, but that's how it all started."

Jonathan watched Garret closely, suddenly very aware of the risks Garret had taken through the years. If Sabatini ever found out about Garret's family, he wouldn't think twice about using them as leverage to get to Jonathan. For that reason, though the two men talked about their lives, personal names and faces were kept out of the mix.

"Do you think I'm doing the wrong thing?"

Garret shook his head. "I know I'd do the exact same thing if I were in your shoes."

Jonathan glanced in his rearview mirror. "So, what are we going to do about him?"

Garret looked down at his watch. It was one thirty in the morning. "See that motel up ahead?"

"Yeah," Jonathan acknowledged hesitantly.

"Turn in."

"What?" Jonathan questioned, looking at Garret as if he had lost his mind.

"Just do it," Garret said firmly.

Jonathan took the next left-hand turn and pulled into the parking lot of the run-down motel.

"You go in and get a room," Garret said. "I'll stay here and see what happens."

Jonathan shook his head, then opened his mouth to say something, but Garret didn't give him the opportunity.

"If you want my help, then we do it my way. Understand?"

Jonathan had placed his life in Garret's hands more times than he could count. If there was anyone whom he trusted completely, it was Garret Woodard. Jonathan shrugged his surrender, then hopped out of the car and made his way to the small motel office. Once he was safely inside, he shot a quick glance back toward the parking lot, but there was no sign of the BMW.

"Thirty-nine a night, or two hundred and sixty-five a week. You break it, you pay for it. No loud music and no drugs," the old man behind the counter said, not bothering to look up from his newspaper.

Jonathan shot a wary glance around the office as he reached for his wallet. The smoke in the room was so thick that it looked like they were in San Francisco at dusk. He finally made out a picture of the Miami coast. It sported a cheap frame and sat above an old desk that was in complete disarray.

"I just need a room for the night," Jonathan said as he pulled a hundred-dollar bill from his billfold. It was all the money he had left.

The older man was eyeing him carefully now over his paper. "I don't have change like that on hand." He pointed over to his safe. "Won't have it till morning."

Jonathan glanced nervously back over his shoulder at the parking lot; his stomach felt like it was being run through a meat grinder. Without a minute's hesitation, he tossed the man the money. "Consider it a generous tip then."

The older man jumped up, sending his newspaper flying. "Would you like some extra towels or blankets or something, sir?"

"Just the key, please, and quick."

The old man furrowed his brow, suddenly eyeing Jonathan warily.

"I'm sorry," Jonathan began, seeing his mistake. "I'm just tired. You know, been traveling all day."

A broad smile quickly spread across the older man's face. "I understand. Me and my wife took a trip to the Grand Canyon last summer. Took two days of almost constant driving. I almost nodded off several times. The wife had to keep poking me in the ribs to keep me awake. Sure was worth it though," the old man rambled on.

Jonathan glanced anxiously out the window.

"Never seen such a big hole in the ground as that. The wife wanted to get on one of them there donkeys and ride down to the bottom, but I said there was no way I was getting—"

"The key," Jonathan broke in. His nerves now completely shot.

"Let's see," the man began, as he scanned the Peg-Board behind him for a key. "Looks like room sixteen is still open. The sink drips, but it's got a nice view of the pool—course there's no water in the pool right now on account of the fungus episode. Seems the board of health is a real stickler on things like that."

Jonathan wanted to leap across the counter and grab the key himself.

"Here you go. Let me know if you need anything else," the old man hollered as the door closed behind Jonathan.

"Now what?" Jonathan asked as he hopped back into the car. "We can't stay here tonight. They know we're here."

Garret just smiled one of his smiles that usually indicated he was two steps ahead of the situation. "Just get your things."

* * *

When Clifford Craddick and Blaine Sabatini broke down the door to room sixteen, Jonathan and Garret were in a semi on their way west. They had climbed out the bathroom window not long after checking in and made their way on foot to a small diner. From there they hitched a ride with a trucker. Four hundred miles down the road the trucker let them out at a café truck stop.

Jonathan rubbed his eyes, then stretched out his arms. "That was the best I've slept in months."

Garret nodded. "I figured as much. You were snoring like a freight train for most of the ride."

Jonathan took a sip of his orange juice, then picked up his menu. "Just so you know, the rest of this trip is on you."

Garret lowered his menu just enough to peek over it.

"I spent a hundred dollars at the motel."

Garret shook his head. "Well, at least the roaches got to enjoy the room."

Jonathan laughed out loud. Then, almost instantly, his face fell. "Do you think he'll follow us?"

Garret set his menu on the table, then motioned over to the waitress. "I don't think we should stick around long enough to find out."

"Where's my family, Garret?"

"They're safe, Jon."

"What if we get separated?" Jonathan persisted. "Garret, I need to know."

Garret glanced up as the waitress approached to refill their glasses and take their order, then he hesitantly looked back to Jonathan.

"Maplecove, North Dakota."

Jonathan visibly relaxed. "Thanks, Garret."

"Thank me two weeks from now when this is all over—after you've seen them and I'm on an extended beach vacation off the coast of Mexico."

Jonathan nodded, then looked up at the waitress. "Since my friend here is buying, I'll have a breakfast steak, two fried eggs, and a side order of hash browns. Maybe one of those big cinnamon rolls, too," Jonathan added as he hungrily eyed the items in the glass display counter across the room.

"Unless you plan to stick around and pay your meal off by doing dishes, you better change that to two breakfast sandwiches to go," Garret corrected.

"Don't expect him to be a big tipper either," Jonathan said, glancing up at the waitress.

The waitress smiled. "Trust me. He wouldn't be the first around this place."

* * *

Clifford Craddick split a sunflower seed open, spit the shell into a cup that he had propped up on the dashboard, then reached into his suit coat pocket and pulled out a cigar. After a couple of minutes the entire car was filled with smoke. Blaine could feel his lungs burning. He coughed into his fist, then rolled down the window to get a gulp of fresh air.

"Too strong for you?" Craddick asked as he continued puffing away.

"How long do we have to sit here?" Blaine snapped.

"You'll sit here until I tell you it's time," Craddick said with a warning glance.

Blaine pulled his lips into a tight line, then stared back out the window into the darkness.

"We almost had him last night. Shouldn't we still be tracking him?"

Craddick's face lit into a wicked grin. "Oh, don't worry. We're tracking him all right."

Blaine turned back to him. "We're just sitting here," he protested.

Craddick raised an eyebrow. Blaine could tell that the man's patience was running thin, but so was his own. Sitting in a dark parking lot with a man who was constantly chewing on sunflower seeds and chain-smoking smelly cigars was not exactly what he had in mind when he signed on for this job. Blaine gave Craddick a quick once-over. He was middle-aged with a thick neck and a large double chin. To call him slow-witted might be exaggerating a bit, but the lackey wasn't exactly Einstein. Blaine would have dismissed him altogether had it not been for his notorious temper. Though Craddick had managed to keep it in check around him, Blaine had heard stories that left him a little edgy.

Both Blaine and Craddick turned as a silver Lincoln pulled into the vacant parking lot. Blaine, who was slouched down in his seat, sat straight up.

"It looks like our wait is over," Craddick said with a grin.

"They've got Jonathan Schmitt?" Blaine asked incredulously.

Craddick turned and gave Blaine a long, appraising look. "Better than Schmitt." Craddick opened his car door and climbed out, and Blaine quickly followed. The two of them walked to the front of their vehicle and watched as the other car pulled up right in front of them. The Lincoln had its headlights off, but as soon as it stopped in front of them, the driver hit the lights, putting the two of them on center stage. Blaine could feel his heart begin to pound. There was no turning back; he was in this now.

Blaine watched as the car doors opened and three men climbed out. Once their doors were closed, one man slowly walked forward, leaving the other two standing by the car. At first the man was nothing more than a dark shape, but as he came into the beam of the headlights, Blaine took a quick intake of air.

"It's been a long time, boy."

Blaine stood there gaping at the man before him. It was like looking in a mirror. The older man had a few strands of gray streaked through his dark hair, and a two-inch scar just above his right brow, but other than that, the resemblance was eerie. Blaine had seen a few pictures of his father, but none of them prepared him for seeing the man in the flesh.

He had an air of power about him that Blaine had not expected. Even Craddick's countenance seemed to change. At first Blaine read it as respect, but it was more than that. It was unquestioning loyalty, tinged with fear.

"Aren't you going to say something?" Antonio Sabatini asked with a short laugh.

Craddick slapped Blaine's shoulder. "This is why you came isn't it? Go ahead, kid. Say hello to your old man."

Blaine's knees were weak, but somehow he managed to walk over and extend his hand to his father. Antonio Sabatini looked down at the outstretched hand with a frown. Then a slow smile spread across his face and he pulled Blaine into a firm bear hug, pummeling him several times on the back. When the two finally pulled back, Antonio slapped Blaine's cheek affectionately, then turned to his companions.

"He's a good-looking kid. Looks just like his old man."

The other men laughed, then nodded in agreement, but Blaine was only vaguely aware of them. He found himself staring at his father, an unexpected onslaught of mixed emotions whirling inside him. "Why don't you boys go down and get a couple of steaks at Tony's and let me and Blaine have a talk."

"Whatever you say, Antonio," Craddick said as he motioned the other men over to his car.

Blaine watched as Antonio's other two men walked into the beam of the headlights. These two men and Craddick were a hodgepodge of ages and sizes, but they did have one thing in common—they weren't the type Blaine would want to meet in a dark alley. Blaine watched as the men climbed into the car, then he turned back to his father. Antonio was looking directly at him. At first his mouth was pulled down in a frown, but when their eyes met, his lips quickly lifted into a broad grin.

"Let's go for a drive."

* * *

For the first fifteen or twenty minutes of the drive, Antonio asked Blaine question after question about himself. He seemed to want to know everything about him, from his little league days to his first steady girlfriend. Blaine did notice that Antonio was very careful to sidestep anything that would lead to talking about Julia, Blaine's mother. Each time her name was mentioned a look came across Antonio's face. Blaine couldn't quite put a name on the expression.

"Are you hungry?" Antonio asked as they neared an Italian restaurant.

Blaine looked down the street to the restaurant. All the lights were out, and the strip of street in front of it was empty.

"I don't think they're open," Blaine said as he glanced down at his watch. It was one o'clock in the morning.

Antonio grinned, then tapped the driver on the shoulder. The driver picked up a phone and quickly dialed. By the time they parked in front of the small restaurant, several lights had already been turned on. Blaine turned to look at Antonio questioningly, but his father only smiled and shrugged.

* * *

"How's your steak, sir?"

Blaine looked up at the man next to him. His hair was still slightly ruffled from just climbing out of his warm bed.

"It's great, thanks."

The man looked over at Antonio. "Can I get you anything else, Mr. Sabatini?"

Antonio reached into his suit coat pocket and pulled out his billfold. Blaine's mouth almost dropped open when he saw the neat stack of one hundred-dollar bills. Antonio filed through them slowly, then pulled out two. He held the bills out to the restaurant owner just as flippantly as if they were fives.

"Everything was delicious as usual," Antonio complimented.

The man accepted the compliment almost as readily as he did the money.

"Anytime, Mr. Sabatini. Anytime."

Blaine had a feeling that he meant "anytime" literally. Blaine watched as Antonio tucked his billfold back in his pocket, then went back to cutting his steak. For the next few minutes the two of them fell silent as they ate.

"You look like your old man," Antonio finally began, though he didn't look up, "but I wonder how much of your mother you have in you." His eyes rose to meet Blaine's.

"That's funny," Blaine answered calmly. "My mother used to wonder how much of my father I had in me."

The intensity of Antonio's gaze instantly lightened.

"I'll say one thing for Julia. She was beautiful. I don't think I've ever met a woman that could rival her."

Blaine nodded, then took a bite of his steak.

"She kept you hidden pretty good all these years. I tried to track you down, but it was like you both just disappeared."

"She didn't want to be found."

"And you?"

"I'm here, aren't I?"

"I've done a little checking on Nicolas Pierce since you showed up. Seems you spent quite a bit of time in and out of juvie out in Montana."

Blaine shrugged but didn't comment.

The intensity in Antonio's eyes returned. "So, why are you here?"

Blaine took a quick drink of his water to wash down his food, then pushed his plate away. "I've spent my whole life hearing stories about you. I figured it was about time I found out who you were for myself."

Antonio leaned back in his chair, eyeing Blaine dubiously, as if needing more of an explanation than that.

"I want in," Blaine blurted out.

"You want in on what?" Antonio asked, feigning innocence.

Blaine rubbed his fingers together greedily, then playfully gestured across at the restaurant. "*All* of it." His eyes grew suddenly earnest. "Look, I'm not asking for any special treatment. I'll start at the bottom if I have to."

"All this comes at a price."

"I know that."

"Do you?" Antonio asked, his tone almost amused, though his countenance seemed deadly serious.

Blaine's eyes deepened until they looked like two black holes. "I wouldn't be here wasting your time if I didn't."

Antonio's eyes seemed to be searching Blaine's soul. Blaine had to fight the urge to squirm under such intense scrutiny. Finally, Antonio pushed back from the table and called out to the restaurant owner. "If my boy comes in again, you make sure you take good care of him. He's one of the family."

Chapter 1

"Just do it," Reegan coaxed.

Elizabeth shook her head, then set the college brochures back on the table. "I don't know. It's *so* much money. Besides, you'll be starting school in a little over six months, and we'll need every spare dime we can get to make sure that you get *your* education."

"Mom, I talked with Mrs. Finegan and my school counselor yesterday. Both of them think I can get a scholarship. My grades are high enough—well, all except last semester, but even with that my overall GPA should be fine if I pull straight As for the rest of the year. And with my AP classes I could start college as a sophomore—or maybe higher if I test out of other basics once I get there."

Her mother didn't quite look convinced.

"Mom, you were two semesters away from graduating when you quit. You need to do this. You deserve it."

"Reegan, that was fifteen years ago."

"*So?* You could do it. Besides, I could get a part-time job to help out with the bills."

Elizabeth was already shaking her head, but Reegan plunged ahead. "Mike's Grocery had a help-wanted sign in the window a couple of days ago, so I stopped in just out of curiosity. Mike said that it's only fifteen hours a week, but he's willing to pay fifty cents over minimum wage if I can start right away."

"Reegan, I don't know," Elizabeth said hesitantly.

Reegan put her hand on her mother's shoulder. "Mom, I can't hide out in this house my whole life."

"I know," Elizabeth said, placing her own hand over Reegan's, her eyes full of both love and trepidation. "I know." Then she stood, her expression suddenly resolute. "Come on. We better get going or I'm going to be late for work and you're going to be late for school."

"What about the job?" Reegan pressed.

"Well, if you want the fifty cents extra you better get moving before someone else beats you to it."

Reegan threw her arms around her mother. "Thanks."

"How come you never thank me when I let you do the dishes? That's a job, too, you know," she teased.

"I don't remember a paycheck being involved with that particular job."

"Three meals a day, a roof over your head, and—"

"The clothes on my back," Reegan supplied with a smile. "Lecture one hundred and three. Committed to memory. Would you like me to recite lecture one hundred and four, entitled 'As Long As You Live In My House'? Another good one. Not as entertaining as 'When I Was a Kid,' but still highly educational."

Elizabeth swatted playfully at Reegan's backside, but Reegan just jumped out of the way, then turned to smile. She couldn't believe how much her mom had changed in the last couple of weeks. Then again, maybe it wasn't so much that she had changed. Maybe Reegan was just seeing her through different eyes.

"Are you working late tonight?" Reegan asked.

Elizabeth nodded reluctantly. "Mr. Haskle asked me if I would work late every night this week. He's short-handed right now, and besides—" Elizabeth paused as she picked up the college brochures, "if I'm going to be starting college again, we're going to need all the extra money we can get."

* * *

Reegan didn't get a chance to stop in at Mike's Grocery before school, so as soon as it was over she made a beeline straight to the little store. Mike Burgess was at the back of the store taking inventory when she entered. He immediately lifted his head to see who it was.

"Reegan! I was hoping you'd come back," he admitted with a broad smile.

"Is the job still available?" Reegan asked anxiously.

Mike reached for a green vest hanging on a coat hook, then tossed it over to her. "It's all yours."

Reegan beamed over at her new employer. "When do I start?"

"Right now," he said. He gave her a quick tour and a description of what needed to be done. She spent the next forty minutes sweeping, dusting, and tidying up the merchandise on the shelves. Mike assisted a number of customers, then the store became rather quiet. Mike approached Reegan with a tired smile. "That probably does it for our usual after-school rush. I think I'll kick back and read the paper for a while."

Mike grabbed a newspaper, then disappeared into the back room while Reegan continued at her tasks. The little bell on the front door rang just as she was about to start on the windows. She turned toward the door just as Seth and Wayne entered.

"What are you doin' here?" Wayne asked, clearly caught off guard.

"I work here," Reegan said, heading back behind the counter.

"Since when?" Seth blurted out.

"I just started today."

Seth's face instantly split into a huge grin. "Well, well, well. I think our work just got a little easier."

Reegan could feel her stomach twist into a queasy knot as she watched him wander over toward the shelves.

"Can I help you, kids?"

They all turned as Mike emerged from the back room. "I thought you might need some help with the cash register," Mike said, turning to Reegan.

"Thanks," Reegan said, relief flooding through her.

Just then another customer entered the store, his eyes immediately falling on Wayne and Seth. "Hey, boys," the man said, his voice booming and his face lighting into a broad grin.

"Hi, Mr. Phillips," Seth said, extending his hand as the big man walked toward him.

"I hope you're takin' good care of that arm of yours," Mr. Phillips said, slapping him on the shoulder. "If you play baseball this next season the way you played football this fall, we might have a real shot at the state championship."

Seth smiled. "You can count on it."

"Coach Richards has already cleared a spot in the trophy case," Wayne added.

The man laughed. "Good. I hear you've got several schools interested in you," he added, returning his attention to Seth.

Seth shrugged, his ego visibly growing with each word. "A few."

Reegan glanced at Mike who had stepped behind the counter next to her. His brows were lowered and his eyes focused on Seth. Something in his expression gave Reegan the distinct impression that he didn't buy Seth's all-American, good-boy image like the rest of the town.

"Well, good luck with the scouts this spring, not that you're going to need it." Then Mr. Phillips slapped Seth's shoulder in parting and wandered over to a sales rack.

Seth followed the man with his eyes, then turned back to Reegan and Mike. "Hello, Mr. Burgess," he said, his plastic smile reminding Reegan of a politician just up for reelection.

"What can I do for you two?" Mike asked tightly.

"Actually, I don't think you have what we needed," Seth said nonchalantly.

"Maybe that's because you cleaned us out the last time you were in," Mike stated, his expression remaining passive.

All the color instantly drained from Wayne's face, but Seth never flinched. "Actually, I've been doing most my shopping online lately. You can get some real steals that way."

Reegan watched Mike's Adam's apple bob, as if he were fighting to keep his cool. Mike wasn't a big man, maybe five nine, if that, and well into his forties, with his idea of exercise being a nap at the lake while the fish nipped at his pole. Physically he was not at all threatening, but right now Reegan could see no trace of his usual jovial disposition.

Seth smiled coolly, then turned to Reegan. "We'll see you around."

Reegan wanted to crawl under the counter. She glanced over to see Mike's reaction, but his eyes were still glued on Seth. Once the two of them left, Mike turned to Reegan.

"Come in at ten on Saturday, and I'll teach you how to run the cash register. I'd show you tonight, but I've got to close up early because my in-laws are coming in from Minneapolis."

Reegan nodded, feeling guilty for not finding the courage to confirm his suspicions about Seth and Wayne. "Thanks again, Mr. Burgess. I really appreciate the job."

Mike looked around the store, then nodded his head in satisfaction. "Well, I appreciate the help. *But*," he began hesitantly, "if you intend to continue working here…"

Reegan held her breath.

"You'd better start calling me Mike."

* * *

Pulling her coat close around her, Reegan headed out the front door of the little store. Though it was still relatively early, the streets seemed exceptionally dark. She looked up at the sky. A little sliver of a moon peeked out from a cluster of clouds, though most of the stars remained hidden. Reegan glanced back toward the store. She could see Mike through the window doing a couple of last-minute things before closing up. He had the radio on and was singing along with the tune, or at least *attempting* to. Reegan smiled, then turned back toward the street. Though Mike had offered to drive her home, she didn't feel like imposing on his generosity. Besides, her house was only a five-minute walk from the store.

With the smell of a brewing storm filling the air, Reegan snuggled her face into her scarf, then started for home. If she hurried she could get there and get her homework done before her mom got home from work. She didn't want to give her mom any reason to change her mind about the job.

After only a couple of steps, Reegan felt a chill run through her worse than the nip of the cold January night. It was a feeling that crept up her spine and sent her skin crawling. Somebody was watching her. She could feel their eyes on her. Reegan's body stiffened as her eyes darted into the shadows. Though her instincts were screaming for her to run, her legs felt like they were cemented to the pavement.

"Hey, Reegan."

Reegan jerked around toward the alley, immediately recognizing the three figures who stood there, even in the dim light. She let her breath out hard.

"What are you doing?" she asked, not even attempting to hide the irritation in her voice.

"We just wanted to walk you home," Seth began innocently. "Wouldn't want you to run into the wrong sorts out here in the dark."

Tera, who had joined them since their visit to the store, laughed, which brought a giant smirk to Seth's already cocky face.

"So did you bring us anything from work?" Seth asked.

Reegan crinkled her nose at him in open disdain. "Look, I've got to get home."

They all jumped, then turned as the lid from a garbage can down the street crashed to the pavement. Reegan could feel her heart begin to pump all over again as she searched the darkness.

"Somebody is out there," she whispered, her throat constricting.

Seth shook his head, not really caring. "It's probably just a dog."

"I don't see one," Tera admitted.

Seth pulled her in close to him. "Don't worry. I'll protect you." His face lit into a wry grin.

Then the two turned and started down the alley away from where the sound had come. Reegan turned to follow them, then quickly glanced back over her shoulder. For a moment she just stared into the darkness. She couldn't quite shake the feeling that someone else was there.

"Reegan, come on," Wayne whispered as he reached out his hand.

Reegan turned toward Wayne, though she didn't take his hand, then slowly made her way through the alley. Seth and Tera met them on the other end of the dark street.

"We're all going to my house to watch some movies. My mom's in Bismark visiting my aunt. What do you say?" Tera asked Reegan, shooting a grin back toward Wayne that caused her dimples to deepen.

"I can't," Reegan said quickly.

Tera immediately threaded her arm through Reegan's and pulled her off to the side, out of earshot of Seth and Wayne. "Come on, Reegan," she whispered. "Wayne wants you to come."

"Tera, I don't want to hurt his feelings—or yours. It's just—" Reegan stopped, searching for the right words. "It's just not going to work. Any of this."

Tera's eyes opened wide as the realization hit her. "*You* think you're too good for *us?*" she snapped.

Reegan opened her mouth, but Tera cut her off.

"Just forget it. Go on back to being the nobody you were before you started hanging with us," she said, storming back to Seth and Wayne.

"What's goin' on?" Wayne demanded, seeing Tera's reaction.

Reegan could hear Tera mumble something to the two guys next to her, which instantly won a broad smirk from Seth.

"Who is he?" Wayne demanded, starting toward her, his eyes smoldering hot with jealousy.

Reegan took a step back under the intensity of his gaze. "What are you talking about?" she asked weakly.

"The other guy," he demanded.

Reegan glanced over at Tera, but she seemed perfectly content to sit back and watch.

"There's no other guy," Reegan said, fighting to keep her voice even.

For a minute the rage in Wayne's eyes lifted just enough for Reegan to see the vulnerability underneath.

"Then *why?*" he asked, his voice almost pleading.

"Wayne, I—I'm sorry."

Wayne's eyes were like two ice cubes in a pool of blue. Finally, he turned and stalked off into the night.

"Go see if you can cool him down," Seth told Tera.

She nodded, then gave his arm a quick squeeze before starting down the road. Once she turned the corner and was gone, Reegan could feel her shoulders relax as if an actual burden had been lifted.

"I wondered how long it'd take you to dump him."

Reegan lifted her eyes to Seth, who had silently walked over next to her.

"I've got to get home."

Before she could move, Seth reached out and took her by the arm, a smile slowly creeping across his face.

"You're not like the rest of the girls around here."

"No, I'm not," Reegan said tightly.

"Most of them would die for the opportunity you're getting," he said as he reached up and touched a strand of her hair.

"I'm not that type of girl," Reegan said, an involuntary shiver slithering across her shoulders.

"That's right, and I'm sure you'd like to keep that good-girl image, wouldn't you?"

Reegan could feel heat instantly rise to her cheeks. "Don't threaten me."

"I wasn't threatening anyone," Seth said, his face the epitome of innocence. "I'd be the last person who'd want to see your reputation ruined by a nasty rumor, especially if it could be avoided," he said, running a finger along her cheek.

Reegan turned to leave, but Seth tightened his grip.

"I wonder what Coach Richards or your college recruits would think if they knew you'd probably fail a drug test," Reegan said, unable to control the quiver in her voice.

Seth visibly flinched. "No one would believe you."

"Drug tests don't lie," Reegan said, forcing herself to remain calm.

Reegan could feel her skin prickle with fear as she felt his steady glare envelop her. "You're playing a dangerous game, Reegan, *very* dangerous." Then he turned and walked away.

Reegan didn't waste a second; she turned the opposite direction and ran down the alley.

* * *

By the time Reegan made it home, her nerves were shot. She immediately locked the door and turned the dead bolt. She would have used the chain at the top of the door, too, but she didn't want her mom asking any questions when she got home. Reegan walked to the refrigerator, pulled out the orange juice, then poured herself a generous glass. Over the past few hours her throat had started to feel a little scratchy and irritated.

Forcing herself not to think about Seth's threats or the eerie feeling she'd had earlier, she walked into the front room, sat down on the couch, and opened her *World History* book. Not more than five minutes later she heard her mom's car pull into the driveway. She could feel her body instantly relax. She quickly got up and undid the dead bolt, unlocked the door, and swung it open. After she did, she immediately sucked her breath in. Standing in the doorway was a heavily muscled man she'd never seen before. She instantly grabbed ahold of the door in case she needed to slam it shut.

"I'm sorry," the man began, "I didn't mean to scare you."

Reegan gulped down hard as she stared at him. He seemed to take up the whole doorframe. "Can I help you?" she asked, her voice noticeably shaken.

The man smiled down at her, but then his eyes darted to the room behind her. "I'm with the power company. We're just letting the residents know we're working in the area tonight. We've had some power outages. Have you had any problems?"

Reegan shook her head, still tightly clutching the door.

For a moment the man just stood there, his dark blue eyes seemingly going right through her. "Well, sorry to have bothered you. Have a good night." Then without another word, he turned and started down the driveway. Reegan couldn't shut the door fast enough. This time she fastened the chain too.

* * *

Reegan lay in bed that night staring up at the ceiling. Several times she climbed out of bed and made it halfway down the hall to her mother's room, then came right back. She knew that if she told her mom about the stranger and the incident in town earlier, her new job would be over. She also knew that if her mom was concerned enough, it could mean another move. Reegan only had four months left until she graduated. This was the longest that she had ever spent in any town. Right now, more than anything, she wanted to be able to graduate here. *Well, maybe not more than anything,* she thought. Reegan turned over on her side, her gaze falling on a tattered picture of her father propped up on the nightstand by her bed. What she really wanted was to see her father again, to have him in the stands when she stood up on the platform to accept her diploma.

Reegan let out a long, sad sigh. What she wanted and what she could have were two totally different things. There was no telling if her dad was even still alive. Reegan ran her fingers across the picture, then glanced out her window into the night. The stars were still hidden behind the building storm, but the moon had not yet surrendered. It still struggled to break through the clouds. Reegan nodded her head, then smiled down at the picture. Her father was alive. She knew it. How she knew it, she didn't know, but she did. Someday she *would* see him again. Sitting up and fluffing the pillow behind her head, she lay back and closed her eyes, content for now to dream about that day.

* * *

At a little after one thirty in the morning, Reegan sat up with a start. Her heart was pounding so hard that it could have rivaled the drum section of any band. She was breathing heavily and sweating profusely. Her eyes frantically darted around her room as she struggled to regain her bearings. Even once it registered that she was safe in her own room, her heart continued to thunder in her chest. Slowly she turned and looked over at the window. The wind howled as it rattled the thin single-pane glass. Reegan climbed out of bed and walked over to the window, anxious to occupy her thoughts with something other than the nightmares that had plagued her sleep. She pushed the sheer curtains back and looked out into the night. The only light to be seen came from the streetlights that dotted her neighborhood. The moon was now completely hidden behind a thick blanket of darkness. The snow had not yet begun to fall, but the brewing clouds foreshadowed its intensity. This was going to be a big storm. Reegan shuddered, her body damp with perspiration.

"Reegan, are you all right?"

Reegan whirled around. "*Mom?*"

"I'm sorry. I didn't mean to frighten you," she said as she walked over and put her arms around her daughter. Almost immediately she pulled back. "What's the matter? You're soaked."

Reegan shook her head. "It's nothing. I just had a nightmare. What about you? What are you doing up?"

"The storm woke me. Since I was already up, I thought I'd check on you. Are you sure you're okay?" Elizabeth asked, the concern returning to her voice.

"I'm fine, Mom, really."

Elizabeth scowled, apparently not completely convinced. Then her eyes went to the window. "Maybe you should skip school tomorrow and stay home. I don't want your cold getting any worse."

The one thing Reegan did *not* want to do was sit around alone in an empty house all day, especially with the odd events of that evening.

"Mom, I'll be fine. Besides, I've got a big test tomorrow that I can't miss."

"I could take the day off."

"You? Take a day off work?" Reegan clutched at her heart as if faking a heart attack.

"Very funny," her mom shot back. Then she tilted her head, appraising her daughter thoughtfully. "You definitely have your father's sense of humor."

"I'm sorry," Reegan said softly, her face immediately contrite.

"For *what?*"

"I must be like a constant reminder of him."

"The joy of watching you grow up to be like him far outweighs the pain."

Reegan fell into her mother's arms. "I miss him."

"I know," Elizabeth whispered. "I miss him too."

Chapter 8

Blaine stared blankly out the window into the darkness. All the clutter and congestion of the big city had long since melted away. Now, by the light of the moon, he could see only stretches of trees and intermittent farmland with an occasional town or gas station to break up the monotony. Smog and ozone alerts were replaced with wide-open expanses and crisp fresh air, but Blaine was only vaguely aware of any of that. His mind was a million miles away.

"What did you think of your old man?"

Blaine turned to look at the man next to him. Craddick had a cigar clutched in his teeth.

"He's very powerful."

"You don't know the half of it," Craddick said with a touch of pride, as if working for a man like that somehow rubbed off on him.

"You ever going to tell me where we're headed?"

Craddick reached over with his free hand and thumped a map while his other hand remained propped on the steering wheel.

"Some little town called—" Craddick had his double chin stretched out as far as it would go in the direction of the map.

"The road!" Blaine demanded.

Craddick had swerved at least three feet over on the shoulder of the highway, flipping gravel out from under the car. He immediately yanked the steering wheel back in the opposite direction, overcorrecting so much that he almost sideswiped a car coming from the opposite direction. Blaine collapsed back in his seat, his heart pumping blood through his veins in giant surges.

"Scared of a little fender bender?" Craddick teased once he got the car back under control.

"A *little* fender bender?" Blaine blurted out, reaching over and grabbing the map. His eyes immediately went to an area circled in red. "Maplecove?"

"That's it. We should be there within the hour."

"Yeah, if we don't end up as roadkill," Blaine mumbled under his breath. "By the way, how do you know he's headed to Maplecove? We lost him back at that cheap motel."

If Craddick looked smug before, he was the epitome of insolence now. "We just wanted him to think we'd lost him. Some of our men trailed him to an old diner. A little bit of green and the waitress spilled her guts. I guess she overheard Garret mention—uhh—"

"Maplecove?" Blaine finished impatiently.

"Yeah, yeah. Anyway, since they ditched their car, Garret and Schmitt have been hitching rides, which is slowing them down."

"If we know where they're at, then why not take them down now?"

"Your old man rotted in a cell for nine years because of Schmitt's big mouth. He's interested in more than just taking him out."

Blaine wrinkled his forehead. "So what's in Maplecove?"

"Jonathan's wife and kid."

Blaine nodded, understanding only too well. "Revenge."

"It's the name of the game," Craddick said smugly, grinning.

Blaine glanced over at Craddick once the man turned and looked out the window. If this man ever did have a heart, he thought, it had long since shriveled and died.

* * *

Blaine tossed his duffel bag on the bed, then plopped down right next to it. He would have laid back and closed his eyes had he not reeked of cigar smoke. Though his eyelids felt like they were fighting gravity, he dug through his bag and pulled out some clean clothes. Craddick had slipped out, saying that he was going to go check out downtown Pinewood to see if anyone knew Elizabeth or Reegan Richards. Blaine shook his head, guessing that Craddick would end up at the local bar instead.

After ten minutes, Blaine emerged from a steam-filled bathroom feeling like a new person. He had on a warm pair of sweats and a clean white T-shirt. His black hair was slicked back, and he had taken a few extra minutes to shave his three-day-old stubble. He tossed his damp towel over the back of the open bathroom door, sat down on the edge of the bed, and pulled his duffel bag over to him. He reached his hand down to the bottom of it, underneath all his clothes, and pulled out his 9mm Glock. Tossing it over in his hand, he checked the clip. It was fully loaded just as he had left it. Blaine looked over at the door, then quickly slid the gun under his pillow. There was no telling what tomorrow would bring, but one thing was certain—he was going to be ready for it.

It was well past midnight when the door flew open and the light flicked on. Blaine sat straight up in bed, shielding his eyes from the light. He had to fight the urge to draw his gun.

"Blaine," Craddick began, his voice loud and slurred. "I want you to meet my new friends."

Blaine's eyes immediately went to the two men standing next to Craddick. Calling them men might be a stretch, but then again they were probably no more than a few years younger than he was.

"This is Seth and Wayne," Craddick offered, slapping both boys across the shoulders.

Seth nodded his head toward Blaine. Wayne, on the other hand, just stood there sizing him up, though he didn't look like he could have walked a straight line if his life depended on it.

"They know Reegan," Craddick offered with a crooked smirk.

"You been seein' Reegan?" Wayne blurted out, his blood-shot eyes challenging Blaine. "Reegan's *my* girl."

"Yeah, right," Seth guffawed. "She blew you off, man."

Wayne turned to Seth, shoving him hard. Craddick quickly stepped in between the two before it turned to blows.

"Okay, boys, settle down," Craddick said, slapping them amiably on the shoulders like a football coach rallying his team for the big game. "It looks like you're taking your anger out on the wrong person."

"That's right," Seth agreed, eyeballing Wayne.

Although Blaine had never met Reegan Richards, after watching these two, one thing was sure—her choice in friends was not very impressive.

Wayne jerked Craddick's hand off his shoulder, then he turned to Seth. "I'm out of here."

He turned and stalked to the door, but just before opening it, he turned back to Blaine. "You stay away from Reegan. You hear me?"

Blaine held up his hands feigning innocence. "Hey, she's all yours." Then as soon as the door slammed, he turned and smiled at Seth. "Looks like your friend's got a nasty temper."

Seth shook his head in disgust. "That girl's twisted his mind, got him acting like some wounded pup."

"But not you?" Craddick asked quickly.

Seth snorted in derision. Then he stopped, his eyes suddenly wary. "Hey, you guys never did say how you know Reegan. Is she some friend of yours or somethin'?"

Craddick pulled a cigar from his pocket, lit it, and looked at Blaine. "She a friend of yours?"

"No friend of mine," Blaine said, his voice impassive.

Craddick lifted his gaze to Seth, his lips pulling into a menacing grin. "Looks like Reegan Richards doesn't have a lot of friends around here."

Seth's face broke into a crooked grin.

"We would be real grateful if you could tell us where we could find her though," Blaine said, keeping his face expressionless.

"*How* grateful?" Seth asked, the greed in his eyes instantly flashing.

Craddick laughed. "I think I know your language, son." He reached into his coat pocket and pulled out his wallet. "This grateful," Craddick announced holding up the money. Seth reached out to snatch the bills, but Craddick just smiled and pulled them back. "Slow down, boy. You haven't told me anything yet."

Seth pulled back, trying to downplay his eagerness.

"She lives in Maplecove."

"We already know that," Craddick snapped.

"She works at Mike's Grocery," Seth continued. "She should be there tomorrow morning. I think the store opens at eight thirty on Saturdays."

"Tell you what," Craddick began, reaching back into his wallet and pulling out several more bills. "If you keep your mouth shut about all of this, including not telling your buddy, I'll double my first offer."

"How do I know that once you find her you'll keep your word?" Seth asked warily.

"Hey, if you don't want my money…" Craddick said flatly, tucking his wallet back into his coat.

Seth reached out and grabbed his wrist. "No, no. I'll do it."

Craddick smiled. "Looks like this is settled then. Tomorrow morning we'll give Reegan Richards a surprise she'll never forget."

* * *

"What about the boys? They know what we look like now. They could go to the cops once this whole thing goes down."

"What boys?" Craddick asked innocently, that all-too-familiar grin flashing across his lips.

Blaine looked at Craddick hard. This whole thing was like a giant spider web. Everyone that got caught in the web was food for the spider.

"So, what's the plan?" Blaine asked hesitantly.

"Tomorrow you're going into Mike's Grocery to persuade Miss Richards into taking a walk."

"And just how am I going to do that?"

"You're a good-looking kid. You figure it out. Now get some sleep," Craddick said as he kicked off his shoes.

"What if Jonathan and Garret get here before we get her?"

"They won't. They're still trying to play it safe, taking their time, thinking we might be following them."

"It's taken you years to find Jonathan Schmitt, but suddenly you're on him like glue. What's the deal?"

"You ask too many questions," Craddick barked, apparently not appreciating the reminder of his past failures. "Get some sleep. You're gonna need it."

Blaine lay in bed, though sleep was the last thing on his mind. Craddick was in the double bed next to his, lifting the rafters with all his snoring. He had passed out not ten minutes after Seth had left. Blaine's stomach began to turn. Seth and Wayne were not exactly model citizens, but he didn't like the idea of them getting entangled in all of this. Blaine turned over on his side. His stomach had been cramping for at least thirty minutes. He would have blamed it on something he ate, but he knew that wasn't it. His life was about to do a one-eighty tomorrow, and after that, there was no going back.

Blaine glanced over at the window. He could hear the wind building momentum outside. The temperature had also dropped significantly. Though it had not yet begun to snow, it was only a matter of time before the heavy clouds released their burden. Blaine shook his head. If things continued in the direction that they were going, tomorrow promised to be treacherous in more ways than one.

chapter 9

Reegan watched as her breath puffed into tiny white clouds in the early-morning air as she made her way toward Mike's Grocery. Despite the sore throat that she had awakened with, she felt like whistling, something she rarely did. Having severed her relationship with Maplecove's so-called *in crowd* brought a measure of relief that Reegan had not expected, but amply welcomed. Seth's implied warning after their altercation the previous night still bothered her, but she was trying to push any thought of that out of her mind. She had just crossed over onto Main Street when she came to an abrupt stop, surprised to see Tera, Seth, and Wayne standing on the porch of Mike's Grocery. Reegan let out a long sigh then took a deep breath and quickly walked the rest of the way to the store.

Reegan expected them to say something as she climbed up on the porch, but no one said a word. Tera glared at her, obviously still mad about being brushed off Thursday night. Wayne showed the effects of a long night of drinking. His face also showed emotions. Anger was clearly there, but this morning it seemed to be tempered by rejection. Seth, who was rarely seen around town on a Saturday morning before noon, was grinning from ear to ear, something in his eyes leaving her instantly chilled. Reegan quickly forced her eyes away and pushed open the door. Mike was at the counter. She could tell at a glance that he had been watching the whole thing from the window. Not that there had been much to see. It was all kind of weird.

"Hi, Mike," Reegan said, forcing her voice to sound cheerful.

"Hi, yourself, young lady. Do you like chocolate-chip cookies? My wife thought you might need a batch, with it being your first week of work and all."

Reegan smiled. Apparently Mike and his wife were cut from the same mold. "Thanks, but maybe later. I'm not very hungry."

Mike glanced out the window at the three who were still planted on the porch despite the freezing weather. Then he turned to Reegan with a warm smile. "Well, come on over here, then, and I'll show you how to run this old thing."

Reegan hung her coat on the rack by the door and walked over to the cash register. *Old thing* was right. The cash register looked like a relic from the past that might be found hidden in the dust of an antique shop. According to Mike, it had been in his family since the little store was built back in the forties. Actually running it was not all that complicated, but Mike still took a solid ten minutes explaining everything. He looked like a little kid showing off his most prized possession. When he was finally done, he turned it over to her, snagged a couple of cookies, and headed to the back room to finish his inventory.

Reegan walked over to the shelves and began straightening them. She had only tidied the top shelf of a food rack when the little bell on the door rang. She turned around half expecting it to be Wayne, but instead a complete stranger stood in the doorway. He was tall and lean, but broad through the shoulders, which was clearly evident even through his coat. His jet-black hair was slicked back, which to Reegan was a complete fashion don't, but the rest of him made up for that one slight imperfection.

"Hi," Reegan said, forcing her face to remain impassive, though that was almost impossible.

He stepped inside and closed the door behind him, shutting the bitter wind out. His eyes quickly searched the whole store until they finally came to rest on her. He gave her a quick once-over, then stepped to a display of hardware goods without a word. The first good-looking guy Reegan had seen in *forever,* and he came equipped with absolutely no manners. Reegan rolled her eyes. That was it! Once she graduated, she was *so* out of here.

"Reegan, do you need any help?" Mike asked as he poked his head from around the back door.

The stranger immediately lifted his head and looked over at her.

"No," Reegan called back. "I've got it."

The young man continued to stare at Reegan for a moment, then finally his face broke into a smile.

"You work here?"

Reegan went to point at her green vest before she realized that she had forgotten to put it on. Instead she looked over at him and nodded.

The stranger shrugged. "I guess I just didn't expect—I mean—you're—" He stopped and shot a glance out the window. "Do you know anything about spark plugs?"

Reegan crinkled her forehead. "Do I *look* like I know anything about spark plugs?"

"Honestly?" he asked, raising his brow.

Reegan could feel her pulse quicken as he walked over to her. He smelled wonderful. Of course, with his face, he could have smelled like dirt, and she would have thought the same thing. Without a word, he reached down and took her hand. Despite her initial assessment of him, Reegan could feel her knees grow weak.

"I don't see any grease under your fingernails, so I'd have to guess no."

"Huh?" Reegan asked, forgetting the original question.

He wrinkled his forehead. "The spark plugs."

"Oh, yeah," Reegan said, finally snapping out of it and pulling her hand away. "Well, you'd be wrong then. I do know a thing or two about spark plugs."

"Like what?" he asked with a smug smile.

"Like—well—they spark," she said lamely.

His face lit into a smile, and Reegan found herself smiling right along with him.

"Let me go get Mr. Burgess," Reegan began. "He knows everything about everything in this store. He'll be able to help you."

"No, no. That's okay," he said quickly. "I'm really not all that interested in buying spark plugs. I would be interested in getting to know the store clerk though. My car broke down a few miles down the road, but I've already called a tow truck. How about joining me for a cup of—"

Though flattered beyond words, Reegan began to shake her head. "I don't even know you," she said bluntly. "Besides, I can't. I have to work."

"Reegan?"

They both turned toward the back room. Mike was pulling on his green vest and walking toward them. "I think it's about time for your break."

Mike extended his hand to the young man next to Reegan. "Mike Burgess."

"Nice to meet you, Mr. Burgess. I'm Tony," Blaine offered with a smile.

"My break?" Reegan interrupted. "But I just got here."

Mike looked shocked. "Federal regulation 224, code three, amendment 29: All hard-working employees must receive a ten-minute break at their boss's discretion. Especially if they volunteer to help out with all this inventory afterwards," Mike quickly added, gesturing toward the stack of boxes in the back room.

"You wouldn't want your boss to be in violation with federal law now, would you?" Blaine pressed.

Mike laughed. "That's right." Then he turned and headed to the back room. "There's some hot chocolate and coffee over on the counter," he called back over his shoulder. "Help yourselves."

Reegan hesitantly walked over and picked up one of the Styrofoam cups. She felt a little awkward. She wasn't in the habit of talking with strangers. Living in a spit-and-you'll-miss-it small town didn't allow for much of a social life.

"Would you like a cup of coffee?" Reegan asked nervously.

"Actually, I'm more of a hot-chocolate man."

"That makes two of us," Reegan began. "Well, except for the *man* part."

"You didn't have to tell me that."

Reegan almost spilled the hot chocolate she was pouring.

"Let me help you," Blaine said as he reached over and took the cup.

"Thank you," she said, very aware of how close he was.

Reegan watched as he shot an uncomfortable glance toward the back room. "Why don't we go outside for a minute?" he said.

Reegan looked at him incredulously, then gestured with her head toward the frosted windows. "If we sit out there, our frozen bodies will be stuck there till sometime next spring."

Blaine, who was taking a sip from his steaming cup, paused to laugh, almost spilling some of the frothy liquid. "I take it you have no aspirations of becoming an ice sculpture."

Reegan laughed. "None."

After a couple of minutes of small talk, Blaine lifted his arm to glance down at his watch. Then, with a disappointed sigh, set his cup on the counter and turned to Reegan. "I guess I better go and see if the tow truck found my car."

Reegan had to force a smile. "I probably better get back to work."

"Maybe the next time I'm passing through we could have lunch or something."

"Like you'll ever just *happen* to be back in Maplecove, North Dakota, population 804—plus or minus the livestock."

"I'll make the effort," Blaine said boldly. Then he held up two fingers like a dutiful Scout. "Scout's honor."

Reegan couldn't quite picture him in a Scout uniform helping old ladies cross the street, but his pouting lips and dark eyes were completely irresistible.

"Okay, if you ever make it back to Maplecove, you know where to find me."

Blaine reached for Reegan's hand, then shook it firmly as if sealing a deal. "It's a date."

* * *

Though the snow had temporarily stopped, an icy blast hit Reegan square in the face as soon as she stepped out onto the porch of the small grocery mart. The shock of the bitter temperatures took her breath away. As she quickly pulled her scarf up around her face, a tight cough was ripped from her chest. From the burning in her lungs, it was obvious that the cold that had pestered her all day had settled in for an extended stay. Reegan shoved her hands into her pockets, then took a quick look around. The street in front of her was barren. Though it was only two in the afternoon, the sun was completely hidden—the culprit a mass of thick, dark snow clouds. The only good thing about the frigid weather was that it looked like Tera, Seth, and Wayne had finally gone home. Reegan shook her head, pushing any thought of them away. Despite the aching in her chest and the soreness in her throat, she found her mind floating back to Tony. Someone who could turn heads with his looks and still hold a decent conversation once he opened his mouth was a rarity around these parts. Add to that wit, charm, and a smile that could make your knees grow weak, and that was a man as close to perfection as it got. Reegan found herself smiling as she thought about their encounter just a few hours ago. Somewhere in the chilly gusts she could almost smell the scent of his cologne.

Reegan had barely stepped off the porch, out of the view of the shop window, when she heard a sound down the alley. She shot a glance down the side street fully expecting to see the three vultures who always seemed to be circling, but to her surprise, the narrow alley looked empty. For a moment she just stood there searching the shadows for the source of the sound. Instead of feeling relief that there was nobody there, an uneasiness fell over her like a dark shroud. She shrugged her shoulders to shake off the feeling, knowing that she was probably just being paranoid, but the uneasiness continued with her. She quickly turned and started toward home, adrenaline surging with each step. Three feet past the entrance to the alley, someone grabbed her from behind. Reegan tried to jerk around to see who it was, but they had her locked in a viselike grip. Before she could even scream, a hand covered her mouth and a bitter smell assaulted her nostrils. Within seconds everything in her world went black.

* * *

Reegan's eyes were so heavy they felt like they had cinder blocks taped to them. She struggled to force them open, but once she did, everything was blurred. Voices floated around in the air, though none of them seemed to make sense. Reegan fought to pull her mind back to reality, but it was like fighting an upstream current. She could tell that she was in the backseat of a car, but she had no idea whose car it was or how she had gotten in it. She struggled to lift her head up, but just moving made her stomach knot. For a moment she thought she might be sick.

"She's awake," a man's voice rumbled.

The voice was vaguely familiar, though Reegan couldn't place it. Slowly she turned her head to look at the person sitting next to her. In an instant her heart began to beat so hard that she could literally feel it pounding against the walls of her chest.

"*You?*" she whispered, her voice tight with fear.

The man in the front seat laughed, then glanced at the man sitting next to Reegan. "Let me formally introduce you to Blaine Sabatini."

Blaine glanced at her, then quickly looked away. "Now what?" he asked the driver.

The man stole a look over his shoulder at Blaine. He seemed to be in his mid-forties, with a round face and a thick neck, but it was his eyes that immediately caught Reegan's attention. They seemed to devour her in one glance, instantly chilling her more thoroughly than the bitter wind ever could.

"Now we get Jon's wife," he said matter-of-factly.

Reegan felt sick. These men were after her family.

"Leave my mom alone," Reegan cried. "My dad isn't here."

"No, but he will be," the man in the front seat said as he broke into a menacing grin. "And we're going to be here waiting for him. Isn't that right, kid?"

"That's right," Blaine agreed coldly.

Reegan could feel her whole body begin to shake. She had to get out of there and warn her mother. She glanced down at her hands. They were tightly tied together at the wrists. Her eyes quickly shot to the door next to her, but, as if he could read her mind, Blaine reached across her and locked the door. Not that it would have mattered anyway. What was she going to do, open the door with her teeth, then stagger through town half drugged with a couple of maniacs right behind her?

"Just sit there and be quiet," Blaine warned. "Then, when this is all over, you can go home."

Reegan could hear the man in the front seat begin to laugh. "We'll send you home all right."

In a body bag, Reegan thought, guessing his meaning. An angry retort came to mind, but she bit her tongue. Antagonizing them was probably not her best option. Right now they needed her, but once they had her dad, she was expendable and she knew it.

"Craddick," Blaine began, "maybe we should take her back to the motel before we get the woman."

Craddick shook his head as he turned the steering wheel toward Reegan's neighborhood. "No. She'll come more willingly if she sees what's at stake."

They were right. Her mom wouldn't hesitate to go with them once she saw that they had Reegan in the backseat.

Reegan felt like a pawn in some twisted game; she had to get out of there before they got to her mom—it was the only way to save her.

Reegan glanced over at Blaine. He had his head turned toward the window. He seemed to be focusing on the storm. The clouds had finally succumbed to their heavy load. Giant flakes were falling from the sky, covering everything in sight with a thick blanket of white. Craddick slowed the car because of the poor visibility and because the windows were starting to fog. He wiped at the front window with his coat sleeve, providing himself a little gap to peer through. With both men distracted by the storm, Reegan slowly sat up in her seat, immediately recognizing the scenery around them. Her heart began to race as a sketchy plan, desperate at best, began to form in her mind. With the blinding snow and her knowledge of the area, maybe she could lose them in the storm. That miniscule sliver of hope seemed to instantly strengthen her resolve. Though her head was still pounding, the fog of confusion was quickly lifting. If she was going to escape, she was going to have to act now.

In a pitch that she had never before hit, Reegan screamed with all she had. The effect was perfect. Blaine's head shot around just in time to meet with Reegan's fists. Tied together or not, they hit him square in the face. Blaine immediately cried out in pain, then reached up and grabbed his nose. Craddick's reaction was no less immediate. He hit the breaks, causing their car to fishtail over the newly fallen snow. Blaine's attention now focused forward as he shouted at Craddick to be careful. Reegan groped for the door lock with her fingers. It took two tries, but she finally got it. Before Blaine noticed what she was doing, Reegan threw the door open. She closed her eyes, took a deep breath, and jumped.

Hitting the pavement with a thud, she rolled several times. The impact knocked the wind out of her, but her thick coat and the snow on the pavement saved her skin from being ripped to shreds. When she finally came to a stop, she staggered to her feet. If she was injured, there was too much adrenaline pumping through her to feel it. As she started toward the closest house, her feet slipped out from under her. With her hands tied together, she could do little to break her fall, her jaw taking the brunt of the blow. When she finally got up, she could taste blood in her mouth. Glancing over her shoulder, she saw Blaine jumping out of the car. He was only a hundred feet from her. For a moment, Reegan just stared at him, too petrified to move. Then her instincts seemed to take over. Her eyes quickly scanned the area around her. The house was too far away; she had to hide quickly. Behind her neighborhood were about eighty acres of thick virgin forest. Though running through it would be treacherous, there would be plenty of places to hide.

Reegan ran to the thick stand of trees. She had explored these woods enough to know that there was a stream that ran right through the middle of it. On more than one occasion she had sat next to the creek on a hot summer afternoon and dangled her feet in the cool water. Now that same water promised to be dotted with patches of ice. She prayed she wouldn't have to wade through it. Maybe Blaine would lose her in the storm and stop looking, but something told her that wasn't going to happen.

Forcing those thoughts from her mind, she plunged headlong into the front line of trees. On the other side of these woods was the little dirt road that led to the Graham farm. If she could make it through the woods without being followed, she would be able to hole up there for a while until she figured out what to do. Reegan could hear a tree limb snap somewhere behind her. Blaine was following her into the woods. Reegan ran faster, though she knew that if she tripped and fell, Blaine would be on her in seconds. Continuing to go deeper into the woods, she ran as fast as she could until her lungs burned for oxygen and her legs throbbed with pain. She jumped over fallen trees and side-stepped large rocks, struggling to keep her balance with her hands tied together and her head still slightly foggy from whatever drug they had used to knock her out. Several bare tree limbs tore at her skin and snagged her clothing.

Reegan knew that she would not be able to keep up this pace much longer. The adrenaline that had surged through her when she'd leapt from the moving car was starting to wear off now, and her whole body was feeling the effect of the beating it was taking. Maybe she could use the storm to her advantage. Though the snow was coming down so hard that she could barely see two feet in front of her, there were still small patches of exposed ground, sheltered by the enormous elm trees towering above. Desperate not to leave an obvious trail, Reegan stepped on the dirt patches as she looked for a place to hide.

A thick entanglement of brush stood just to the left of her. Without giving it a second thought, Reegan dove under the dormant shrubbery. She tucked her feet up next to her, trying to hold herself in a tight fetal position, and held her breath. Blaine couldn't be more than a couple hundred feet behind her, if that. Reegan looked down, her eyes going to several drops of red blood in the fresh powder. The bright red spots stood out like a large neon sign against the white snow. Reegan reached up and wiped at her face. There was at least a two-inch gash on her chin that was still dripping with blood. Reegan's breath caught. Even if he couldn't see her tracks in the snow, he would easily follow the trail of blood right to her. She had to get out from under the bush. Just as she was about to spring to her feet, a boot brushed up against the snow covered bush she was hiding under. It was too late. He was already to her. Her whole body trembling with fear, Reegan quickly looked around, searching for something, *anything,* she could use to protect herself. Spotting a large stick half hidden in the snow, Reegan grabbed for it with her bound hands and jumped to her feet all in one motion. She closed her eyes and swung with all she had at the man in front of her. The stick connected, followed immediately by a thud. When she opened her eyes, Blaine was crumpled in the snow face-first. Reegan felt sick as she stared down at his motionless body. A small part of her wanted to reach down and feel for a pulse, but a bigger part told her to run. Throwing the stick to the ground, she ran toward the creek, thinking only of the Graham farm that lay just through the woods on the other side. Once there, she could follow the dirt road back to town to get help.

Minutes later, Reegan watched as the falling snow hit the creek, then melted into the freezing water. Little pieces of crystallized snow floated on the top of the creek, while bigger chunks of ice lined the embankment. The little creek was nothing substantial, twelve feet wide and three to four feet deep near the middle, but with temperatures like this, it stopped Reegan cold. She listened to the water bubbling and churning as it passed over rocks and rotting tree limbs while her eyes ran the length of the creek searching for a better way around. When there wasn't one, she took a deep breath and stepped into the creek. The pain was immediate. It felt like she had stepped into the blue flame of a welder's torch. She bit down on her lip, forcing herself to move deeper into the creek. Before it was all over, she would be waist-deep in temperatures cold enough to turn moving water into ice.

The current wasn't very strong, but Reegan's legs were quickly going numb, and she was having a hard time keeping her balance. Near the middle, the water was so cold that she found herself gasping for breath. She staggered forward, her eyes locked on the bank and her steps deliberate so she wouldn't slip on the smooth rocks that made up the bottom of the creek. One false move, with her hands bound, and she would slip beneath the surface of the freezing water. Reegan could feel her whole body shudder with the thought. If she didn't make it across and they caught her, she would not be able to get help for her mother.

Though her legs and feet were almost completely numb, she forged forward with renewed determination. Then, just three steps from the incline of the embankment, Reegan heard the snap of a tree branch. As she whirled around, her eyes searching the woods behind her, she slipped on a patch of mud and silt in between the smooth rocks beneath her feet. She went down. The freezing water that enveloped her stifled the cry of panic that was ripped from her chest. With pain shooting through her body in a measure that she had never before experienced, she screamed under the water, sucking the icy liquid into her burning lungs. With limbs flailing, frantically attempting to escape the water's grasp, she finally broke through the surface and gasped for air.

Pain pricked her entire body like a thousand sharp needles as she struggled to her feet, staggered up the bank, and collapsed onto the cold, wet ground. Her strength was depleted. She could feel all the blood draining from her face as she struggled to remain conscious. Just before she surrendered consciousness, a hand reached down and turned her over. She lay in a wet and muddy heap staring up at the figure before her. The man's chest was rising and falling, his torso wet and muddy, but Reegan's eyes seemed drawn to the stream of blood slowly trickling down his forehead.

Chapter 10

Reegan's eyes snapped open as soon as she heard his voice, her body immediately tingling with fear. Though she lay perfectly still, her eyes quickly darted to the figure across the room. She could feel her breathing quicken, though she fought to control it. Blaine was standing at a window with his hand on the curtain, parting it just enough that he could peek outside. He was speaking quietly into a cell phone, but Reegan couldn't hear what he was saying. Forcing herself to remain calm, she slowly glanced around the motel room. There were two double beds, a well-worn dresser, and a small bathroom. The bathroom door was partially open and, from what she could see, no one was in there. The thought of being alone in a motel room with this man made her sick to her stomach, but at least the other man wasn't there.

"I've got to go. She's awake," Blaine whispered into the phone.

Reegan's whole body began to shake, or maybe it had been shaking all along and she was only now noticing it. Her eyes immediately shot to Blaine, then held him as he crossed the room heading toward the door. She could feel her body recoil at just the sight of him, repulsed by the very qualities that before had attracted her.

"What are you going to do to me?" Reegan whispered, not sure she really wanted to know.

For a minute their eyes locked. Reegan almost looked away under the intensity of his gaze, but more than anything, she needed to see his reaction.

"You're going to need something to drink to fight off your fever," Blaine offered shortly.

Reegan was only vaguely aware of the heat coming from her body.

"Why, if you're just going to kill me?" The words came out of her mouth before she could stop them.

Blaine continued to watch her, his eyes dark and emotionless. Finally he turned and opened the door. Reegan struggled to control her breathing as she watched the door close behind him. Once he was gone, she turned her attention back to the room. On the dresser across from her bed was a television, and next to it was a telephone. Reegan's eyes locked on the phone. That was it, her way out of all of this. She sat up and swung her legs over the side of the bed. With legs that felt like jelly, she started across the floor. She'd only made it halfway across the room when the door swung open and her captors entered. She froze.

"Where do you think you're going?" Craddick taunted as he closed the door.

Reegan could feel her already unsteady legs begin to tremble. "I was just . . ."Craddick looked over at the phone and smiled menacingly. Reegan's heart jumped into her throat as she watched him calmly walk over and pick up the receiver. Triumphantly, he held it up for her to see. The cord had been cut.

"You're not dealing with a couple of country bumpkins, girlie," Craddick began as he slowly walked toward her. "We know exactly what we're doing." He was within inches of her now. Reegan could feel her stomach knot. Craddick reached his hand out and gently touched her cheek with the back of his hand. Then, from out of nowhere, he reared back to strike her. Blaine jumped forward and grabbed his wrist.

"Leave her alone," Blaine threatened, his voice like ice.

Craddick looked almost as surprised by Blaine's reaction as Reegan. "Listen here, boy," Craddick snapped, yanking his hand free. "I don't care who your daddy is. On the road we do things *my* way."

Blaine's eyes flashed, but then, almost as an afterthought, he shrugged his shoulders in surrender. "Okay, do it your way."

Reegan stared at the two of them in horror.

"You'll just have to explain to Antonio why she's roughed up," Blaine added calmly. "Personally, I thought he made it quite clear that he plans to handle this one himself."

Reegan could tell that Blaine had hit a cord. Craddick's eyes were blazing, but under his facade, she could almost see him squirm. Someone who could make Craddick squirm was definitely not someone Reegan wanted to meet. Craddick turned and gave her a once-over.

"Sure you're not just goin' soft for a pretty face?" Craddick asked, his voice as cold as the storm outside their door.

"This job is my chance to prove myself," Blaine said tightly. "Do what you want with her when this is over, but until then, keep your hands off." Then Blaine's eyes narrowed and his jaw flexed. "Otherwise you'll be answering to more than just Antonio."

Craddick's eyes blazed. "I won't have a punk kid threatenin' me."

Before either man could say another word, several sharp knocks came from the other side of the door. Craddick glanced down at his watch, his lips instantly broadening into a wicked grin.

"Looks like you're about to get that chance to prove yourself," Craddick stated sarcastically.

Blaine started toward the door as Craddick grabbed Reegan hard by the arm and pushed her toward the bathroom.

"I told Seth to bring his friend along, too," Craddick said, his voice hushed. "Take care of both of them."

"Seth and Wayne . . . They're a part of this?" Reegan breathed in disbelief, her eyes wide and her stomach twisting in revulsion.

Craddick's lips twisted into an evil smirk as he shoved her into the bathroom.

Reegan wanted to scream, but the look in his eyes sealed her mouth tighter than tape ever could. Then he shut the door, leaving her alone in the small room, her body trembling. She pushed her ear up to the door, straining to hear the conversation on the other side. Though it was muffled, she could hear Craddick greeting Seth and Wayne like soldiers returning from a victorious battle. Seth sucked it up with unabashed arrogance, asking several times if there was anything else Craddick needed help with. Reegan shuddered to think what else Seth would be willing to do for a price. Once the money was exchanged, Craddick escorted the two of them to the door. The door was barely shut behind them when Craddick's voice lowered somewhat.

"Take care of them. And don't leave any evidence behind." Then his tone became as sharp as a razor blade. "But remember, if you fail, it won't make any difference that Sabatini's your old man."

As the door opened and shut again, Reegan slumped to the floor, tears coursing unrestrained down her cheeks. Her body felt numb, her limbs unmoving, and her mind frozen as the shock of the situation completely enveloped her.

There was nothing she could do to help Seth and Wayne now. In a few minutes they would be left to the mercy of a man depraved enough to take life just to prove himself. Reegan could feel a wracking sob released from somewhere deep within her; with a knowledge as dependable as the sun's rising each morning, she knew that her mother would be next.

* * *

Reegan sat on the bathroom floor for the next twenty minutes, the last of her tears exhausted. When Blaine first left, her mind had been so consumed with what he was about to do to Seth and Wayne that she didn't contemplate what Craddick would do to her. Now her mind could think of nothing else. Her eyes raced around the room searching desperately for something with which to defend herself. Other than a tub with a mildew ring midway up, a sink with a leaky faucet, and a rack on the wall behind the toilet that held a scanty stack of dingy towels, there was little else in the room. Reegan's eyes then rested on a plastic trash can next to the toilet. She crawled over and pulled it into her arms, then fell back in despair. Her effort only revealed that it was the one thing in the room that the maid *had* cleaned. Discouraged to the point of exhaustion, she set it back down. As she did, something behind the toilet caught her eye. A small piece of broken glass from a bottle or tumbler had been tossed halfheartedly toward the garbage. It now sat behind the toilet obscured from view. Reegan quickly picked it up, her heart racing as she did, but before she could stuff it into the pocket of her jeans, someone began to pound on the bathroom door.

"Get out of there," Craddick barked.

With her hands instantly shaking so violently she almost dropped it, Reegan placed the glass into her pocket and stood. When she opened the door, Craddick was already across the room, pulling his coat over the pistol that was strapped to his chest.

"As soon as Blaine gets back, we're going for a little drive," he said, shoving a second clip into his coat pocket.

They both turned as the door flew open. Blaine stood in the doorway, the wind swirling snow around him like a miniature tornado. He quickly stepped inside and closed the door behind him.

"Well?" Craddick asked, his voice raised in mockery.

Blaine brushed the snow from his coat, unbuttoned it, and slowly took it off. Reegan sucked her breath in as she stared at him in horror. Bright red drops of blood streaked his white T-shirt. Reegan could feel the blood drain from her face. For a minute she thought she might faint, but the fear that was surging through her wouldn't allow it. Blaine didn't even look at her, instead his gaze fell on Craddick.

"It's done," he said, his voice holding no remorse.

"You killed them?" she mumbled, her voice no more than a whisper.

Craddick looked at Blaine for several seconds, the smirk on his face revealing his approval. "I guess you've got more of your old man in you than I gave you credit for."

Reegan could feel her fear instantly turn to rage. "You monster!" she screamed.

Craddick turned to her, his eyes flashing a deadly warning. "Scream again, and it'll be the last sound you ever make."

Reegan was still delirious with rage, but she had no doubt that Craddick would make good on his threat. There would be a time for justice, something inside warned her, but this was not the time.

"Get yourself cleaned up," Blaine snapped, motioning Reegan toward the bathroom. "I put some dry clothes over on that chair for you."

Reegan glanced over at a neat pile of clothes placed on a chair by the bathroom door.

"We don't have time for that," Craddick barked.

"I've got to change anyway. I'm not going anywhere with this splashed across my chest," Blaine countered, gesturing toward the blood. "And look at her. Do you really want to take the chance of someone seeing her like that?"

"All right," Craddick grudgingly relented, "but make it quick. I talked to Sabatini when you were gone. He said Jonathan should be here any minute." Craddick turned to Reegan. "What are you waiting for?" he barked. "*Move!*"

Reegan lifted her hands to show that they were still tightly bound together.

Blaine walked quickly to her, pulling a switchblade from his pocket. Reegan stood her ground, her eyes filled with hate. Blaine cut the rope with one clean swipe of the lethally sharp blade. Then he grabbed her arm, his eyes holding her more firmly than his grip.

"Don't try anything stupid."

She glared at him, though she didn't say a word. Blaine finally released his grip and waved her toward the bathroom.

Once Reegan shut the door, she had to steady herself against the counter. Anger tinged with fear was surging through her in waves, each swell peaking higher than the last. She quickly set the clothing down on the edge of the tub, took a deep breath, and glanced down at the raw skin around her wrists. Gingerly, she began to massage life back into them. Once she was done, she lifted her eyes to the mirror. She almost did a double take at her appearance. A stream of dried blood from the two-inch gash across her jawline ran under her chin and down her neck. Her face was flaming red with fever, and she had a semicircle of mascara under each eye. Reegan reached down and turned on the faucet. She cupped her hands together, allowing the water to overflow in her hands. Then, using her fingers as a cup, she drank the cold water in several greedy gulps. When she finally came up for air, she splashed the remaining water on her face. Though it made her chin sting, it felt wonderful on her hot cheeks.

After drying her face on a towel, she glanced over at the pile of clothes. She quickly changed from her damp clothing into Blaine's dry ones. Though his clothing felt baggy on her, she was grateful for something warm to wear.

"Hey, get out of there."

Reegan turned to stare at the bathroom door as Craddick pounded on the other side. As her heart instantly began to race, matching his pounding beat for beat, she instantly remembered the shard of glass still in the pocket of the damp jeans discarded on the floor. With trembling hands, she quickly retrieved it, tucking it safely into her pocket. Then, with a deep breath to steady herself, she slowly opened the door.

"Come on," Craddick began, grabbing her hands and callously retying the ropes over her open sores. "It's time to dangle some bait in front of your old man."

Chapter 11

"What about the woman?" Blaine asked as he handed Craddick the note.

"There's no time for that now," Craddick said, shooting a sharp glance back at Reegan.

Reegan could feel her whole body flood with relief. She may not have succeeded in getting away from them, but her flight through the woods had stalled them just enough to save her mom.

"Jonathan will be here any minute," Craddick growled. "I'd love to stick around and take care of him myself, but Antonio wants him in one piece."

The euphoria that had surged through Reegan's body was instantly severed. She watched helplessly as Craddick got out of the car and walked toward the thick stand of forest leading to her own backyard. She looked down at her hands, which were bound tight. This time Craddick had also tied her feet and taped her mouth shut. They were taking no chances. She had already struck one powerful blow to their perfect plan; they were not about to give her another opportunity.

To Reegan's complete horror, as soon as Craddick disappeared into the woods, Blaine opened the passenger door and climbed out. He quickly opened the back door and climbed in next to her. Reegan's heart was racing. She tried to scoot as far away from him as possible, but there was nowhere to go. She was trapped. Her eyes filled with terror and revulsion as she watched him reach for her hands. Then with one quick swipe from his knife, he removed the rope. Reegan instantly reached up to gouge his eyes, but he caught her by both wrists. From the look on his face, Reegan could see that she had caught him off guard.

"Just calm down. I'm not going to hurt you," he said, slowly releasing his grip.

Reegan glared at him with utter contempt, though her body was trembling so fiercely she could barely control it. She had seen the fresh stains splattered on his shirt. Now he was telling her to calm down—that he wasn't going to hurt her! Reegan would sooner be thrown in a tank of man-eating sharks.

"I'll get some ointment or something to go on your wrists tonight," Blaine said as he pulled a second rope from his pocket. He shot a quick glance out the window before retying the second rope around her tender wrists. He tied the rope firm enough that she couldn't slide it off, but loose enough that it didn't dig into her flesh as the last one had. When he was done, he slowly pulled the tape from off her mouth.

"Why are you helping me?" she asked, her eyes searching his.

"Look, I'm not . . . like him," he said.

"No, you're just the parasite that feeds off people like him," Reegan snapped.

A look flashed across Blaine's face, but Reegan couldn't read it.

"That mouth of yours is going to get you in trouble," Blaine said, his voice suddenly sharp. "You better watch out for Craddick. He'll kill you in the end, but he'd just as soon knock you around in the meantime."

"Oh, so you're okay with the end result. You just don't want all the extras on what little conscience you do have," Reegan spat out sarcastically.

Blaine reached out and grabbed Reegan's arms. His face was within inches of hers. His jaw was tight, and his eyes blazed like a hot August sun.

"Stay away from him. Do you hear me?"

Reegan swallowed hard, then bobbed her head, her throat too tight to speak. Blaine glanced down at his hands. He almost looked a little surprised at his own intensity. Then his face relaxed along with his grip.

"Just stay away from him."

Reegan nodded, the anger inside her finally giving way to fear. She watched anxiously as Blaine reached into his coat pocket and withdrew a bottle of water.

"Hurry up," he said, as he held the water to her lips.

Reegan didn't question him this time. Her body was hot with fever, and without water to cool it, she would soon be in serious trouble. She drank the water in several quick gulps, some trickling down her face. When she was done, Blaine shoved the empty bottle back into his pocket, then reached out to put the tape back on her mouth. Reegan glared at him. He might have given her a little water and loosened her ropes, but she wouldn't forget what he had done to Wayne and Seth. Blaine gave her one last look, then climbed out of the car and opened the front door.

For the next ten minutes, with Blaine back in the front seat, Reegan's mind raced through every minute chance of escape she had. When Craddick finally climbed back into the car, brushing snow from his coat, his round cheeks flushed from the bitter wind, Reegan was no closer to a plan than when he had left.

"Let's get out of here," Craddick said. He reached over to crank up the heater, then glanced back at her. "Now we get to see if Jonathan cares more about his little girl than his own sorry hide." With that, he put the car in drive and pulled away.

* * *

Jonathan thought that he would have felt elated the closer he got to Maplecove and his family, but once he spotted the wooden city sign, half buried in the snow, his shoulders slumped.

"Maybe this isn't such a good idea," he mumbled.

"What?" Garret exclaimed, glancing over at his friend in shock. "You're not backing out now, are you?"

Jonathan looked back out the window, letting his breath out hard. "What am I thinking, coming back? Haven't I already messed up their lives enough?"

"Whoa, wait a minute. Last I checked it was Antonio Sabatini who caused all this, not you. You've done everything in your power to protect your family."

"Until now," Jonathan said stubbornly. "I could be leading that pack of murderers right to them."

Garret looked in the rearview mirror at the empty street behind them. "Do you see anyone back there in that mess? Because all I've seen for miles is snow."

Jonathan shook his head, still not completely sure that he was doing the right thing. Though putting his family in danger was by far his biggest concern, it was not his only one.

"What if she—"

"Remarried?" Garret filled in gently, seeing the look on Jonathan's face.

Jonathan looked back, searching Garret's face for any sign one way or the other.

"She didn't."

The elation that Jonathan felt was surprisingly short-lived. Not only had Elizabeth raised Reegan without him, but she had also spent all these years alone, just as he had.

"Look, Jon," Garret began, "you're not going to get another chance to do this. Your wife and daughter are exactly five minutes from here. Say the word and I'll turn this rented piece of junk around, but this is your one shot. If it's not now, it's never."

Before Jonathan could answer, both men were distracted by a Jeep parked in front of a small grocery store. A flashing blue light sat perched on top of the Jeep while a uniformed officer stood talking to a man under the covered entry to the store. Jonathan turned to stare back at the scene as they passed. Though it was probably nothing more than a local incident, an uneasiness settled over him.

"Come on. Let's go," Jonathan urged, trying to shrug off the feeling.

As they pulled up in front of the house, Jonathan looked expectantly to the front door. His heart was beating, his palms sweaty, and his nerves wracked, but the thought of seeing his family again seemed to force everything else from his mind.

"What are you waiting for?" Garret said with a smile. "Get up there."

Jonathan reached for the door handle, then quickly turned back to Garret. "Listen, Garret—"

"Save the mushy stuff for your wife," Garret said, waving Jonathan toward the house. "Trust me, there will be plenty of time to thank me later. Like when this piece of junk breaks down and you have to push."

Jonathan climbed out of the car and darted toward the house. The wind tore at him, seeping easily through his thin black jacket, but he felt none of it. His mind was a flood of emotions. What would she say? How would she react when she opened the door to see him standing there after so many years? Jonathan took a deep breath to steady his nerves as he stopped in front of the door, but before he could raise his hand to knock, the door flew open and a figure plowed right into him. Jonathan took a step back, slipped on some ice and—arms swinging to regain his balance—went flying. With a thud that knocked the wind right out of him, his back smacked down on the wooden porch. For a minute he lay there, hoping to regain his senses. Then, as if somehow drawn, his eyes went to the woman standing before him. She was staring down at him with her jaw slack, as if she were seeing a ghost.

"Elizabeth." His voice was no more than a whisper. "It's me."

Elizabeth's face was a contortion of shock and utter devastation. For a minute no words seemed to come, then looking like she was on the verge of collapsing, she said, "They took her, Jon. They took Reegan."

* * *

Jonathan tried to steady his hand as he read the note that had been stabbed into Elizabeth's kitchen table with a switchblade.

Jonathan,

The game's over! You lose. If you want Reegan to live, come alone. Monday night, 7:00 P.M. You know where to meet me.

Jonathan set the note down, then lifted his eyes to Elizabeth. He almost had to look away. His wife could barely stand, she was so distraught. The anger that had raged through him when she first told him about Reegan quickly turned to guilt. If he had just stayed in hiding none of this would have happened.

"Jon, what are we going to do?" she asked, her face twisted with grief.

For the first time in more than a decade, Jonathan stood and pulled his wife into his arms. "It's going to be okay," he whispered as he stroked her soft blond hair.

Almost as if on cue, Garret got up and excused himself, mumbling something about calling in backup.

"I can't lose her," Elizabeth choked out between sobs.

Jonathan pulled back to look at her, his eyes instantly fierce. "We're not going to lose her. It's me they want. They're just using Reegan. Once I'm there . . ." Jonathan stopped. He couldn't finish. As much as he wanted to comfort his wife, he couldn't lie to her. Antonio Sabatini craved revenge like a man dying of thirst craved water. He would never willingly let Reegan go. She didn't just happen into his plan—she was as much a part of it now as her father.

"We'll find her, Elizabeth," he finished gently. "We'll find her."

"We don't even know where to look," she answered with a helpless shake of her head.

Jonathan picked up the paper. "No. I know exactly where they're taking her."

Garret stepped back into the room. Jonathan let go of Elizabeth and turned to face his friend. "Garret, call the agency. We need help."

"They're already here," Garret said reluctantly.

"*What?*" Jonathan asked, staring at Garret in confusion. "What do you mean they're already here?" Jonathan searched his face, but Garret couldn't even look him straight in the eye.

"When we found out that Sabatini was still alive," Garret began slowly, "we had to do something."

Jonathan could feel blood instantly flush warm across his face. "You set me up? This whole thing?" He felt like he had just been plowed into by a dump truck. The man he had trusted with his life for years had betrayed him. "You told me about my mother, knowing full well that I would come and that Sabatini would follow?" The look on Garret's face was all the answer he needed. "How could you do that to me?" Jonathan shouted, his shock quickly turning to rage.

Elizabeth reached out and touched his arm. "Jon, this isn't going to help us find Reegan."

Once Jonathan turned to his wife, his countenance instantly softened. She looked so vulnerable, like an injured bird trapped and cornered. She had already been through so much; he would do anything not to add to her pain. Jonathan glanced back at Garret, his face still hard, but his tone was noticeably tempered. "How did you know that I'd come here after I went to see my mother?" Before Garret could answer, Jonathan's eyes opened wide, his mind struggling to digest the obvious. "She helped you. She was a part of this. That's why she had the key to the box with her at the hospital. That's why she wasn't surprised when I came. She had it planned."

Garret nodded slowly. "Your mother knew you were tired of running. She was afraid it would just be a matter of time before you tried something like this on your own. When we approached her with our plan, she was relieved."

"This was a pretty big gamble you were willing to make with my family."

"You were willing to make the same gamble just to deliver an old family heirloom," Garret countered softly. "You tell me that we didn't make the right decision, Jon. But if you're honest with yourself, you'll know this was the only way to keep you safe permanently."

Jonathan turned and walked toward the window, staring out at the white blur of snow. Then he turned back to Garret, his face hard. "If you already have agents here, why didn't they stop that maniac from taking my daughter?"

"I don't know," Garret admitted tightly, obviously upset with how they had handled this. "But we're about to find out. Agent Wesley will be here in five minutes. He's been down at Mike's Grocery getting all the information he can—which probably isn't much."

Jonathan shook his head. So his gut reaction when they'd passed the grocery store had been dead-on. "You tell that *weasel*—"

"Wesley," Garret corrected.

"I know what I said," Jonathan shot right back. "You tell him he can stay there. If he can't handle staking out a dinky town like this, then he'll be no use to us where we're going."

"Where are we going?" Garret asked hesitantly.

"Back to where this all started, an old alleyway in Jersey City."

Chapter 12

Owen Wesley looked like an undercover agent. He was neither tall enough to stand out in a crowd nor striking enough in feature to draw attention. His hair was a cross between a dishwater blond and a weak brunet. The agent that stood beside him seemed to be his exact opposite. He looked like a slightly smaller version of the Incredible Hulk, minus the green skin. Jonathan would have sooner pegged him as a bouncer at a nightclub than an FBI agent. Garret had introduced him to Jonathan as Shane Hickman, but both Garret and Wesley kept calling him Lefty. When Jonathan asked them about it, both men smiled.

"After one hit from his left fist, there's no need for the right," Garret said, reaching over and holding up the man's iron fist.

"No one really calls me that but these two," Agent Hickman offered, extending his hand to Jonathan.

Jonathan shook his hand, grudgingly relieved to have a little muscle on their side.

"I am sorry about your daughter," Hickman offered, his voice not nearly as intimidating or threatening as his size.

Jonathan nodded. He was still brooding over being set up, but there was no time to concentrate on that now. Every second they wasted was time that could be spent going after Reegan.

"I talked to Reegan the first night of our stakeout," Hickman continued.

"You talked to Reegan?" Elizabeth blurted out.

"I think I—*we*—scared her a little," he said apologetically. "First when Wesley knocked off a garbage can lid when we were following her, then later that night when I was posing as a utility worker."

"Why didn't you warn her?" Jonathan demanded.

Hickman lifted his eyes to Garret, then lowered his head slightly.

Jonathan shook his head. "You didn't want to tip off Sabatini," he grumbled, the sting of the betrayal instantly resurfacing. Jonathan had to get his mind elsewhere. He didn't have the time or the energy for this. "All right, this is how it's going to work," Jonathan began. "I'm going to get on a plane and go to Jersey. I'll fly into JFK instead of La Guardia, since Sabatini will probably expect me to fly into the closest airport. Then I'll take a taxi to Jersey. Wesley and Hickman can—"

"Whoa boy, hold on," Wesley interrupted. "I know Reegan's your daughter, but we're in charge here. You're not trained to—"

"You mean I'm not trained like you *professionals?*" Jonathan snapped sarcastically. "The same three professionals who let my daughter fall into the hands of trained hit men?"

Wesley's jaw tightened, and his narrow eyes deepened in intensity. "Now wait a minute," he snapped.

"No! You wait," Jonathan snapped right back.

"What did you have in mind, Jon?" Garret interrupted, stepping in and putting a hand across Wesley's chest.

"This is completely against policy," Wesley protested, obviously stung that Garret was siding against him.

Garret turned to him, only the muscles in his face betraying his impatience. "Let's at least hear what he has to say."

Wesley's eyes continued to smolder, but when he saw that Garret had no intentions of budging, he finally surrendered.

"Like I said, I'll fly to New Jersey," Jonathan continued.

"I'm coming with you," Elizabeth broke in.

"Absolutely not!" Jonathan exclaimed, turning to the woman next to him.

In a split second the vulnerability that had softened her blue eyes vanished. "I *am* going. For all these years I kept Reegan safe. *Me!* Alone. Then the four of you, three of which are supposedly trained FBI agents, show up and Reegan disappears." Her eyes cut through the four of them as cleanly as a doctor's scalpel. "I'm not going to sit idly by waiting to see what those lunatics do to my daughter. So whether you like it or not, or agree or not—frankly I don't care—you better get used to the idea because I *am* going and that's the end of it." With that she turned on the balls of her feet and stormed into the other room.

Jonathan blew his breath out hard. "I guess she's going."

Garret nodded. "I guess so. One good thing about it—with her around, there might not be any need for Lefty."

* * *

Jonathan watched as a steady flurry of snow continued to pour down from the sky. Elizabeth was still in the house quickly gathering the few things that she would need for the trip. Though Garret sat in the front seat of the car and Jonathan in the back, neither of them said a word to each other. The silence between the two seemed to override even the howling of the wind.

"Look, Jonathan," Garret finally began, "I know you're mad, and I can't say I blame you."

"Save it, Garret," Jonathan grunted as he continued to look blindly out the window. "Let's just concentrate on getting Reegan back."

Garret reached for his wallet and pulled out two thousand dollars in hundred-dollar bills. Then he reached across the seat and handed it to Jonathan.

"What's this for?"

"You're going to need some money if you're going to Jersey," Garret said, his voice matter-of-fact. He started to say something else, but instead let out a long sigh and turned back around.

Jonathan took out his gun and extended it to Garret. "This will never make it past airport security. I'll get it back from you when you get there," he said flatly.

Garret took the gun while Jonathan looked expectantly toward the house, then anxiously down at his watch. With the details of their plan ironed out, it was time for action. Garret would drive Jonathan and Elizabeth to the airport where two airplane tickets were already waiting. Elizabeth had successfully assured all of them that nothing short of actually locking her up would stop her from coming. To a small degree, Jonathan was relieved. At least if he had her with him, he wouldn't have to worry about her trying to get Reegan on her own or Antonio's men coming back and taking her too.

Garret would stay behind and handle the local police as well as issue a missing-persons all-points bulletin. After that he would join them at their agreed-upon rendezvous point. Wesley and Hickman would handle the ground cover. They would take the route most likely used by Reegan's abductors, just in case the news bulletin proved fruitful and Reegan was spotted. Neither Jonathan nor Garret took any stock in that scenario, but they couldn't take any chances. If Antonio's men slipped up, Wesley and Hickman would be there. Jonathan was still mulling over the details of his plan when Elizabeth opened the car door and slipped in next to him. The fire that he had seen in her eyes just minutes before had since been extinguished, leaving behind only uncertainty and fear.

"What if we're too late?" Elizabeth asked, her voice strained.

Jonathan could feel his own throat tighten. "We won't be," he said, forcing his words to sound infallible. He swallowed hard. Having Elizabeth within inches of him after so many years of separation was almost too surreal. He watched her steadily as she turned and stared blankly out the window. The years had been kind to her. Though she had obviously experienced her fair share of heartache and stress, she was still beautiful. Her blond hair, now cut midway up her neck, fell softly around her face, drawing immediate attention to her startling blue eyes. Jonathan swallowed hard, remembering the sheer agony that he had seen in them when she first told him about Reegan. As he looked at her now, still so frightened, he wanted desperately to reach out and take her into his arms, but somehow he couldn't. In that instant he felt more alone than he had felt in years. Here was his wife, the woman that he had loved his whole life. But did he really know her? How much had they both changed?

"Did you get a picture?" Garret asked, turning to look at her over his shoulder.

Elizabeth reached into her coat pocket and pulled out a wallet-size photograph. "I've got it. It's recent too. We just had her senior pictures taken."

Before she could hand it to Garret, Jonathan reached out his hand. "Please. The last time I saw her, she was six."

Elizabeth's eyes grew tender as she slowly handed him the picture. "She's not a little girl anymore."

Jonathan looked down at the picture, remembering when he had held his little girl in his arms, buried his face in her long dark hair, and kissed her good-bye. Now he held a picture of a young woman, fully grown, with only the haunting blue eyes and long dark hair still remaining to prick his memory. "She's beautiful," he whispered, suddenly feeling very empty. He had not been there to see her grow and develop into the woman she now was.

"She looks like your mother," Elizabeth said gently. Then a hint of a smile crossed her lips. "But she definitely has your stubborn temperament."

"After watching you stand up to Wesley today, I'd say Reegan didn't have a genetic chance," Garret teased Elizabeth dryly.

Jonathan shot a sharp glance at Garret, but then smiled despite himself. Elizabeth had always been the calm one of their little family, but mess with someone she loved and she could spit fire.

"Let's get going," Jonathan said with a sigh. "It's time I met my daughter."

* * *

By the time their airplane was midway to Kennedy International Airport, Jonathan's stomach felt like he had filled it with a bucket of bolts and nails. He swallowed hard, then reached over and took Elizabeth's hand. He didn't have to look at her to see how she was doing; her hand was trembling every bit as much as their plane had through the turbulence.

"Elizabeth, maybe this isn't such a good idea," Jonathan began hesitantly. "I know you want to—"

Elizabeth cut him off in midsentence. "Jon, we've already settled this. I'm coming with you."

Jonathan searched her face for several seconds. Her eyes were round and fierce, deepening in shade even as he watched. Though it didn't happen much, Jonathan knew that when she got like this, there was no changing her mind. He held up his hands and braved a smile. "Okay, okay! I surrender."

His teasing melted her scowl in an instant. She smiled at him weakly, then reached up and touched his face. "I've missed you."

Jonathan was completely taken off guard by her sudden tenderness. "I know. I've missed you too."

"I'm sorry about how things ended."

Jonathan shook his head. "You made the right choice in leaving."

"Did I?" she asked sadly.

Her words sparked a passion in Jonathan. He'd been waiting to hear them for years. He wanted to tell her that maybe they had made a mistake, that maybe they could be together even now. But could they? Jonathan looked into her eyes and realized he had nothing to lose by finding out if she had wished the same over the years. "Do you ever wonder if maybe we could have made it work?" he asked slowly, gauging her reaction.

Elizabeth's brow creased, but she nodded her head thoughtfully. Were they really strangers? It would keep their minds off Reegan to discuss something else, and now that Reegan knew about her father, perhaps it was time to revisit the past. Finally she nodded her head thoughtfully, almost wistfully. "Every day."

Jonathan let out his breath slowly. "So, where do we go from here?"

"I don't know," she admitted honestly. "It's been a lot of years—so much has happened."

"Maybe that's where we should start. I wasn't there with you when you took Reegan to her first day of kindergarten or when you taught her to drive a car. Some nights I would lie awake in bed and imagine all of those things . . . then other times I'd do just about anything not to think about it."

"Because it was too painful?" Elizabeth offered knowingly.

He nodded.

Though Elizabeth's eyes were filled with tears, a smile itched at her lips. "Well, you might be grateful you missed teaching Reegan to drive. That first day she plowed right over the neighbor's mailbox and came within inches of the neighbor. I was sure we were going to have to be relocated again—and that time it had nothing to do with Sabatini."

Jonathan laughed, then sat back, completely content to listen as she reminisced.

The flight passed, as well as their layover in Minneapolis, as they talked about their years of separation. They were surprised that, although they'd both had the opportunity, neither had remarried, and though they'd stopped attending church for the same reasons of self-protection, neither had forsaken their religious beliefs. During the conversation, Elizabeth had surprised Jonathan, slowly leaning over and kissing him tenderly on the lips, then leaning her head on his shoulder in a moment of quiet.

"Do you ever wish you would have married Mr. Money Bags?" Jonathan asked hours later, his voice lighthearted, but his question serious.

Elizabeth lifted her head to look at him. Then on impulse she leaned in and kissed him. It wasn't like the kiss she'd given him before, and the intensity surprised him to the point of speechlessness. When she pulled back, her eyes went from him to an older woman across the aisle. Following her eyes, Jonathan also turned to see the woman.

She was clucking her tongue and staring at them, obviously appalled. Jonathan quickly turned back to Elizabeth, his face flushed and his expression instantly sheepish.

"Do you think it would help if I told her that I hadn't kissed my wife in more than a decade?"

Elizabeth glanced over at the woman whose face was still drawn into a tight pucker. "I don't think so," she said with a smile. Then, almost as quickly as it appeared, her smile vanished and a shadow crossed her face. Jonathan didn't have to ask where her mind had gone. Throughout the entire journey, even as he became reacquainted with his wife, he had been unable to fully distract his mind from one horrifying thought—their daughter's life was now being used as ransom for his own.

* * *

Jonathan held onto Elizabeth's hand as they made their way through the crowded airport terminal. With only his duffel bag and Elizabeth's small carry-on, there was no need to stop at the baggage claim. Instead they headed straight for the doors. Jonathan's senses seemed heightened. He felt as if a thousand eyes were trained on his back, just waiting for the right moment to strike. This was Sabatini's terrain, and Jonathan felt like a child blindly making his way across a trail lined with asps. He tried to shrug it off as paranoia, but he couldn't help but think that Antonio already knew he was there. Jonathan fought the urge to scan the crowd. Instead he clutched Elizabeth's hand and quickened his pace.

Once they were outside, the two of them raced to the closest cab, handed the driver their luggage, and hopped in. Elizabeth shot Jonathan a nervous glance.

"Do you think they're here at the airport?"

"We'll take the long way around just incase," Jonathan began. "It'll be a lot harder to follow us right through downtown Manhattan."

Once the cab driver climbed in, Jonathan quickly handed him a slip of paper with an address scribbled on it. As the cab bolted from the airport, Jonathan finally turned back toward the crowd, his eyes hesitantly searching for the faces he somehow knew were there.

Chapter 13

Jonathan stared numbly at the monstrous buildings that towered above them as their cab plodded through the congested streets of Manhattan. He would have had to crane his neck just to see the lofty summits of the skyscrapers, their peaks blending into the overcast sky that encroached on them. Though he had been through this city countless times in his life, it now seemed as foreign as a walk on the crater-scathed surface of the moon. He watched as a steady stream of cars and pedestrians crammed the busy city streets and sidewalks, the blaring of horns echoing through the metropolis. As chaotic as it was, somehow everything in the city seemed to belong—everything, that was, but him.

Jonathan nearly flinched as Elizabeth turned to face him. He quickly managed a smile, though the look in her eyes told him that he had not been quick enough. He expected her to question his expression, but instead she reached over and touched his arm, then looked back out the window. The two of them drove for the next hour in almost complete silence. Fear seemed to be the common bond between them. Fear that they might never see Reegan again, fear that an evil man might destroy what was left of their family, and finally, when this was all over, the fear that they might not be able to pick up the pieces and go on.

Jonathan shot a quick glance over his shoulder at the cars behind them. Being on edge in a situation like this was a given, but there was something nagging him that he couldn't quite put his finger on. Something was wrong. He had tried unsuccessfully since boarding the plane back in North Dakota to shake the feeling, but it continued to plague him like a festering sore. Suddenly Jonathan was pulled from his thoughts by a hand on his shoulder.

"What is it?" Elizabeth asked, unable to mask the trepidation in her voice.

Jonathan turned around to face his wife, who shifted in her seat to look out the back window. "Are we being followed?" she asked anxiously.

Jonathan caught a glimpse of the cab driver scowling at them in the rearview mirror.

"You two in some kind of trouble?" he asked, quickly scrutinizing the two of them.

"Not us," Jonathan answered nonchalantly. "But you might be. NYPD five cars back. I think he saw you almost sideswipe that blue sedan."

The cab driver swore under his breath, then, after a quick glance in his side-view mirror, took a sharp right turn down a side street.

"One more ticket and I lose my license," he admitted as he accelerated. "Hold on."

The cab driver's admonishment was unnecessary. After several sharp curves into small back alleyways at breakneck speed, dodging garbage cans and debris as well as a few parked cars, Elizabeth and Jonathan were both clutching the seats in front of them with death grips. With their knuckles chalk-white, the cab driver flew across a busy main street. Amid squealing brakes and loud car horns, he then broke off into another narrow alley, swerved in front of a garbage truck that was lifting a hefty metal dumpster, and slammed on his brakes. As Jonathan and Elizabeth gasped for air and leaned back in their seats, the cab driver turned around to face them. He was grinning from ear to ear as if he had just won the Indy 500.

"I think I lost him."

"Ya think?" Elizabeth asked in exasperation. "You could have killed us."

Jonathan just shook his head. "Did I mention the fact that dead passengers don't tip very well?"

That won a quick laugh from the cabby. "I'll have to keep that in mind next time." Then, after a quick glance behind them, he started down the alley.

Elizabeth leaned close to Jonathan and whispered, "Was there really a cop behind us?"

Jonathan shook his head. "No, but if someone was tailing us, I have no doubt we shook 'em."

Elizabeth turned and looked at the long alley behind them. "I'll be glad when this is all over."

Jonathan wrapped his arm around Elizabeth and pulled her next to him, feeling her body relax even as he did. He wanted so much to tell her that everything was going to be okay, but he couldn't find the words. Though he was sure that no one was following them, something still wasn't right. When the driver pulled up in front of the motel and climbed out to get their baggage from the trunk, Jonathan was still wrestling with his own uneasiness.

"When's Garret supposed to meet us?" Elizabeth asked.

Jonathan looked down at his watch. "Not long. He told me . . ." Jonathan stopped.

"What's wrong?" Elizabeth asked, eyeing him curiously.

Jonathan shook his head hesitantly. "Nothing."

Elizabeth raised an eyebrow, not letting him off the hook.

"It's just that Garret is usually emphatic about me having an entourage of agents whenever there's even the slightest hint of danger," Jonathan admitted reluctantly. "I can't believe he sent the two of us out here alone."

"It was your idea. Besides, everything happened so fast. Maybe he had a lapse of judgment, but under the circumstances…"

"If anything, Garret works best under pressure."

"What are you saying?" Elizabeth asked, watching him apprehensively.

Jonathan shrugged it off, feeling guilty at the mere thought. "Forget it. I think I'm the one who's having the lapse in judgment."

"Are you sure?" Elizabeth asked wearily.

"Garret's the best. He's risked his life for me more times than I'd like to remember."

They both turned as the cab driver opened Elizabeth's door. Jonathan handed him the money, then slung his duffel bag over one shoulder before picking up his wife's bag.

"Next time we're walking," Elizabeth whispered as they headed toward the lobby of the spacious hotel in front of them.

Jonathan ran his hand across the back of his neck. "What's a cab ride through New York and Jersey without a little whiplash?"

* * *

After bolting the door to their room, Jonathan placed their duffel bags on the bed and crossed to the window, thoroughly scanning the busy street below them.

"You don't honestly believe they could have followed us? If they were following us in the first place," she amended.

Jonathan turned to face her, his eyes deadly serious. "Underestimating them has ended more than one life."

"I'm well aware of what these men are capable of," Elizabeth said dryly.

Jonathan felt another stab of pain. After all the years of running to protect his family, in the end, Antonio had found them anyway. The irony was almost more than he could take. He turned back to stare blankly out the window, his frustration and guilt quickly turning to anger. In an effort to bring justice to one man, Garret Woodard had used him and his family as live bait. The very notion was infuriating.

"What time is Garret supposed to meet us?" Elizabeth asked as she started toward him.

"He should be here any minute—once he got the bulletin out he was going to take a private jet straight to La Guardia." Jonathan looked down at his watch. "With our two hour layover in Minneapolis, I'm kind of surprised he didn't beat us here."

Jonathan looked back out the window, his eyes suddenly drawn to a man sitting at a bus stop across the street. He appeared to be reading a paper, but his eyes were on everything but the black-and-white print. Jonathan watched intently as another man passed directly in front of the first. The second man nodded, then took a seat at the far end of the bench just feet from the man with the paper. A minute later, both men stood and began walking toward the entrance.

"Get your things," Jonathan commanded, already halfway across the room.

"What's wrong?" Elizabeth asked, her face mirroring his fear.

"They're here."

"But how did they—"

"I don't know," Jonathan broke in as he grabbed the duffel bag that held his things, including the box intended for his daughter. "But we're not going to stick around long enough to find out."

"Maybe we should just let them take us so we can find out where they're keeping Reegan," Elizabeth said.

"We can't. The second they have me, they'll kill her. We have to get out of here."

Slowly opening the door and scanning the empty hallway, the two of them began to run toward the elevator. Just three feet in front of it, the light to their level lit, indicating that someone was headed to their floor. The two of them stopped cold.

"The stairs," Elizabeth offered breathlessly, pointing to a door next to the elevator.

Clutching Elizabeth's hand, Jonathan threw open the door and started down the stairs. After only a couple of steps, his feet froze. He leaned over the banister slightly and saw one of the men that had been on the bench outside. Though the man was climbing the stairs two at a time, he was still three flights down. Jonathan and Elizabeth turned, then raced toward the roof two stories above them. They could hear their pursuer gaining on them with each step. Out of breath and gripped by fear, they burst through the door to the roof. Jonathan's eyes locked on a second set of stairs on the far side of the roof.

"Over there," he yelled.

They ran as fast as they could across the tar-stained roof, and after throwing open the door and barreling through, they came to a screeching halt. There, in the stairwell just a few stairs from the top, was the second man Jonathan had seen entering the building. The man said something in between deep breaths, but his words were drowned out by

Elizabeth's blood-curdling scream. Jonathan yanked Elizabeth back outside, his attention immediately going to the building next to theirs. Though a full floor shorter, and with an eight-foot gap between the two buildings, it seemed to be their only option. Jonathan turned to Elizabeth, grabbing her firmly by the shoulders.

"Do you trust me?"

Elizabeth glanced from Jonathan to the gap between the two buildings, her eyes round with terror, before turning back to face him. She reached out and gripped his hand, then quickly nodded, her eyes more intense than he had ever seen them.

With their eyes locked on the roof of the other building, the two of them began to run. Jonathan could feel his lungs burning as his legs thundered toward the roof's ledge and the sheer drop below. As they took their last step and the leap beyond, Jonathan could hear the blood rushing through his ears, drowning out everything but Elizabeth's high-pitched scream. After a split second of flight, their bodies hurtling over the deadly drop below them, the two of them crashed onto the adjacent roof. Though the wind had been knocked out of him, Jonathan staggered to his feet, pulling Elizabeth up with him. Something told him they'd just experienced a miracle. Then, without once looking back at their pursuers, they hurried toward the door leading to the staircase and disappeared inside.

* * *

Jonathan looked around the dimly lit restaurant, his eyes scanning every face, hoping that he wouldn't recognize anyone and, more importantly, that no one would recognize him. Several couples were talking quietly over their candlelit dinners, totally oblivious to anything around them but each other. His eyes went to the waiters who were doting on their customers, hoping for a night of tipping big enough to pay their car payments. Jonathan knew. He had been in their shoes. In fact, that was how he had met Elizabeth, stealing her right from under Charley Madison's nose on the very night the man had planned to propose.

Jonathan shook his head as his eyes went to the woman next to him. If he had not acted quickly that night, Elizabeth would be sitting here now with another man. That thought made Jonathan feel both guilty and sick to his stomach. If he had left her alone she would have married someone that could have taken care of her.

"Are you sure we're safe here?" Elizabeth asked anxiously, her eyes also taking in every inch of the restaurant.

"We're safer here than in some secluded back alley. Trust me—I know."

"What if Garret didn't get the note?"

Jonathan shrugged, thinking back to the street kid he had entrusted the note to. Jonathan had instructed the boy to deliver it to the bellman at their hotel, with explicit instructions for the bellman to give it to Garret Woodard. "Let's hope he did. If not, we're out fifty bucks."

Elizabeth looked down at the gourmet meal before her, picking at it with her fork. "After you pay for this, we'll be out more than fifty bucks."

"After how the agency used us, this is nothing," Jonathan snapped.

He could tell by the look on her face that his anger wasn't helping matters. He reached across the table and took his wife's hand. "I'm sorry. Tell me about Reegan," he began, hoping to occupy her thoughts.

Elizabeth visibly relaxed, but before she could speak, a waiter approached Jonathan. He bent to speak in his ear while slipping him a note. Jonathan opened the folded note and quickly read its message.

"Well?" Elizabeth pressed once the waiter was gone.

Jonathan pushed his chair back. "It's from Garret. Come on, let's get out of here."

As they stood to leave, the same two men who had chased them across the roof of the hotel entered the restaurant. Both Jonathan and Elizabeth spotted them instantly.

"What do we do?" Elizabeth cried, her voice high and panicked.

Jonathan shot a quick glance around the room. The only other way out of the restaurant was through the kitchen. Without a word, he grabbed Elizabeth's hand and started for the swinging doors that separated the kitchen from the dining area. A quick look over his shoulder confirmed that Sabatini's men were following right on their heels. As they started through the kitchen, Jonathan heard a large crash behind them. Not taking the time to stop and see what had happened, he and Elizabeth barreled through the kitchen amid a slew of shouts from the Italian chefs they'd nearly trampled, then threw open the back door and plunged into the street. As they raced down the narrow alley that ran behind the restaurant, neither of them slowed their pace enough to look back at the chaotic scene still unfolding behind them.

chapter 14

Jonathan peered into the darkness of the vacant warehouse, quickly scanning every shadow for the smallest hint of movement. Thin lines of moonlight streamed in through the dirty windows on the far wall, but other than that there was no other source of light. Once his eyes finally adjusted, Jonathan could see the outline of several wooden crates scattered across the room, as well as fifty-gallon metal barrels pushed up against the walls. Other than that, the run-down factory looked empty. From the markings of graffiti and gang insignias on the outside of the building, he guessed it had been vacant for quite some time. Jonathan could feel Elizabeth's grip tighten around his arm.

"Why are we meeting him *here?*" she asked breathlessly as she peered past the doorframe into the darkened room.

Jonathan turned to face her, suddenly wishing that he had not brought her, that he had been more insistent that she stay in Maplecove. And yet, at the same time, she might have been in just as much danger there.

"The alley we're meeting Sabatini in on Monday night runs behind this place. Garret's probably keeping an eye on the alley from here."

"As long as Sabatini and his men aren't doing the same thing," Elizabeth shot back.

Jonathan could feel the muscles in his back and neck tense. He reached over and grabbed Elizabeth's hand, then took a step through the doorway. Elizabeth didn't budge. Jonathan turned back to face her.

"Are you sure you trust him?" she hissed anxiously.

"Who?"

"Garret," she whispered fervently. "He admitted he set you up. Maybe he just made up the part about bringing you out in the open to smoke out Sabatini. Maybe he brought you out of hiding because he sold you out. You said yourself it was strange he didn't fly with us or send in other agents." Elizabeth stopped, allowing her words to sink in. "How else do you explain those men finding us at the restaurant? Garret was the only one who knew we'd be there. Now he wants to meet us *here* where no one would know if we just— disappeared."

"Garret's not a dirty cop. I might be upset with how he handled all this, but I'd still trust him with my life," he said adamantly.

"But do you trust him with mine—or Reegan's?" Elizabeth asked, tightening her grip.

Before Jonathan could answer, a loud clang rang out from the darkness. It sounded like metal smacking into metal. Jonathan grabbed Elizabeth's hand just as the outline of a man rose from behind a stack of metal barrels.

"Run," Jonathan cried as the two of them turned toward the empty parking lot.

"Jonathan, wait! It's me," the man called out.

Jonathan froze, his heart forcing blood through his veins like a raging river. He slowly turned around to face the approaching figure. Within seconds Garret was to them. Though Jonathan could feel his whole body flood with relief, he could feel Elizabeth's stiffen.

"You two okay?" Garret asked, taking a quick look at the deserted parking lot behind them.

Jonathan nodded as Garret ushered them into the warehouse and closed the door with an echoed thud.

"Wait here," Garret said as he walked back toward the metal barrels.

Jonathan could hear Elizabeth's erratic breathing as she moved in close beside him.

"It's going to be okay," he whispered, quickly turning his own attention back to Garret, who was returning with two flashlights.

"Come on, I'll show you where we're set up," Garret said, handing Jonathan a flashlight, then walking toward a set of metal stairs leading up to the second floor.

Jonathan and Elizabeth followed suit, Jonathan using his flashlight to help them better view the room they were in. The middle of the warehouse was two stories high, rising all the way to the roof, but all along the perimeter of the second floor were crossbeams supporting metal walkways and drop ladders. The metal staircase that they were approaching led to a small office area on the second floor, but other than that one corner, the rest of the second floor was open ceiling, surrounded only by the walkways.

Jonathan could feel Elizabeth's grip tighten as they ascended the stairs behind Garret. As they reached the top, Garret knocked on the door twice. Within seconds the door opened. Elizabeth sucked her breath in, startled by the figure standing in the doorway. He was dressed in black from head to toe with a pair of night-vision goggles over his eyes. As soon as he saw Elizabeth's reaction, he pulled off the goggles, revealing a pair of light blue eyes and a crop of blond hair.

"Sorry. I didn't mean to scare you," he said, extending a pair of night goggles to each of them.

Garret and Jonathan turned off their flashlights, then the three of them wordlessly followed the agent through the doorway. After putting on the goggles, Jonathan glanced around the room. Besides the agent that met them at the door and Garret, there was a third agent sitting on a wooden crate tapping away at a laptop. Other than an almost imperceptible nod of his head, his attention stayed on the computer screen.

"This is Agent Larsen," Garret offered, gesturing to the man in black who had opened the door for them.

Jonathan nodded, then stuck out his hand. "I appreciate everything you guys are trying to do," he said frankly, shaking Agent Larsen's hand.

The man shrugged. "I thrive on assignments like this. I'd choose a stake-out over a desk job any day of the week."

Jonathan shook his head, his heart still racing. "You can have it. If this is ever over I'd be perfectly happy behind a desk in a four quad. I could use a few years of boredom."

"Sounds pretty good to me too," Garret admitted.

Agent Larsen grinned. "I'll take a post at the front entrance until you need me," he offered.

"Notify us immediately if you see anything," Garret said as the agent picked up his assault rifle.

They all watched as the man cracked the door slightly and slipped through. Once the door was closed, Garret turned to Jonathan and Elizabeth, motioning them toward a small office on the far side of the room. As soon as they were in the windowless room and the door was closed, Garret pulled off his goggles and turned on the light.

"You look like you've had a long day," Garret said with a hint of a smile as Jonathan stripped off his own goggles and ran a quick hand through his disheveled hair.

Jonathan could feel his temper instantly ignite. "No thanks to you! Twice today we could have been killed, once at the hotel, then again at the restaurant." Jonathan could feel the burning in his face and knew that his blood pressure was probably skyrocketing. "What were you thinking sending us here alone?"

Garret reached over and placed his hand on Jonathan's shoulder. "As I recall, my friend, it was you who suggested coming here alone in the first place. Quite forcefully in fact."

"I was out of my mind with worry for my daughter," Jonathan erupted.

"I know," Garret said calmly. "That's why I didn't send you here alone."

Jonathan stared at Garret, his face registering his confusion, but his anger not subdued. "What are you talking about?" he demanded irritably.

Garret turned to Elizabeth. "Do you remember the lady who saw you kissing on the plane?"

Elizabeth's eyes narrowed. "How did you know about her?"

"That was Agent Crain, a twenty-year veteran of the FBI. And trust me," Garret began with a crooked smile, "she got a pretty good laugh out of that particular assignment." Jonathan shook his head while Elizabeth's mouth fell slack, but Garret just folded his arms in satisfaction. "The taxi driver who picked you up at the airport and took you to your hotel—" Garret paused for effect, looking at the two of them, "also an agent. We planted him at the airport to wait for your plane. When you were at the restaurant—"

"*The waiter?*" Elizabeth interrupted.

"No. We didn't know you'd be going there, so we didn't have time to plant him in that kind of a position, but the customer who stuck his foot out and thus directed Sabatini's men into the dessert cart . . ." Garret shrugged. "Well, you get the idea."

Jonathan shook his head, relieved that his trust in Garret was well-founded.

"If I would have come with you, it would have been like pasting a bull's-eye on your forehead," Garret offered, his tone matter-of-fact. "Sabatini told you to come alone. He knows I'm an agent. He wants revenge, but he's smart. He's not going to risk his freedom for it. He would have just slipped underground and taken you out the first chance he got."

Jonathan let his breath out hard.

Garret slapped him on the shoulder. "We're going to get her back, Jon. Trust me, we're going to end this once and for all."

* * *

A little after nine, Jonathan and Elizabeth, accompanied by Agent Larsen, slipped out of the abandoned warehouse and cautiously made their way to where a cab was waiting down a side street. Neither Jonathan nor Elizabeth was surprised to see the same cab driver that had picked them up at the airport. With only twenty-four hours before the meeting with Sabatini, every precaution was to be taken.

"You two happen to lose something," the agent behind the wheel offered, holding up their duffle bags. "The agent back at the restaurant picked them up once Sabatini's men cleared out of there."

"Thanks," Jonathan said, shaking his head as he took both bags. "We ran out of there so quick I didn't even think to grab them."

"No problem," the agent offered with a smile.

While en route to the apartment building that would serve as a temporary safehouse for the two of them, Agent Larsen informed them that two other agents would be staying in the apartment with them through the night.

Jonathan looked over at Elizabeth with a shadow of a reassuring smile, though his own stomach was still a knot of anxiety. After several detours to ensure that they would not be followed, they finally pulled up to a gate securing an upscale high-rise apartment complex.

"Here's the keys to your apartment," Agent Larsen began, handing Jonathan a set of keys. "For the next twenty-four hours, you are Michael and Lori Fisher, who are housesitting for Professor Allen Burton. The professor and his wife are supposedly on sabbatical in London for the summer." Agent Larsen handed Jonathan a security pass. "This will get you through the front gate. The other two agents I told you about are already in your apartment. I need to go back to the warehouse for a couple of hours and take care of a few things, but after that I'll stake out your apartment from over there." He pointed to a little delicatessen across the street.

"I'll be driving through the night to maintain my cover," the agent who was posing as a cab driver began, "but I'll stay in the area and drive by every chance I get. If you need me," he continued, handing Elizabeth a business card, "call."

"With us, along with the security officer that the complex already employs, you'll be fine," Agent Larsen assured them.

"We appreciate it," Jonathan stated, climbing from the cab.

"We'll see you two in the morning," Agent Larsen said as the door closed.

Jonathan let out a laborious sigh. There were still several hours before morning; what those hours would hold, they could only wait and see.

chapter 15

Jonathan stared blankly into the freezer, though his mind was on everything but food. Finally, he pulled out a half gallon of vanilla-bean ice cream and plopped it on the counter. Then he searched three different drawers before retrieving two spoons. He handed one spoon to Elizabeth, then sat down on a stool next to her. Elizabeth leaned to the side to see the living room where the two agents were sitting, then turned back to Jonathan.

"Do you think Sabatini's men will find us here?" she asked quietly.

With only one spoonful missing to mar the top of the ice cream, Jonathan set his spoon down and walked to the cabinets. "I don't know. I don't understand how they could have followed us to the hotel this morning," he admitted, his face showing his frustration as he returned with a jar of peanut butter. "Then again at the restaurant. We were so careful." He added a scoop of peanut butter to the ice cream, then began to smear it across the top.

"Maybe they were able to follow us," Elizabeth said, getting to her feet and going to the refrigerator.

Jonathan pulled a face. "Were you in the same cab as me? No one could have followed us."

"Maybe they have an inside connection—someone working for the agency."

"It's possible, but—"

"But what?" Elizabeth asked, returning with a bottle of chocolate syrup.

Jonathan jabbed at the gooey concoction with his spoon, his mind retracing every moment of the last few days. "I don't know. Maybe—maybe, they bugged us somehow."

"Bugged what?" Elizabeth asked, squirting a generous amount of chocolate syrup on top of the peanut-butter swirl. "We flew to Jersey. All we brought with us is our duffel bags, and we haven't had those out of our sight . . . well, except for a short time at the restaurant . . . but Sabatini's men wouldn't have been able to plant something in them without that undercover FBI agent seeing them."

Jonathan shook his head. Though he didn't have an answer, the thought continued to pester him.

"What about before we came to Jersey?" Elizabeth began. "Maybe—"

Jonathan could feel the hair on the back of his neck stand on end. "Where's my duffel bag?" he asked suddenly, an incident that had happened just days before now leaping out at him in warning.

"In the bedroom," Elizabeth said anxiously. "Why? What's the matter?"

Jonathan didn't take the time to answer. Instead he shot to his feet and ran toward the living room. Then, as if stopped by an invisible barrier between the kitchen and the living room, Jonathan froze. There, slumped on the couch were the two agents assigned to protect them.

"What's the matter?" Elizabeth cried, standing to come to his side.

"Stay where you are!" Jonathan yelled, his eyes going to a curtain across the room, where, with the aid of the moonlight streaming from behind, he could see the slight silhouette of a man. Jonathan could feel the instinct of self-preservation, coupled with an even more compelling need to protect the woman he loved, explode within him, leaving his limbs trembling. He took a step toward the man, his fists clenched and his heart racing, when a second man came at him, hidden by the wall that separated the kitchen from the living room.

"Remember me?" the man sneered, grabbing Jonathan hard by the arm and jabbing the barrel of a pistol into his ribs. "That pack of gum you've been carrying around in your duffel bag has proven quite effective," the man gloated. "We've been able to track your every move."

Jonathan's eyes focused on the man who held him. "Dr. Bailey," he muttered between clenched teeth.

"You remember," the man taunted. "Only, Dr. Bailey is the poor guy I 'met' just before I found you."

Jonathan's eyes shifted as a man he didn't recognize stepped from behind the curtain.

"Elizabeth, run!" he screamed.

The last thing Jonathan saw was the butt of a gun being raised.

* * *

"Wake up!"

Pain gripped Jonathan as soon as his eyes opened, seizing him with such magnitude that he began to retch.

"He's awake," the voice barked.

The next thing Jonathan felt was a bucket of freezing water being tossed into his face. The cold water took his breath away, bringing his mind instantly back to reality. He slowly pulled himself to a sitting position, the effort causing an intense shock of pain that seemed to radiate through his skull. He lifted his hands to his head and held it until the pain subdued to a bearable level, then he slowly glanced around the room. It was dark and damp like a cellar, with walls made of cinder block and cement. A single lightbulb with a long string hanging below it was the only source of light. The string was swaying slightly as if it had just been pulled.

"Hello, Jonathan."

Jonathan's eyes lifted to a man just entering the dimly lit room. Though Jonathan's vision was blurry from a swollen eye, the recollection was immediate.

"Sabatini," Jonathan said coolly, his heart thumping within his chest.

Antonio Sabatini began to cluck his tongue, his face showing mock concern as he descended the few stairs that led into the room. "What happened to your face?"

Jonathan tried to keep his face passive, but fear was climbing his spine like an animal of prey.

"Where's my wife and daughter?" Jonathan demanded, his voice a cross between rage and terror.

Sabatini folded his arms, his face holding a caustic smile, his eyes displaying something altogether different. "It really pains me to see you like this," Sabatini cooed, ignoring Jonathan's question. He gestured across the windowless room they were in. It was then that Jonathan noticed the two other men in the room. They were on either side of him. Jonathan recognized the one to his right immediately. It was the man who had posed as a doctor. He had a sneer on his face and an empty bucket in his hand. The second man— the silhouette behind the curtain—he had seen for only a split second before being knocked senseless. The man now had his arms folded, rippling muscles bulging out from his shirt. Jonathan's attention went back to Sabatini. Sabatini's eyes had narrowed, and the muscles along his jaw were flexed. "Pains me, that is, to see you trapped in a room like this." He paused, his eyes filled with hate. "But try spending nine years in a room about a fourth this size."

"You killed a man in cold blood," Jonathan spat out before self-preservation and common sense could stop him.

The consequence of his words was immediate—a blow to the face that nearly lifted him off the cold cement floor. For a second all he could see were flashes of light spinning in front of him as his eyes rolled into the back of his head. Somewhere echoing through his brain, Jonathan could hear Sabatini screaming at the man who had struck him.

"Don't kill him! Not yet! Not until I know for sure," Sabatini raged.

Jonathan struggled to sit up, his vision temporarily showing double.

"Gionni, get him cleaned up," Sabatini barked.

Jonathan could hear Sabatini's footsteps followed by a door slamming heavily.

"All right, you heard him. Let's get him cleaned up," Gionni, the man who had posed as the doctor, ordered.

Jonathan was dragged to his feet and shoved in a chair, where he was then doused with a second bucket of water.

"You've been a lot of trouble, Jonny boy," the bigger man sneered.

"What did you do to my wife?" Jonathan demanded.

The man grabbed Jonathan by the collar with one massive fist. "I'll tell you what we *will* do to her when we—"

"Mario!" Gionni shouted, cutting him off.

The bigger man's face immediately registered his mistake.

Gionni looked away in disgust, turning his attention back to Jonathan. "You cooperate and you might get to see her again," he said, his voice tight.

"She got away," Jonathan breathed, looking at the two of them expectantly to see their reaction.

The expression on their faces supplied all the affirmation he needed. Jonathan sat back against the chair, relief flooding over him like a soothing elixir.

"She didn't go far enough," Mario said, reaching up and touching a large purplish-blue knot on his forehead. "And when I catch her—"

"Enough," Gionni demanded, pulling a nylon rope out of his jacket pocket and tossing it to Mario. "We don't need her. By this time tomorrow we'll be out of the country." He threw the rope to Mario. "Tie him to the chair."

Jonathan slowly allowed the air to escape from his tense lungs, relieved that at least his wife was safe. His daughter's future, though, was far less certain. Not wanting to think about that, Jonathan's mind went back to what he had heard Sabatini say just minutes ago—*Don't kill him until we know for sure.* Know what? Jonathan had already testified against Sabatini. He had also turned the pictures from his photo shoot over to the police—pictures that clearly identified Sabatini as the killer, as well as two other men who were still in a high-security prison as accomplices. What else could he possibly have or know that Sabatini would go to such risk to get?

When Jonathan was secured in the chair, the two left, bolting the door shut from the other side. Jonathan slowly looked around the room, his head swimming with the effort. There was nothing in the small basement room but the chair he was sitting in and four dirty walls. He tried to pull his wrists free from the rope, but it was no use. They wouldn't budge an inch. He let his breath out hard, his mind soaking in the reality. He wasn't getting out of this place on his own. The only door was bolted shut and probably guarded as well. He was tied to a chair and, even if he wasn't, there was nowhere to go. His only hope lay in Elizabeth getting back to the warehouse to tell Garret. He closed his eyes, praying that somehow his old friend would find him.

* * *

Jonathan's head rose off his chest the second he heard the bolt being slid from the lock. He blinked twice to try to get his eyes to focus, though the effort was not rewarded. His body stiffened as the door opened and Sabatini entered. Jonathan expected the two other men to follow, but they didn't. Instead Antonio closed the door behind him, leaving the two of them alone.

"What do you want from me?"

Sabatini smiled. "Funny you should ask," he said as he slowly descended the stairs.

Jonathan could feel his heartbeat quicken with each step.

"The pictures you took that night in the alley," Sabatini began, keeping his expression passive.

"I gave the pictures to the—"

"I know that," Sabatini snapped. He took a couple of steps toward Jonathan, fighting to control the tension that was written all over his face. "A couple of my boys stole the pictures from an evidence locker after the trial and destroyed them."

Jonathan wrinkled his forehead. "Why? You'd already been convicted at that point."

"Never mind that," Sabatini said impatiently. "Did you keep the negatives?"

"The negatives?"

"Yes!" Sabatini barked, unable to subdue his tone.

Jonathan's mind was drawing a blank, but he couldn't let Sabatini know that. Something told him that the wrong answer could mean his life.

"What do you want the negatives for?" Jonathan asked, trying to buy time.

Sabatini thrust his face within inches of Jonathan's. "Don't try to play me, Schmitt. Just answer the question."

Jonathan's mind was racing. The negatives Sabatini was talking about also held the shots that Jonathan had intended to use in his photo exhibit. Once he had witnessed the murder and found out that his whole life would be turned upside down, he had tossed the negatives in a box with all of his other photos. What Elizabeth had done with them, he could only guess. Usually the agency told them to burn any memorabilia dealing with their former lives, but from the look in Sabatini's eyes, telling him that would not be wise.

"I've still got them," Jonathan said evenly.

Sabatini pulled back, though he kept his eyes wary, as if deciding whether or not Jonathan was telling the truth.

"Where are they?"

"Where's my daughter?"

Sabatini's eyes flashed, but this time he held his temper. "I'm losing my patience."

"I'll have to take you to them."

"Just tell me where they are," Sabatini demanded, the veins in his neck bulging.

Jonathan shook his head, his face as rock-hard and challenging as Sabatini's.

"Not even if it means your daughter's life?"

Jonathan flinched, which brought a broad smile to Sabatini's lips. "That's right, Jon, her fate rests in your hands now." He slowly turned and walked up the stairs. Just before he closed the door, he turned back to Jonathan. "Sleep well," he said, his tone thick with sarcasm. Then he slipped through the door, bolting it shut behind him.

Jonathan sat alone in the room, Sabatini's words still sending a chill through his entire body. He tried to force his mind elsewhere, concentrating instead on the negatives. Why Sabatini wanted them, Jonathan didn't have a clue, but he had no doubt that Sabatini would go to any extreme to get them, including killing Jonathan's only child.

* * *

Elizabeth crouched behind a metal dumpster two blocks away from the apartment complex, her heart pounding in her chest and her limbs quivering like jelly. Dropping to her knees because her trembling muscles could no longer support her, she strained her eyes in the darkness, searching for Sabatini's men. She knew she had to get to Garret—it was Jonathan's only hope—but she had to be certain that she hadn't been followed. If they caught her, Jonathan wouldn't have a chance. After only just being reunited with her husband, the thought of losing him again was unthinkable. She took a deep breath, grabbed ahold of the dumpster for support, and pulled herself to her feet. Down another two hundred feet, the alley opened up to a main road. She could see a gas station just across the street. If she could make it that far, she could use the pay phone to call for help. Checking the darkness one more time to be sure that no one had followed her, she slipped from her hiding spot and darted down the narrow street.

Once inside the phone booth, Elizabeth quickly dialed the number printed on the business card given her just hours before. With her hands shaking, she slid two coins into the pay phone and dialed. Five minutes later a yellow cab squealed to a stop in front of the phone booth. Elizabeth jumped into the backseat, then reached over and locked the door.

"What happened?" the agent blurted out.

"They broke into the apartment. They took Jonathan," Elizabeth said, trying to hold back the tears.

"What about the agents with you?" he asked as he peeled away from the curb and started down the road.

"I think they were alive when I left, but just barely," Elizabeth offered, wiping at her eyes.

The agent behind the wheel pulled out a cell phone and began to dial. "Do you know where they were taking him?"

"I don't know." Elizabeth began crying.

As the agent began to talk into his cell phone, Elizabeth turned and stared out the window; this whole thing felt like a horrible nightmare. She wished she could just open her eyes and it would all be over. She wiped at the steady stream of tears that was now sliding down her checks, blurring her vision.

Fifteen minutes later she was in the abandoned warehouse watching Garret pace back and forth in the room, trying to digest everything that she had just told him.

"The man said he had bugged Jonathan?"

"I think so," Elizabeth said, trying to remember. "He said something about tracing him all this time through a pack of gum."

"This changes things," he began thoughtfully, "but it doesn't completely wipe out our plan." Garret rubbed at his face with both hands, then looked silently up at the ceiling, as if thinking his plan through. When he lowered his eyes back to Elizabeth, who was still visibly shaken, he took a step toward her. "Mrs. Schmitt, I know how terrible this is for you, and I understand how you feel."

"You couldn't possibly know how I feel," Elizabeth said, shaking her head and staring at him in disbelief. "This is just another case for you. But for me—" Elizabeth stopped. Her voice suddenly choked with emotion. "This is my family."

"I know," he said, his eyes filled with compassion.

They both turned as someone knocked on the door. Elizabeth quickly wiped at her cheeks as Garret reached over and flipped off the lights, then opened the door. Once the man was in the room and the door was shut, Garret turned the lights back on. Agent Larsen was standing before them.

"What's the situation, sir?" he asked Garret.

"They planted a tracking receiver in a pack of gum Jonathan had in his duffel bag. That's how they've been one step ahead of us through all of this," Garret offered.

Agent Larsen turned to Elizabeth. "I'm sorry about your husband, ma'am."

Elizabeth nodded as she watched Agent Larsen put his night-vision goggles back on.

"If you need me, let me know," Agent Larsen said, turning to Garret. "If not, I'll take a night post."

Garret nodded, then turned to Elizabeth, strapping on his own goggles. He pointed to a sleeping bag that had been spread out in the corner. "I know it'll be hard, but try to get some sleep."

Elizabeth nodded, though she knew sleep was very unlikely.

Chapter 16

Reegan lay trembling on the bed, her body glistening with perspiration. Though she knew Blaine was sitting right beside her bed, she no longer cared. Her throat was completely raw, but it was her chest that ached with each violent bout of coughing. Her fever had escalated throughout the day, but had finally broken ten minutes ago, leaving her damp and shivering.

"Where are we?" she asked weakly.

"Just out of Madison, Wisconsin," Blaine said as he lifted a cup of water to her lips. "You need to drink."

Reegan drank the water greedily. "Where are you taking me?" she asked, wiping the moisture from her lips with the back of her hand.

"New Jersey."

Blaine reached into his pocket and pulled out a bottle of pills. He popped it open and handed her two. She hesitated for only a minute before putting them in her mouth. If they were going to kill her, they would have already done it. After taking another sip of the water to wash down the pills, she watched as Blaine got up and walked over to a duffel bag, pulled something out of it, and walked back to her. As soon as he sat back down, he took her hands in his and carefully cut the ropes. Both of her wrists were swollen and throbbing. He squeezed a generous amount of antibiotic cream across his fingers, then gently applied it to her wrists. The whole time that he worked, Reegan never took her eyes from him. There *was* a weak spot in Craddick's plan, and she was looking right at it.

"Craddick won't be back for a couple of hours," Blaine said. Reegan could see the disgust in his eyes as he spoke. "By then he'll be too smashed to care that I took the ropes off."

Reegan forced a smile. "Thank you for the water, and for freeing my hands. I know you're taking a big risk in helping me." It sounded wooden, but it was enough for Blaine to look her in the eyes, albeit cautiously. "I promise I won't tell Craddick about any of this," she added, then held her breath, praying that he wouldn't see through her.

Blaine watched her for several seconds but didn't speak. Finally he stood and made his way toward a chair across the room.

"You were right. You're not like him." Reegan could feel her stomach turn even as she said the words.

"I know what you're doing," Blaine said, his eyes seemingly darker than usual.

"What do you mean?" Reegan stammered, her pulse quickening.

"Don't try to run. If you do, Craddick will hunt you down and finish the job. He's just waiting for a good excuse."

Though her body was still warm, Reegan suddenly felt chilled to the bone. "I won't," she said weakly, unable to control the quiver in her voice.

For the next ten minutes the two of them sat in silence with only the blaring of the television to cut the tension. Reegan was certain that Blaine had purposely turned it up so that no one in the adjacent rooms would overhear them. Once or twice, when his gaze fell on the television screen, Reegan snatched a quick glance at him. His dark charcoal eyes rested on the screen, but from the indifferent expression on his face, Reegan guessed that he wasn't really watching. Every once in a while he would flex his jaw, then reach up and rub at the dark stubble on his face; but other than that one nervous gesture, the rest of his expression was unreadable. Reegan was beginning to doubt her strategy. Who was she trying to kid? Thinking that this maniac would turn against his own flesh and blood and help her was nothing short of delusional. She would have to come up with another plan. Reegan pulled the blanket around her shoulders and stared up at the ceiling, silently praying that she would live to see the morning.

Hours passed before Craddick finally staggered into the room. Blaine had been right—other than briefly glancing to see that she was still there, he immediately plopped down on the bed and passed out. Blaine was still sitting in the chair across the room, but once Craddick fell asleep, Blaine pushed the chair up against the door and sat back down, barricading them all in. Reegan's hopes were instantly crushed. Even if he did fall asleep, there would be no way to get past him. She closed her eyes, trying to stop the tears that were brimming. She felt thoroughly exhausted, both emotionally and physically. Though her mind was screaming for her to stay awake, her body was unwilling. With the horrible images of the day promising to haunt her dreams, she slipped into a fitful and restless sleep.

Craddick awoke the next day with bloodshot eyes and breath that could fuel a tanker. After shoving Reegan into the backseat of the car, he climbed into the seat next to Blaine, tilted his head back, and in five minutes was snoring. That had been a little over two hours ago. Reegan looked over at Blaine. His eyes were equally red, though not for the same reason. Apparently he had spent a good deal of the night wide awake, making sure that Reegan didn't go anywhere. Now, as he drove the car across the slick roads of Wisconsin, the lack of sleep pulled heavily on his features. He rubbed at his dark eyes, then yawned broadly, stretching his arms out across the steering wheel. Reegan found herself relishing a measure of satisfaction from his discomfort. She looked down at her hands. Though they were still tied together, her feet and mouth were void of any restraints. Craddick hadn't wanted anyone seeing her being carried to the car. Instead he had walked behind her, his assault pistol buried in the thickness of her coat, reminding her with each sharp jab what would happen if she ran.

Reegan glanced back out the window. In the last thirty minutes, the clouds that had covered a large portion of the northeast the last few days had finally lifted, allowing the sun to shine down in full force. The result was a blinding reflection off the crisp white snow. Reegan's eyes shifted to Blaine as he flipped down the visor above his head and slipped on a pair of dark sunglasses. Using the distraction to her advantage, Reegan slowly shifted so that her body was mostly positioned behind his seat. She held her breath, praying that he wouldn't notice, then she looked back out the window. After only a few minutes she could feel Blaine's eyes on her. She turned to look at him, but as soon as she did, he immediately angled his head away from the rearview mirror to the road ahead. Before he could have another opportunity to sneak a glance at her, she quickly pulled the sharp piece of glass from her pocket.

"Are you hungry?"

Reegan's eyes shot to Blaine as he held up a bag of pretzels. "No. I'm fine," she stammered, clutching the glass so tightly in her hand that it almost pierced her skin.

Blaine watched her for several seconds before turning his attention back to the road. Reegan could feel her shoulders fall in relief. Though her stomach was gnawing clean through to her backbone, food would have to wait. Time was of the essence now. Though Craddick still had his head craned in an awkward position, with a trickle of drool at the corner of his mouth, his snoring had stopped.

Reegan began sawing discreetly on the ropes, stopping several times when Blaine shifted restlessly in his seat, or when she could no longer suppress a cough. Though the pills Blaine had given her both last night and then again this morning had stopped the fever, her cough still persisted. She continued to carefully cut the rope until it had thinned to nothing more than a few intertwined strands. Waiting until Blaine fumbled through the bag for another handful of pretzels, she cut through the last fiber of rope. With the restraint severed and the glass still secured in the palm of her hand, she quickly adjusted the rope so it looked like it was still attached, then lifted her eyes to the darkly tinted windows and the scene beyond. Though the sun was out in full force, heaping mounds of snow still lined the interstate. The result was slush and mud splattered across every car that passed. Reegan would have tried to signal someone in a passing car, but she knew the tinted windows were too dark. Before she could do anything, Craddick began to stir. With a moan, he grabbed at his neck, which obviously had a nasty crick in it, straightened in his seat, and wiped at the spittle on his chin.

"Find some out-of-the way place to pull over," Craddick growled.

Blaine looked down at his gas gauge. "I need some gas anyway."

Craddick rubbed at his neck, then turned to face Reegan. If anything, a night of hard drinking had only added to his foul mood. "It makes no difference to me *how* I deliver you to Sabatini." Then he tapped the gun concealed beneath his coat. "You keep that in mind."

At that moment all the resolve within Reegan seemed to drain. Craddick must have seen the change in her because his lips lifted into a smug grin.

"That's right. You scrap any idea of runnin' because I'll be right behind you if you do."

Reegan turned her head, refusing to let him see the defeat she was feeling. Instead, she watched from the side window as Blaine exited the interstate and headed toward a run-down gas station on an adjacent access road. An auto salvage yard, almost a quarter of a mile farther down the road, appeared to be the only other business around. A snow-covered field with a dilapidated tractor provided the only backdrop to the two businesses. Reegan took a glance over her shoulder at the interstate now behind them. She had been so preoccupied with inconspicuously getting the ropes off that she had paid little attention to where they were.

"I meant what I said," Craddick barked.

Reegan jerked back around to face him.

"If you run, I'll catch you," he finished, his voice a methodical whisper. Then he turned back around as Blaine pulled into a parking spot on the side of the building next to the restrooms. Without another word, Craddick jumped out and headed into the men's room. Blaine quickly scanned the area around them, then, satisfied that no one was around, turned in his seat to face her. The hard lines above his brow softened.

"I'm sorry about him."

This time the softening in Blaine made her instantly furious. Somewhere in his warped, twisted mind he knew this was wrong, but he was still doing it. As far as she was concerned, he was worse than Craddick.

"Come on," Blaine began, reaching over and opening his door. "I'll walk you to the restroom before I fill the tank."

Reegan's heart leapt. This was it, her chance to escape. She quickly glanced down at the rope to make sure that it still looked intact, then stood as he opened the door. Blaine reached over and grabbed her just above the elbow. He held her close to his side, but as far as Reegan could tell, he wasn't holding a gun. The two of them then walked briskly toward the door marked for women.

"I'll wait for you out—" Blaine stopped, his attention instantly drawn to a car pulling into the gas station and heading straight for the vacant spot next to them. His body went instantly rigid. "Reegan—*don't,*" he whispered. Though his voice was calm, it carried a clear message.

Blaine tightened his grip on her arm as two muscular men dressed in black leather climbed out of a car not five feet from them. Reegan's mind was screaming for her to do something, but her body seemed immobilized with fear. Then, out of the corner of her eye, she saw one of the men turn and look at her. It was now or never. Almost before the thought had completely formed, Reegan sprang into action.

"So who's the woman you've been seeing?" Reegan demanded. She shot a quick glance over at the two men, who immediately turned to face them.

"You can keep her for all I care, because I'm done with you," Reegan shouted, glaring at Blaine, whose jaw went instantly slack.

Reegan yanked her arm free, then turned and stormed straight toward the front of the gas station. She heard Blaine start after her, but after a quick glance over her shoulder, she saw one of the large spectators step directly in his path.

"You heard the lady," the man grumbled. "She's no longer interested."

"So beat it," the second equally muscular man growled.

Just then the door to the men's room flew open and Craddick emerged. His eyes shot from Blaine to the two men next to him. "Hey, what's going on?" he demanded.

Reegan started to run. She rounded the corner at full speed, praying she wouldn't slip on the icy walk, then ran past the front door of the gas station heading straight for a stack of firewood for sale on the far side of the parking lot. If Blaine and Craddick reacted as she suspected, they would look for her inside the gas station first. Right now, with every second counting, she needed to do the unexpected.

A split second after she ducked behind the pile of wood, Craddick and Blaine rounded the corner. Craddick had his gun drawn, but quickly tucked it inside his coat as he burst through the front door of the gas station. Blaine was right behind him. Reegan was just about to stand when Blaine stopped in his tracks and turned back toward the parking lot. Reegan did a quick intake of breath as his eyes zoomed in on the bulky pile of wood she was hiding behind. Just as he was about to take a step toward her, someone inside the gas station started shouting. Blaine whirled back around, his focus instantly riveted on the scene unfolding inside. With his hand reaching inside his coat, he barreled through the front door.

Reegan was on her feet as soon as Blaine crossed the threshold. She ran blindly across the parking lot, momentum and fear more than any rational thought pushing her forward. She was only halfway across the slushy paved lot, heading toward the auto salvage yard, when a loud bang resounded from behind her. Reegan clenched her teeth, waiting for the hot lead that was sure to rip through her flesh. Instead, someone inside the gas station screamed in pain. Reegan ducked her head and ran, not once slowing enough to look back.

Chapter 17

A tall wooden fence topped with loops of barbed wire encircled the entire premises of the auto salvage yard. Reegan ran to the front entrance and pulled on the gate, but it was chained shut with a large metal padlock. Fighting the urge to look back toward the gas station, she ran to the far side of the fence to hide. After rounding the corner, she plastered her body against the fence. She stood there for several seconds, struggling to catch her breath in between wracking coughs. Though the distance between the two businesses was no more than a quarter of a mile, her already aching lungs felt like they were on fire.

Reegan scanned the access road, but there wasn't a car in sight. She looked back over at the interstate. To get to it, she would have to go out into the open and climb a steep embankment knee-deep in snow. Reegan turned, allowing her eyes to run the length of the fence. Toward the far corner, outside the back fence of the salvage yard, there was a beat-up truck minus all four wheels and the hood. Reegan took another quick breath and ran toward the truck.

Desperate for a place to hide, she climbed onto the open engine, then hoisted herself to the roof of the truck. From there she could see right inside the salvage yard. Trucks and cars that had been smashed down to twisted metal took up almost every square inch of the yard, leaving only enough room for a small building situated near the center. But it was a large pile of worn tires inside the fence, just feet to the left of where Reegan now stood, that drew her attention. Her eyes then locked on the razor-sharp wire looped across the top of the fence. With her stomach contorted every bit as much as the twisted metal, Reegan stretched her foot out, carefully placing it in between the sharp, jagged edges, and pressed down on the wire. She took one last frantic look toward the far end of the fence before turning her attention back to the tires. Then, before she could change her mind, and with every muscle in her body braced for impact, she leaped toward the mound of tires.

After a split second of soaring through the air, Reegan's body smacked into the side of the enormous pile of rubber, then tumbled end over end before hitting the ground with a hard thud. This time adrenaline would not temper the pain. Once she had enough oxygen to breathe, the first sound out of her lungs was a scream. As she lay prostrate on the ground, gripped with pain and only vaguely aware of several tires bounding in different directions, someone began to rattle the front gate. Reegan raised her head, her labored breaths suddenly coming in rapid, unabated gulps as her eyes locked on the gate. She sat there motionless, a paralyzing terror exploding inside her. They were coming after her just as Craddick had promised.

With the sound of her own breathing flooding her ears, she staggered to her feet, almost regretting that not even fear was able to dull the pain that now raged through her body. Several streams of blood ran down her legs which had been ripped open by barbed wire, but it was her shoulder that made her head swim with agony. From the way it hung limply to her side, it only took a moment to surmise that it had been dislocated. Clutching it with her good arm and gritting her teeth, she staggered across the junkyard.

Reegan angled toward several rows of smashed vehicles piled three and four deep, trying unsuccessfully not to cry out from the excruciating pain that erupted with each step. After slipping behind a large stack of crushed cars and slouching to the ground to surmise the damage to her legs and shoulder, she heard a loud thud across the salvage yard. She could feel her body tense while her heart fluttered wildly. She slowly peered around the smashed metal in time to see several tires bounding in different directions. *They're here!*

Somewhere off in the distance, Reegan could hear the gentle whine of a police siren, but it was too late. Unless the sirens scared them off, it would be only a matter of minutes before Blaine and Craddick found her. In desperation, Reegan jerked her head back around, her eyes searching for something she could use to defend herself. Then, almost instantly, she froze. Just to the left of her she could hear the low rasp of heavy breathing followed almost immediately by a snarling growl. Turning her head so slowly that it almost felt like she wasn't moving at all, Reegan came face to face with a large, black Doberman pinscher. Saliva glistened across the black rim of his mouth, while the muscles across his sleek body were pulled taut in preparation for his attack.

"Whoa, boy," Reegan stuttered breathlessly, clumsily staggering to her feet. "I'm not going to hurt you."

Without taking her eyes from the dog, she began to back up, but after only two steps, she backed into something.

"Reegan, don't move."

Startled, she jumped, simultaneously letting out a scream. She started to turn, but Blaine grabbed her good arm and held her firmly.

"Back up," he whispered, close enough that she could feel his breath on her neck.

"Forget it. I'd rather take my chances with the animal in front of me," she snapped, her voice instantly cold and defiant.

"Just do it," Blaine demanded.

Reegan took one step back as she watched the Doberman pinscher take a step toward her. She had no doubt that the dog was fully capable of pulling her limb from limb, but the man behind her was certainly capable of no less. She was just about to take another step backward when the dog lunged at her. As a scream erupted from her throat, Blaine stepped in front of her, pulling his gun from under his coat. Reegan thought at first that Blaine was going to shoot the dog, but instead he aimed the gun just above the dog's head and fired, the shot pinging as it ricocheted off a pile of metal. The Doberman pinscher yelped, then cowered back several steps, frightened by the reverberating echo.

"Back up!" Blaine demanded, his voice sharp.

Reegan hesitated for only a second before slowly staggering backward with Blaine following closely. Once they reached the end of the demolished cars, the two of them started toward the small office. Each jarring step sent a surge of pain through Reegan's shoulder that almost took her breath away. As soon as they reached the building, with Reegan's attention returning to the guard dog, Blaine pulled his sleeve up over his hand, broke the window on the office door with his fist, and carefully reached in between the protruding pieces of glass and unlocked the door. With the now-recovered dog slowly creeping toward them, they both slipped into the building and slammed the door shut. Reegan wasted no time. She immediately sprang for a phone on a nearby desk. Blaine was to her in a split second, his hand slamming the phone back down. Reegan scrambled to the far end of the office, but Blaine stood where he was, his eyes going instantly to her shoulder.

"You're hurt," he said, immediately starting toward her.

"Leave me alone!" Reegan screamed.

Blaine stopped, his face suddenly sober. "Reegan, I'm not going to hurt you."

"You could tell Craddick you never found me," Reegan began in desperation, her body in so much pain that she knew she would never be able to fight him off. "You could say I got away. You could say anything, but *please,*" she begged, tears now glistening as they spilled down her face. "Please, let me go."

"Craddick's dead."

Reegan stared at Blaine blankly. "*What?*"

Blaine stepped forward, but instead of going toward her, he slouched into a chair. "I shot him," he said, his voice barely audible.

Blaine could have been speaking Japanese and it would have registered more quickly than what he was saying now.

"When I went into the gas station, he had his gun aimed at the gas attendant. I identified myself and told him to freeze, but he just stood there, his gun cocked and his finger reaching for the trigger." Blaine stopped. From the look on his face, he was reliving every detail.

"What do you mean, you identified yourself?" Reegan asked, her voice slightly elevated.

Blaine's eyes lifted, though he almost looked surprised to see her standing there. "I'm an undercover cop," he said slowly. "I'm working on special assignment with the FBI."

Reegan stared at him, her jaw suddenly slack. For a minute she wanted to shout for sheer joy, but the image of Wayne and Seth's blood on Blaine's chest siphoned out her breath. She began to shake her head adamantly. "Liar!"

"Reegan, it's the truth."

Before Blaine could protest, she lunged for the phone. Blaine was on his feet in an instant.

"Don't," he said, his voice almost pleading. "Sabatini put a bounty on your father's head big enough to entice almost anyone. I can't be certain that someone on the inside won't jump on it. Not only that, but it'll blow my cover, and we'll never nail Sabatini." Blaine stopped, his eyes searching hers. "If that happens, your dad's a dead man."

They both turned as the sound of the sirens increased, stopping right in front of the salvage yard. Blaine was to the window in an instant. With a quick shake of his head, he turned back to Reegan.

"You can't go with them." His eyes were round and intense.

Reegan shook her head, her eyes narrowing. "I don't believe you. You're just saying all this to get me to come with you. You're not a cop. Cops don't shoot innocent people in cold blood."

"I didn't kill your friends, though we did put them in protective custody for now. That night, after I left the motel, I followed them to an alley behind that bar in Pinewood. I could hear them plotting out how they were going to break in and steal a case of beer. When I approached and told them I was an undercover cop, Seth punched me in the nose. Apparently he thought I was on this high-security assignment just to take down a couple of penny-and-dime thieves."

Reegan shook her head, still not believing, but Blaine added, "It was *my* blood on the shirt. Think about it, Reegan. Which way was the blood splattered?"

"How should I know?" she snapped in frustration.

"Think, Reegan, think!" he pressed, his eyes suddenly intense.

Reegan had been so repulsed and horrified that night when Blaine came back to the room that her mind had taken in little more than the bright red blood, concluding instantly that Wayne and Seth were dead. Now the image of the stained shirt filled her mind, details jumping out that she had been too distraught to notice before. Within seconds Reegan's breath caught. The blood had streamed down his shirt, not splattered across or smeared. Tilting her head slightly, she stared at Blaine as if in a numb stupor.

"You're a *cop?*"

Blaine slowly nodded his head, the tension across his shoulders showing instant relief.

Questions were forming so fast in Reegan's mind that she could barely juggle them all. "Why didn't you…when were you going to—"

"Look," Blaine interrupted, taking a quick glance out the window, "I'll tell you everything you want to know. But right now, we need to get out of here."

* * *

"This is going to hurt."

"Have you ever done this before?" Reegan asked, her eyes round as she looked at the man next to her.

"Do you really want me to answer that?"

"Just do it," Reegan blurted out, diverting her eyes from Blaine to one of the walls of the barn that was now serving as their temporary hideout.

Blaine took her firmly by the shoulder. Then, in one jerking motion, he popped her shoulder bone back into the socket. Reegan screamed, the sudden shock of pain making her knees grow weak. Blaine caught her around the waist.

"It's done," he said gently, immediately leading her to a bale of hay so she could sit down.

Reegan sat down on the bale, her body shaking involuntarily and her stomach queasy. Though her shoulder still throbbed, setting it had ebbed the pain significantly.

Reegan's attention then went to Blaine. Though learning
that he was an undercover cop had relieved her fear, it did
little to pacify the indignation she was feeling.

"Why didn't you tell me?" she asked accusingly.

Blaine dragged over another bale of hay, then sat down
facing her. "I know this might sound unfair to you, but we
needed you to look scared. If I'd told you the truth, and
Craddick had caught on, he'd have buried us both."

"So you put me through all of this—chasing me through
a freezing river in sub-zero weather, making me think that
Seth and Wayne were dead, and allowing my shoulder to be
dislocated in a fall that easily could have broke my neck—
just so you could eventually, *maybe,* if he didn't kill me in the
process, arrest Craddick?" Reegan blurted out, her face
growing redder with each word.

"No," Blaine said evenly. "So I could help the FBI bring
your father home."

Reegan stiffened, any comeback instantly snatched
from her.

Blaine let his breath out. "I'm sorry. Maybe it *was* a
mistake."

"No," Reegan jumped in, her voice instantly placating.
Though she didn't like the means of the plan, the end result
was exactly what she did want. If going through all of this
made it possible for her father to come home, it was
undoubtedly worth it. Reegan tilted her head to the side,
quickly appraising Blaine, who had turned his attention to a
wall lined with shovels, rakes, and other assorted, neatly-kept
farm equipment.

"Is Sabatini really your father?"

Blaine stiffened. Though he had to know that the question would come, it still left him noticeably jarred. He
continued to stare at the tools placed meticulously across the

wall of the barn, though he no longer seemed to be seeing them. For a minute Reegan wasn't sure that he was going to answer. Then, with his face showing a mixture of shame and resentment, he turned back to face her.

"I wish I could say he wasn't—" He stopped, his face suddenly showing more shame than resentment. "But I can't."

Reegan didn't know what to say. Before her sat a man who was doing everything in his power to put his own father behind bars. If her emotions were at the surface, his must be raging. Blaine stood, obviously no longer comfortable with the conversation. Reegan also felt an immediate desire to change the subject.

"Now what?" she asked restlessly.

Blaine turned back to her, his eyes instantly dropping to the ugly red stains across the bottoms of her ripped pant legs. "Before we do anything, I better take a look at your legs."

Reegan glanced down at the dark blood that had seeped through her pants. Though the throbbing pain of her shoulder had overshadowed the pain from the lacerations, it had not bested it by much. Reegan winced as Blaine lifted her pant leg. The blood had dried, causing her pants to stick to the open wounds. Now, with the material pulled free, the sticky, clotted wounds reopened.

Blaine let out a discouraged sigh. "Some of these are pretty deep. You're going to need stitches. We're going to have to get you to a hospital."

"We don't have time for that," Reegan said rashly, quickly pushing her pant leg back down. "We need to make sure that Sabatini doesn't find my father."

"I'll handle it. As soon as I drop you off at the hospital—"

Reegan shook her head. "I'm not staying at the hospital. I'm going with you."

Blaine was on his feet in an instant. "That's out of the question. This is too dangerous."

Reegan could feel her temper flaring. "Oh, and tying me up and leaving me with Craddick *wasn't* dangerous?"

Blaine's eyes flooded with guilt, but it didn't stop him. "And that's exactly why I'm *not* going to take you with me now." He extended his hand to help her up, though his face was still unbending. "I'm going alone."

Reegan twisted around so that she didn't have to face Blaine, but instantly discovered what a mistake that was. A sharp pain shot up her arm. She bit down on her lip to keep from crying out.

"Listen, Reegan," Blaine began, his voice noticeably more gentle. "I know you want to help your father, but I promise, the FBI will protect him."

Reegan turned back to face Blaine. "Like you protected me?"

"You're still alive aren't you?" Blaine shot back.

"Only because I got away."

The tightness along Blaine's jawline slowly eased, replaced by a hint of a smile. "I'll have to admit, using that cheating boyfriend ploy was pretty quick thinking. You blindsided me on that one."

Before Reegan could respond, Blaine glanced around the barn, his attention already elsewhere. "We've got to get going."

"How? The police will be searching for that police car you stole back at the salvage yard. They'll spot us the second we hit the road." Reegan arched a brow. "You better hope you're a cop after stealing it."

"I didn't steal it. I merely transferred it from one governmental agency to another."

"I'll bet that's not what those cops thought."

Blaine shrugged while attempting to hide a smile. "They'll definitely have some extra paperwork tonight. But hey, when this is all over, I'll make sure their department gets a brand new car."

"I'm just glad the Doberman pinscher left us and went after them."

"He must have smelled donuts on them," Blaine teased. "You know us cops."

Reegan looked at Blaine curiously. "I never would have guessed you to be an undercover cop."

"Good. Let's hope Sabatini doesn't either." Blaine stood, reaching his hands out to help her up. "Come on. Until we come up with a better option, we'll have to go on foot."

Reegan gawked up at him. "Easy for you to say. You have two good legs."

"Unless you want to ride to the nearest town on a stolen tractor," Blaine began with a crooked smile, "it doesn't look like we have much choice."

Chapter 18

"What in the world did you do to your legs?" the nurse asked as she pulled up Reegan's pant legs.

Reegan shrugged. "I had a little run-in with a barbed-wire fence."

"A *little* run-in?" The nurse shook her head, then reached for a pair of scissors and began slicing Reegan's pant legs up to her thigh. Then she cut them crosswise so that the front of Reegan's legs was exposed. Gingerly she lifted a leg at a time and cut the remaining material at the back of the legs, instantly turning her pants into a pair of shorts. "Let me get the doctor."

Reegan watched as the nurse left the room, returning five minutes later with an ER doctor. He scowled down at Reegan's legs. "Now, *what* happened?"

"I got cut on some wire," Reegan offered.

"What were you doing?" he asked as he moved his rolling chair toward the lower end of the bed.

"I was trying to climb a fence."

"What about your chin?"

Reegan's hand flew up to the day-old cut she had gotten while running from Blaine. With everything that had happened in the last twenty-four hours, she had completely forgotten about it. "I slipped on some ice yesterday."

"Why didn't you come in for stitches?" he asked, eyeing her warily.

"I didn't think it needed it," she said weakly.

The doctor raised an eyebrow but only glanced over at the nurse. "Her chin needs to be stitched also."

The nurse nodded as she readied a tray of needles, gauze, and cleaning solution.

Reegan reached up to feel the clotted blood across her chin. As she did, the doctor's eyes went to her hands.

"What did you do to your wrists?" he exclaimed.

Reegan's breath caught. "I—I must have hurt them in the fall," she said, unable to come up with anything quick to explain the rope burns.

"It looks like you've had something on your wrists," he said, looking her straight in the eyes.

Reegan shook her head, trying to keep her face as passive as possible. "Just a bad fall, that's all."

The doctor nodded his head slowly, but didn't press the issue further. Finally, after thoroughly examining both legs, he stood and turned to the nurse. "Get her cleaned up and we'll get started." Then he glanced at Reegan. "Have you had a tetanus shot recently?"

Reegan shook her head in indication that she hadn't. The doctor scribbled something on the paper held by his clipboard, then left the room without another word.

"Sorry, honey," the nurse said. "But you wouldn't want to end up with lockjaw."

Reegan lay back on the bed and closed her eyes. Getting lockjaw was the last of her worries right now. She was thoroughly exhausted. Her body ached from head to toe, but as she lay there, more than anything, her body yearned for sleep. A couple of minutes and a few shots later, the nurse began to clean Reegan's legs with a copper-colored iodine.

Reegan opened her eyes briefly, but as the shot to numb her legs began to work, she began to relax. It seemed like days since the last time she'd slept.

"The doctor will be back in a minute," the nurse offered once she had finished the prep work.

Reegan didn't even open her eyes. "Thank you," she whispered.

For the next few minutes, Reegan enjoyed the first peace she had felt in days. If she had been left a second longer, sleep would have completely enveloped her. As it was, she barely acknowledged the doctor when he entered. He started with her chin, using small intricate stitches to avoid scarring. Then, when he was finished, he turned his attention to her legs. The medication had completely numbed the area, so the stitching was painless. He did his work in silence, allowing Reegan to give in to her heavy eyelids. She vaguely remembered him finishing, saying that he expected them to heal well. The next thing she heard was someone calling her name.

"Reegan, wake up!"

Reegan looked up into the face above her. "Blaine?" she said groggily. She struggled to sit up. "What are you doing here? I thought you'd be long gone by now."

"What did you tell the doctor about your legs?" he asked anxiously.

"What do you mean?"

"How it happened?" he persisted impatiently.

Reegan stared at Blaine, her anxiety rising sharply. "I told him I cut them trying to climb a barbed-wire fence."

Blaine exhaled audibly. "The police must have notified all the hospitals in the area."

Reegan struggled to her feet, instantly grabbing hold of the bed next to her for support since her legs were still partially numb. "What are you talking about?"

"Your doctor is down the hall talking to a security officer. If my hunch is right, the police are probably already on their way."

Reegan looked down at her wrists. "He must have thought the abrasions were from handcuffs." She looked back at Blaine, her voice panicked. "What are we going to do?"

"We're going to get you out of here," Blaine said, his eyes quickly surveying the room.

"How?"

Blaine rushed over to a drawer marked "scrubs." Without taking time to explain, he pulled a green pair of scrubs over his jeans and cinched them at the waist. Then he took off his coat, pulled a green shirt over his head, and put a matching cap on his head.

"Lay back down on the bed."

"What are you doing?" Reegan asked as Blaine grabbed a blanket and threw it over her.

"Whatever you do, don't make a sound," he said, draping a stethoscope that had been carelessly left on the counter around his neck. "The doctor is just down the hall and around the corner. If he hears us, we'll be sitting in a cell sporting a couple of black-and-white jumpers."

After checking to make sure that the hall was clear, Blaine wheeled the bed out of the room and headed for the elevator. He had only made it a few feet down the hall when a nurse emerged from a nearby room. Her eyes went directly to the covered body, then widened as they came to Blaine.

"Who is this?" she demanded as she quickened her step toward them.

"I'm not sure," Blaine offered, looking down at Reegan's still body. "She didn't say." Then he laughed awkwardly. "Sorry. Just a little mortician humor. When I tell it to my other customers, they laugh till they're stiff."

"Who are you?" the nurse demanded, not impressed by his flippancy.

Blaine started pushing the bed toward the elevator. "I'm new—from downstairs in the morgue," he offered, trying to get past her.

The nurse reached down and pulled the blanket off of Reegan's face.

"Boo!" Reegan whispered.

The nurse let out a shrill scream, then threw the clipboard she was carrying straight up into the air. Not waiting around until the nurse recovered, Blaine reached down and scooped Reegan into his arms and raced down the hall. The elevator was no longer an option. By the time they made it to the bottom floor, a security officer would probably already be waiting for them. Instead Blaine set his eyes on a square box marked "laundry chute."

"You up for a little ride?"

Reegan's eyes went from the laundry chute back to Blaine. "Surely you don't expect me to…"

Blaine didn't answer; instead he lifted the lid with Reegan's feet and dropped her, screaming, into the chute. After a quick glance behind him at the security guard that was now racing down the hall after them, Blaine pushed open the chute.

"Get out of the way," he yelled down to Reegan, who was now at the bottom. He glanced briefly at the security guard, just feet from him, then jumped in and let go.

After free-falling two full stories, his echoing screams following him down the chute, he landed in a huge pile of linen.

"Are you absolutely insane?"

Blaine's head jerked around to face Reegan. She had crawled out of the pile of laundry and was leaning heavily on a commercial-size washing machine for support.

"I might have to plead the fifth on that one," Blaine said, rolling out of the thick pile of laundry to stand at Reegan's side. "Are you okay?" he asked, genuinely concerned.

"You could have gotten us both killed," Reegan protested as Blaine reached over and picked her up into his arms.

"Dirty laundry won't kill you." Blaine smiled. "But if the police catch us, and Sabatini's men find out, they will."

Without another word, Blaine headed to the door. Just outside the laundry room was a short hall and a stairwell. With Reegan's arms wrapped tightly around his neck, Blaine started up the first flight of stairs. As they neared the landing, they could hear someone who was approaching the stairwell above them yelling for them to stop.

"There's no place to go," Reegan cried. "We'll have to give ourselves up."

Blaine's eyes grew round as he looked back down the flight of stairs they had just come up. "Maybe not."

* * *

"The morgue!" Reegan exclaimed.

"Hey, I'd rather hide among the dead than be one," Blaine admitted as he set her down and yanked open the door.

They both turned as the shouts coming from the stairwell grew closer.

"Stick around and let them catch you if you want," Blaine continued, "but I'm going in."

Blaine quickly shut the door behind her as soon as Reegan hobbled through the doorway, then he grabbed a nearby chair and propped it up against the door handle.

"This won't stop them for long," Blaine said as he turned back to the dimly lit room.

"Now what?" Reegan asked, shrugging off a shudder as her eyes went to several metal doors on a refrigerated wall used for temporarily storing bodies. "And don't think I'm hiding in there."

Blaine picked Reegan back up and started for a door on the opposite side of the room.Once they reached it, Reegan reached down and opened the door since Blaine's arms were full. Then the two of them peered into the room. Though it was dark, a sliver of light peeked in from under a large garage door. Reegan looked to the garage-door opener on the wall next to them, but before she could push it, the garage door began to lift. Reegan's whole body stiffened. At that same moment someone began to pound on the door that Blaine had temporarily barred with a chair.

"What are we going to do?" Reegan cried, looking first at the opening garage door, then back at the door to the morgue.

Blaine jerked around to face the doorway they had just stepped through, then immediately stepped behind the door and closed it partway, temporarily hiding them from whoever it was that was entering the garage. Within seconds someone backed a van up to the dock and turned off the engine. Reegan could see a glimpse of the man through the door hinge. He started toward the back of the van to open the doors, but stopped when he heard the pounding coming from the door to the morgue. Reegan could feel her heart race as he turned with an impatient sigh and started their way.

"Don't move a muscle," Blaine whispered as his own body stiffened.

Reegan struggled to control her choppy breathing as the man walked through the doorframe. As soon as he had passed, Blaine slipped noiselessly from their hiding place and started toward the van. By the time they were at the van door, they heard the door to the morgue fly open. Blaine practically threw Reegan in the front seat before jumping in next to her. As he revved the engine and sped out of the garage, Reegan glanced in the side-view mirror to watch the driver of the van and two bulky security guards race out onto the dock. Reegan let the pent-up air in her lungs escape before turning to Blaine.

"Do you realize this is the second vehicle you've *borrowed* in less than three hours? Or is this just another typical day at the office for you?"

Blaine shot a quick glance at her, then shook his head. Reegan watched him as he turned his eyes back to the road. In the last two hours, she had seen a side of him that she'd never have guessed given his well-built facade.

"You're an interesting guy, Agent Sabatini."

"I'll take that as a compliment," he said as he changed lanes. "It definitely beats being called a parasite."

Reegan grimaced. "Hey, at the time I thought you were a hit man."

"Let's just pray that's what Antonio Sabatini still thinks," Blaine said as he dodged off the main road and onto a back street. "If not, my cover isn't going to be the only thing with holes in it."

Reegan could feel the knot that had occupied her stomach the last two days returning. "You can't go to New Jersey alone," she said.

Blaine nodded, though he didn't take his eyes from the road. "Believe me, I no longer intend to."

chapter 19

Though the blizzard had finally subsided, the temperature had only elevated to the single digits. Reegan and Blaine sat in silence in the warmth of the van, watching the moon climb into a sky speckled by countless points of light. Though she tried to fight it, Reegan could feel her eyelids drooping as she watched the stars dance on the smooth surface of Lake Michigan.

"If you want, you can stretch out in the back," Blaine offered.

Reegan's eyelids snapped open. "No. I'm fine," she lied, trying unsuccessfully to stifle a yawn.

"They shouldn't be much longer."

"Do you trust them?" Reegan asked, watching his face for any sign of hesitation.

Blaine managed a smile, but even in the dim light she could see a flicker of doubt in his eyes. He started to speak, but before a full word had formed, a noise to the left of them clamped his mouth shut. They turned to see a motor home followed by a small white car making its way through the trees to the well-hidden spot that Blaine had chosen.

"That's them," Blaine said as he reached for the door handle.

"In a motor home?" Reegan asked skeptically.

Blaine turned back with a smile. "And no, it's not stolen—or *borrowed*."

Reegan smirked, then climbed out of the van, her legs still throbbing as the chilly night air whipped across her exposed flesh. Blaine quickly walked around to her side of the vehicle and wrapped his arm around her waist to help her walk.

"You're trembling," he said, pulling her close.

"I left my coat back at the hospital," Reegan said, her teeth beginning to chatter.

"Come on. Let's get you in where it's warm," Blaine said, helping her toward the motor home.

After only a couple of steps Reegan stopped, her eyes focused on the two men who were just climbing from the white car. "Wait a minute. I've seen that man before. He came to my house the night before I met you. He said he worked for the utility company."

"That was just his cover. Agent Hickman is an FBI agent. The other man with him is Agent Wesley."

They both turned as the door on the side of the motor home swung open. Standing in the doorframe was a woman in her early fifties wearing a white sweatshirt printed with large purple magnolias. She'd matched the shirt with her black polyester pants and thick-soled orthopedic shoes. Behind her was a man of about the same age wearing a Phoenix Suns sweatshirt, khaki pants, and white tennis shoes. The woman smiled broadly at Reegan, motioning them toward the motor home, then hugged herself, rubbing her arms up and down for warmth.

"Now I know why I live in the desert," the woman said as she moved to the side to let Reegan, Blaine, and the two agents enter the living area of the motor home.

After shutting the door, the older man, sporting a generous spread across his midsection and a receding hairline, gestured toward a little table with cushioned bench seats that probably also folded down into extra beds. Reegan shot Blaine a dubious look as she scooted across the vinyl bench seat. Agent Wesley and Agent Hickman took the seats across from them, while the older couple pulled out a couple of fold-out chairs. Now that they were all closer and the light was better, Reegan could tell that the older couple was not as old as she had first thought. The woman smiled at Reegan.

"I'll bet you weren't expecting mom and pops to be your protection?"

Reegan smiled uncomfortably.

"That's the whole idea," the older man added. "The more typical we look, the better for all of us. Who's going to suspect an older couple in a big motor home to be a couple of undercover FBI agents?"

Reegan shook her head. She couldn't help wondering how many sweet little old ladies or fragile old men she'd passed on the street were packing Uzis.

"I'm Agent Christiansen," the woman began, "and this is Agent Perry," she added, gesturing toward the older man next to her.

"Do you know where my father is?"

Agent Christiansen shot an uncomfortable glance at Agent Perry, who reluctantly turned to Reegan.

"We just got word," Agent Perry began, his face grim, "Sabatini has your dad."

Reegan gasped.

"What happened?" Blaine demanded, turning his attention to Agents Hickman and Wesley.

"It doesn't matter now," Agent Christiansen broke in. "What we need to do is concentrate on getting him back." Her eyes deepened in intensity. "We can't take the chance of

Antonio suspecting you. With Craddick gone he's already going to have his guard up." The agent glanced over at Reegan, then took a deep breath, surrendering to the inevitable. "We're going to have to play along."

Reegan could feel her heart begin to thunder as she surveyed all the faces that had turned to look at her.

"No! It's too dangerous," Blaine blurted out, understanding only too well what Agent Christiansen was insinuating. "I can't take her with me. You said yourself that Antonio will be on full alert."

Reegan could feel her stomach turn as she watched the exchange. The tension in the room only confirmed what she had already concluded. If she didn't go with Blaine to New Jersey, not only would her father's life be in danger, but Blaine's would be too.

"I'll go," Reegan said, her voice no more than a tense whisper.

Every head turned in her direction. Blaine began to shake his head, but she didn't give him the chance to speak.

"My father's life is at stake. I'm going," she said, her tone showing her resolve.

"We'll make sure that every precaution is taken," Agent Perry said, nodding his head reassuringly.

Reegan swallowed hard, wishing she were safe at home in Maplecove. Then her hand instantly flew to her face.

"What about the stitches. How will we explain Blaine taking me to the hospital?"

Agent Christiansen's eyes ran across Reegan's face, her brow creased in thought. "The stitches under your chin aren't noticeable. And," she continued with increased confidence, "with a pair of pants to cover up your legs, I think you'll be fine."

"If Sabatini does notice the stitches on your chin, you can say it happened the day before Blaine and Craddick showed up. With Craddick gone, Sabatini won't be the wiser," Agent Perry offered.

Reegan let her breath out, that problem seemingly rectified. "Are we riding in the motor home with you to New Jersey?" she asked, still feeling as if she were in a daze.

Agent Christiansen shook her head. "No. You and Blaine will travel alone in the car that Wesley and Hickman drove up in. The four of us will follow at a safe distance." Agent Christiansen walked over and opened a cupboard over a small sink. Instead of dishes or food, the cupboard housed a high-tech surveillance system. "Your vehicle has already been equipped with two transmitters so we can track you wherever you go, one under the driver's seat and another in the trunk. We would give you both individual devices, but we can't take the chance of Sabatini finding them on you."

Reegan stared at the woman numbly. For a girl that had spent her entire life being sheltered, Reegan felt she'd dropped dead center in the middle of a James Bond movie.

"Though it's not stolen, the car you'll be driving will be reported as such as soon as you're safely to Jersey City—just in case Sabatini checks," Agent Perry offered, his attention on Blaine.

Blaine nodded, the gratitude for their precision evident on his face. "By now I'm sure Antonio knows that Craddick's dead," he spoke up. "I need to make contact and assure him that I'm still bringing Reegan in."

"But you shot Craddick," Reegan began. "What are you going to tell him?"

"The news report we issued on the national news identified the shooter as the gas station attendant," Hickman offered. "He was protecting himself against Craddick and an unidentified man. He fired in self-defense. Craddick was killed, but the other man escaped." Hickman turned to Blaine. "Fleeing from the police should help you account for not immediately contacting Antonio after Craddick was killed."

Blaine's face showed obvious relief.

"We already picked up the gas attendant and put him in protective custody," Agent Christiansen continued. Reegan looked confused. "Not only for his safety," the woman offered, seeing her expression, "but for both of yours as well. If Antonio finds out what really happened…" The woman stopped. There was no need to finish. They all knew what the repercussions would be.

"I can't believe this is happening," Reegan said, resting her elbows on the table and massaging her temples with her fingertips.

"Well, if your father wouldn't have been so stubborn and hot-headed, insisting that he help us handle this case, maybe things would have worked out a little differently," Agent Wesley snapped.

They all stopped—their eyes riveted on the agent, who, up to that point, had remained silent. Though Reegan had no idea what Wesley was talking about, she was instantly ready to defend her father. Blaine beat her to it.

"Agent Wesley, if you'd done your job properly, maybe Jonathan Schmitt might not have felt inclined to do it for you."

Wesley's mouth tightened, while Reegan's fell open.

Disgusted, Blaine scooted out of the bench seat, walked over and opened the door, then pulled a cell phone from his pocket. "I've got to contact Antonio." He gave one more sharp glance at Wesley, then shut the door.

Reegan shook her head. Though Antonio Sabatini stood for everything that Blaine risked his life to fight against, the fact still remained that he was Blaine's flesh and blood. He'd have to face that reality soon. Reegan glanced across the table to Agent Wesley. Wesley's apparent incompetence had only delayed the inevitable.

* * *

Blaine and Reegan drove in silence, neither of them discussing Reegan's father, Antonio Sabatini, or all the unknowns that lay ahead. Blaine had already assured her after his phone call with Sabatini that her father was still alive. The relief she had felt was quickly replaced with terror once the realization of what she had committed herself to finally sank in. Now even the terror had ebbed, returning her to the numbness she'd felt when she'd found out about her father's capture. She glanced over at Blaine. From the look on his face, he was fighting off the anger, guilt, and whatever other emotions she could only guess were tormenting him. Reegan wanted to reach over and touch him, but she didn't. Though she had seen a different side of him today, it seemed he was now retreating into the role that he'd assumed earlier. He had pulled back into a shell, playing the part, and he was determined, regardless of how painful this was for him, to see it through. She only hoped that he would have the strength to actually do it when the time came. Her life, and the life of her family, depended on it.

"I plan to drive through the night," Blaine said, interrupting her thoughts. "You might as well push back your seat and get some sleep."

Reegan could feel her stomach growl. "Is there any chance we could stop and get something to eat first?"

The hardness in his face instantly softened. "I guess it has been a while since we've had anything to eat. You must be starving."

Reegan only nodded.

"I'm sorry. I'd stop for a burger or something, but we can't take the chance of being seen by the police—or Sabatini's men."

Reegan's head shot around to the rear window, the hair on the back of her neck standing on end. "Sabatini has people following us?"

"I don't know. We just need to be careful." The underlying tone in his voice held as much warning as his words.

Blaine glanced in his side-view mirror at the dark, empty road behind them, then pulled over on the shoulder.

"What are you doing?" Reegan exclaimed, her eyes going from Blaine to the road behind them.

"Getting you something to eat." He climbed out, walked to the back of the car, and opened the trunk, then returned a second later carrying a bulging grocery sack and a small ice chest. "I'm not sure what's in here," he said as he climbed behind the wheel and shut the door. "The agency stocked the car with items the couple we supposedly stole it from would use on vacation."

Blaine reached into the sack and pulled out two bottles of water and a bag of chips. He handed them to Reegan, then turned and placed the sack with its remaining contents on the backseat. Then he opened the ice chest and took out two ham sandwiches.

"Well, at least we won't go hungry," Blaine said, turning back around and handing Reegan one of the sandwiches.

Reegan smiled halfheartedly, then took a quick sip of her water. The cool liquid provided a welcome relief to her sore throat. After placing her bottle in the cup holder below the CD player, she glanced over at Blaine. Though he held his sandwich in his hand, his head was slightly lowered and his eyes were closed.

"Are you okay?" she asked, her voice elevated.

Blaine opened his eyes and looked at her in confusion. Then slowly his lips lifted into a weak smile. He held up his sandwich. "I was just saying a prayer."

Reegan felt her face flush. "I'm sorry. I thought you were sick or something."

Blaine smiled. "No. Just praying."

Reegan tilted her head to the side, looking at Blaine curiously as he pulled the car back onto the road.

"What?" he asked, glancing at her, his mouth now full of food.

Reegan shrugged, a little embarrassed. "I'm just surprised that you're—religious."

Blaine swallowed, then took a sip of his water. "Why? Because my father is a convicted murderer and I'm an undercover agent who's posing as a hit man?"

Reegan smiled, liking this side of him. "I guess."

Blaine turned back to stare out into the darkness.

"So, what about your mother?" Reegan asked. "You haven't mentioned her."

"She's incredible," he offered immediately, then a mischievous smile slowly began to spread across his lips. "Of course, I didn't always think that." As he turned back to the road, his smile faded. "My mom didn't know what my father did—what he *was*—until right before she left him. Once she knew, the marriage was over, and to protect me, she moved me as far away from my father as she could—a little town in the mountains of Utah. I found out years later that just before we'd moved there, my mom had given some important information about my father to the police. Information that later, along with your father's testimony, helped put him behind bars."

Reegan raised her brow. "Did your father find out?"

"No. Apparently he thought it was one of the worms that worked for him. A betrayal like that has only one clear sentence in my father's book—the police found the man floating facedown in Lake Superior."

Reegan felt sick. "Did your father ever try to come after you?"

Blaine nodded his head. "He tried, but my mom made sure that finding us was not an option. Before we moved to Utah we both got new names, forged birth certificates, social security cards, everything. That way I could live a normal life." Blaine let his breath out. "When it was time for me to go undercover, the FBI planted information about me under the alias that I was supposedly raised with."

"Wow," she said soberly.

"But of course, I didn't know any of this growing up, and I was too young to remember much of my father. All I knew was that I didn't *have* a dad."

Reegan could feel her throat constrict, knowing exactly how he felt.

"When I got a little older I channeled that frustration into rebellion. At first it was nothing serious—arguing with my mom, then fighting at school . . . that kind of thing."

Reegan nodded.

"Then it was skipping school and stealing." Blaine shook his head, clearly sorry for what he had put his mother through. "My mom left my dad so I wouldn't be exposed to that kind of life—then there I was, slipping into it anyway."

Reegan felt sick. Not only for *his* mother, but also for what she had put her *own* mother through.

"Fortunately, I was eventually able to change my life."

"So, you were raised in Utah?" Reegan had another question itching, but hoped he would supply the answer himself.

Blaine must have read the hint, because he instantly smiled. "Yes, I'm LDS."

She shook her head, appraising the man before her. "Do the surprises ever stop with you, Agent Sabatini?"

"My name's not Sabatini—not anymore anyway. When my mom remarried, my stepfather adopted me. But that's a whole different story."

"Well, I have a little confession of my own."

"What's that?"

"I'm a Mormon too. Well—not an active one exactly. We stopped going when I was pretty young. At the time I didn't know why."

"You would have been too easy to track down if you were openly practicing your religion."

Reegan nodded in agreement. "By the way," she began, her thoughts suddenly elsewhere, "could I borrow your cell phone? I need to let my mom know that I'm all right."

Blaine turned to face her, his expression serious. "Your mom went with your dad to Jersey City."

"She *what?*" Reegan demanded.

"Agent Hickman said she was adamant about going with your dad. She didn't really give them much choice in the decision."

Reegan's eyes opened wide in alarm. "Did Sabatini get her too?"

"No," Blaine said firmly. "He tried, but she got away."

Reegan could feel her whole body relax, though every limb continued to tingle. She shook her head, frustrated, but not at all surprised that her mother had gone after her. Taking a deep breath, Reegan leaned her head back on the headrest, comforted that, though she couldn't see it, the motor home was somewhere behind them. She glanced over at Blaine. His brow was lowered and his eyes dark. She couldn't help but wonder what he was thinking. One thing was certain— tomorrow, as he reunited a father and daughter, he would forever end any connections to his own father.

Chapter 20

Reegan only woke once during the night when Blaine stopped for gas. When he finally nudged her just before dawn, it felt as though she had slept on hard-packed dirt through the winter. She slowly stretched her tender limbs, then turned to the man next to her.

"How are you feeling?" Blaine asked, rubbing his own tired eyes.

Reegan swallowed, then massaged her stiff neck. Though her throat was still sore, the aching in her chest was gone. The rest of her body still felt the effects of the last couple of days, but a heavy night's sleep had alleviated even a portion of that.

"Better," she admitted after a yawn.

"You look like you feel better," Blaine said honestly.

Reegan looked down at the soft sweatpants that Agent Christiansen had given her last night in the motor home. She'd also obtained coats for both Reegan and Blaine since theirs had been left at the hospital. She smiled, remembering the look on Agent Wesley's face when Agent Christiansen had asked him to volunteer his new coat for Blaine. Reegan took a deep breath, sure that if she could just have a nice warm bath, she would feel like a new person. She shook her head thoughtfully. So much had happened in the last month, it was almost like she *was* a different person. She looked over at Blaine as he stretched his own stiff muscles. The thick, dark hair that had previously been slicked back now fell soft and slightly mussed across his forehead and down the back of his neck, while his dark, serious eyes were now reflective, almost plaintive.

"I'm sorry for what my father took from you, for what he took from your whole family," he said, keeping his eyes pointed forward.

Reegan's eyes opened wide at the unexpected comment. She watched as he turned to face her, his expression showing his vulnerability. She was a little taken aback by the genuine expression of empathy on his face. Had he spent the whole night thinking about this? Had he spent a lifetime thinking about it? Somehow that thought instantly deepened the hate that she felt for Antonio Sabatini. How many lives had he destroyed, including those of his own family? How many more would he destroy if they didn't stop him?

"Is that why you're doing this?" Reegan pressed gently. "To try to make up for what he did?"

"I can't undo what he did. But maybe, if I'm lucky, I can stop him from doing it again."

"Do you hate him?"

Blaine's body stiffened as he stared out the window before him. He was silent a moment, cautiously picking through his feelings. "Not anymore. But I did for a long time." Blaine turned to face her, his eyes open and honest. "Hate is a heavy burden to carry." He turned back to the window, his eyes pensive. "When I first moved to Utah, away from Antonio, I hated it and everyone there. I was miserable. So I spent the next couple of years making everyone around me miserable." Blaine's face shone with regret.

"You mentioned a stepfather last night?"

"I hated him most of all," Blaine admitted without flinching.

"And your feelings now?" Reegan asked, watching him closely.

Blaine's countenance visibly changed. "He saved my life. If it wasn't for him and the things he taught me—" Blaine shook his head. "I don't know where I'd be." He turned to look at her, as if he could see into her very soul, as if he could see her pain and guilt and anger. She quickly looked out the window, her eyes stinging.

"Are you hungry?"

Reegan nodded, only now feeling the rumbling in her empty stomach.

"There's some granola bars and apples in the sack, and I think there's some juice in the ice chest."

Reegan twisted around in her seat to gather the items for breakfast, then the two of them spent the next few minutes enjoying their food in silence.

"When you contacted Antonio last night, had he heard about Craddick?" Reegan asked, taking the last sip of her juice.

Reegan watched as Blaine's eyes flashed to the rearview mirror before finally falling on her. Though he tried hard to keep his face passive, Reegan could see the apprehension in his eyes as he slowly nodded.

"And?" Reegan asked, not liking the intensity of his expression.

"He made it quite clear there are to be no more mistakes."

Reegan let her breath out slowly, then glanced across the horizon as the night sky slowly surrendered to the rising sun. Despite the beauty of the breaking day, Reegan couldn't shake the chill that seemed to be climbing her spine.

"It might be a good idea if you ride in the backseat now that it's getting light. If we *are* being followed, we need to keep up all pretenses."

Reegan nodded slowly, his words and the expression on his face only adding to the eerie feeling of impending doom that she couldn't quite shake. "Did you see anyone following us last night?"

Blaine rubbed at his bloodshot eyes. "No, but I don't want to take any chances."

"I should have driven last night and let you sleep. You've been up for two nights straight."

"I'm all right," he said, trying to stifle a yawn.

"You won't be any good to my father like this."

"If we're being followed, how am I going to explain letting my hostage drive while I take a nap?" Blaine asked, lifting one brow.

"If someone is behind us, they'll follow at a safe distance, right?"

"Not so far away that they won't be able to tell the difference between us," Blaine said, reaching over and playfully tugging a long strand of her dark hair.

"I need a hat," Reegan acknowledged thoughtfully, before her eyes opened wide. "Didn't you say the agency packed this car to make it look like it belonged to a couple who were on vacation?"

"Yeah. There are a couple of suitcases in the trunk."

Reegan's head shot around to the front window, quickly scanning the area. "See that clump of trees?" she asked, pointing to a spot a few hundred feet ahead of them. "Pull over."

Blaine glanced in his rearview mirror. Though the shadows of night had not completely faded, the sun was slowly bringing the countryside to life.

"Blaine, trust me. This will work."

Blaine shook his head in frustration, then veered off into the small stand of trees. Five minutes later, with her hair pulled up into a baseball cap and the collar of the coat she had borrowed from Blaine flipped up, Reegan pulled back onto the road.

Blaine handed her a dark pair of sunglasses. "Turn your head like you're changing the station on the radio when someone passes."

Reegan glanced over her shoulder at him as he stretched out across the backseat. Though she was not about to admit it, she had never been so scared in her life.

* * *

The ride through Indiana, Ohio, and into Pennsylvania was a blur. Though Reegan had driven the last four hundred miles while Blaine slept in the backseat, her mind had been able to focus on little more than the impending hours that lay ahead. She glanced over her shoulder at Blaine, who was sleeping as soundly as possible in the backseat. Doubts flooded her mind. Would he actually be able to arrest his own father? Or worse—what if trouble erupted? Reegan reached over and turned on the radio, desperate for something else to occupy her thoughts.

"Where are we?" Blaine asked groggily.

"I'm sorry," Reegan said, turning to face him, then she quickly reached to turn off the music. "I didn't mean to wake you."

"It's okay," Blaine said, slowly pulling himself to a sitting position. He glanced down at his watch. It was almost noon. "I've already slept longer than I planned."

Reegan glanced at his red eyes, knowing that he had to be running on fumes. "We're in Pennsylvania," she informed him.

Blaine reached into the sack of food that he had placed on the floor. After digging through it, he retrieved two bottles of water. He handed Reegan one bottle then opened his own, drinking it greedily.

"You're going to have to stop and get some gas," he said, pointing to a gas station a few miles down the road. "Pull around to the back so we can switch places first."

Once Reegan shed her disguise and the two had changed places, Blaine pulled the car around to the pumps. Reegan slouched down in the backseat nervously scanning the area, but there was only one other car in the parking lot.

"Stay put," Blaine said as he climbed from the car.

Reegan watched anxiously as he filled the tank, then quickly walked inside the station. He returned less than a minute later carrying a small sack. "I think we're in the clear," he said, the tension in his face easing as he climbed behind the wheel.

Without another word, he pulled back onto the street. Once the two of them were safely on the road again, Blaine twisted around and handed her the sack.

"I thought you might be hungry."

Reegan reached into the sack and pulled out two hot dogs that looked like they'd been turning on the warmer for a week. She must have pulled a face, she realized, because Blaine, who was watching her in the rearview mirror, instantly smiled.

"It's definitely not a filet mignon, but I'm pretty sure it's edible."

Reegan bit into the leatherlike dog and forced a grin. "Delicious."

Blaine laughed, immediately easing the strain of the situation. "I wouldn't suggest a career in undercover work. You don't have the face for it. They'd see right through you," he teased.

"You did pretty good—with the lying anyway, *Mr. Boy Scout*."

"Hey, I actually was a Boy Scout."

"And your other lie—the one you told me back at Mike's Grocery about wanting to come back to Maplecove and take me out to lunch?" Reegan asked, watching his expression carefully. "That was all just a part of the job?"

Blaine gave her a long look, his face unreadable. Reegan could see him struggling for something to say. With her cheeks burning, she quickly forced a smile, realizing that the whole thing in the grocery store had been a part of the act. He wasn't interested in her—he was just doing his job.

"Well, I'll say one thing about you—you're good at what you do," she admitted with a smile that she hoped looked more genuine than it felt. Then she turned and looked out the window.

Chapter 21

For the next thirty minutes they drove in almost complete silence. Reegan's stomach felt like it was manufacturing sulfuric acid. She shifted restlessly in the backseat, trying desperately to think of something to discuss other than the meeting with Sabatini.

"So, what do you do for fun in Utah?" she asked, hoping an unrelated topic would ease the mounting pressure.

Blaine shrugged. "When I was younger I used to spend a lot of time fishing and practicing my tae kwon do." He turned to her with a mischievous smile. "That's how I knew how to set your shoulder. Sometimes those tournaments could get pretty intense, and unfortunately, I didn't always come out victorious—or in one piece."

"I'm glad you didn't mention the extent of your medical training before you set my shoulder."

Blaine laughed, then he looked back out the window. "The last few years I haven't had much time for anything recreational. After my mission nine months ago, I went straight to the police academy."

"Why did you decide to become a police officer?"

"It's a long story."

"Even better," Reegan said with a smile.

Blaine smiled back at her, then let his breath out in surrender. "When I was fifteen my stepfather encouraged me

to join a police explorer group. I consented—reluctantly. After
a mini two-week police academy, I spent the next year going
on ride-alongs, seeing firsthand the ins and outs of law enforce-
ment and learning state law—everything from the Miranda
rights to minor traffic violations. I loved it," he admitted
openly. "Especially the time I spent studying the law." A sad
shadow crossed his eyes. "It was during that time that I made
the decision to help the police apprehend my father."

"That must have been hard," Reegan said gently.

Blaine nodded. "It was. After that, I started reading everything I could about the Mafia. At sixteen I took my GED,
started taking online college courses, and two and a half years
later, I graduated with an associate's degree in criminal justice."

"Wow. That's amazing," Reegan said, clearly impressed.
"And how did you end up working with the FBI?"

"I went to them to offer my help because I knew I could
get on the inside. They agreed. It's not every day that a cop
has the kind of inside connections with the bad guys that I
have," Blaine admitted soberly. "So at night, after I had
finished my classes at the academy, the FBI began preparing
me for this assignment. It was pretty intense."

"So, do you think you'll end up staying in law enforce-
ment?"

"I'd like to go back to school. Who knows, maybe
someday be a state prosecutor." Blaine blew the air out of his
cheeks, then shook his head. "I'm glad there are people who
can work the streets, but I don't think I could day after day.
Once this is done—"

"You want to move on and have a more normal life,"
Reegan filled in, understanding completely.

Blaine smiled, realizing for the first time that she *did*
understand. "If we can make it through this, maybe we can
both move on."

Reegan smiled, though her heart wasn't entirely in it. Though she desperately wanted this to be over, once it was . . . Reegan turned to look out the window, letting her thoughts trail off, not wanting to face the feelings she was beginning to recognize. This was not the time. Right now she needed a clear head, and thoughts like these were only clouding it.

"Reegan, we'll get your father back."

Reegan's eyes shot to Blaine, then slowly she began to shake her head, emotion suddenly at the surface. "I don't even know if I'll recognize him when I see him—it's been so long."

"He's your father; you'll know him."

Reegan took a deep breath, regaining her composure. "Have you met him?"

"No. But if he's anything like you, I'm sure he's amazing."

* * *

"Are you sure you're ready for this?" Blaine asked over his shoulder as he drove the remaining two miles to the Italian restaurant in downtown Jersey City.

Reegan could feel her heart pounding in her chest, but she only nodded her head, afraid that her voice might give her away. Blaine had called Sabatini on his cell phone and gotten the instruction to bring Reegan to the same restaurant that Sabatini had taken him to initially.

"If you think this is where they're keeping my father, why not just call in the police now?" Reegan asked. "You said he does a lot of his dealings here and behind the restaurant."

Blaine shot a glance in her direction. "Because it's just a hunch. What if I'm wrong? We won't know for sure until we see him."

Reegan swallowed hard, her mouth completely dry with fear.

"There is one thing we can do," Blaine said, his eyes fixed on the rearview mirror.

"What's that?" Reegan asked expectantly.

"Pray," Blaine said, his expression serious.

"Don't worry. It's already been done," Reegan said, her tone equally somber.

As Blaine pulled down the alleyway that ran behind the restaurant, Reegan felt an eerie sensation rush through her entire body. She realized this was Antonio's playground.

"This is the alley where my father witnessed the murder, isn't it?"

Blaine didn't need to answer, Reegan could *feel* it. Blaine nodded, his face showing that he too felt uneasy. Then he gestured toward the back of a large warehouse at the far end of the alley. "If anything happens to me, you run to that warehouse."

"What about the agents in the motor home?" Reegan asked, shooting a backward glance toward the main road.

"Wesley and Hickman will be at that warehouse with some other agents already in place. Agents Christiansen and Perry will stay at a safe distance in the motor home to maintain their cover."

Reegan wanted to tell him to start the engine and press on the gas, but instead she took a deep breath and forced herself to think about her father. Blaine climbed out of the car and quickly opened her door. She looked up into his face expectantly, but it was unreadable. Blaine reached out and took her by the arm, then pressed his 9mm Glock against the thickness of her coat. Her eyes widened.

"They might be watching," he whispered between clenched teeth.

Reegan could feel her body flood with adrenaline so quickly that her legs began to shake uncontrollably, but Blaine nudged her toward the door. She glanced up at him, but the fear she knew he was feeling wasn't present on his face. Instead, he looked like a boxer getting ready for the bell to ring. Any trepidation or hesitation was covered by a look of unabashed arrogance—the face that Antonio Sabatini would want to see. The expression that he would *expect* to see.

Reegan took a deep breath and held it as Blaine pushed open the back door to the Italian restaurant and entered the kitchen. The aroma of stewing tomato sauce, garlic, and freshly baked bread filled the small room. Sterling silver pots with copper bottoms hung from a metal rack over a counter covered with vegetables. A man wearing a white apron splattered with red sauce was busy adding spices to a large pot simmering on the stove, while a second man was pulling a loaf of hot garlic bread from a large oven. Both men turned as Blaine and Reegan entered the room. Though their eyes went immediately to the gun pointed at Reegan's side, neither of them looked particularly alarmed.

"Where's Sabatini?" Blaine barked.

The man at the stove gestured with his head to a set of swinging doors separating the kitchen from the dining area, then went right back to stirring the sauce. Blaine jabbed Reegan with the barrel of the gun, urging her toward the door. She could feel her breathing quicken with each step. Once the two of them pushed through the doors, her eyes went to a table at the far end of the small restaurant. Three men, who had been deep in conversation, turned to look at them. Other than those three men, the rest of the restaurant was empty. Reegan singled out one of the men, her jaw instantly going slack. Other than a hint of gray speckled through his hair and a lifetime of living on the edge stressing his features, he was a carbon copy of the man next to her. The man leaned back in his chair, his eyes locked on her.

"Hello, Reegan."

Blaine pushed Reegan toward the table. She stumbled forward, almost falling as she neared the three men. Once she had her balance, her eyes lifted to Antonio Sabatini. His eyes seemed to go right through her, leaving her feeling somehow defiled. Then his attention went to Blaine. He seemed to scrutinize his son just as intently.

"Mario, check him for wires."

"You don't trust me?" Blaine asked evenly, holding his arms out as Mario stood to search him.

Sabatini shrugged, then turned his eyes to Mario.

The big man nodded. "He's clean."

Reegan slowly let the air escape from her lungs.

"Gionni, Mario, take the girl to the basement," Sabatini said, his eyes staying on Blaine.

As both men stood, Reegan shot a glance at Blaine. For a fleeting second their eyes met.

"What are you going to do with her?" Blaine asked, trying desperately to sound passive.

Sabatini motioned for Blaine to sit down beside him. "Her old man has something we want, and she's going to convince him to give it to us." He waved his hand impatiently toward his men, who now had Reegan firmly by the arms. As Reegan was pushed toward a staircase leading to the basement, she risked one more parting glance at Blaine.

"Move," Mario barked, pushing her toward the stairs.

Reegan grabbed the railing, fighting the urge to elbow them both and run despite their guns. Instead, she descended the stairs, a feeling of desperation and gloom enveloping her like a dense fog. When they reached the bottom, the bigger guy slid the bolt from the lock and pushed the door open. Reegan's eyes shot to a man tied to a chair on the far side of the dimly lit room.

"You've got some company, Jonny boy," Gionni said, pushing her into the room.

Reegan's breath caught as she stared at the man before her. She could hear the door being bolted behind her, but her eyes remained riveted on the man tied in the chair. He slowly lifted his head. His face was badly bruised, with streams of dried blood coming from a cut above a swollen eye. Her knees grew weak.

"Reegan!" he gasped, his voice no more than a hoarse whisper as he stared at her in wonder.

For a moment it felt like Reegan couldn't breath. She stood there motionless, her mind struggling to grasp what her heart already knew. "Daddy?" she cried, her legs suddenly finding the strength to carry her down the stairs. Once she reached him, she bent down in front of him, cupping her hands gently around his battered face. "Is it really you?" she asked, her eyes quickly taking in every inch of his face.

Jonathan nodded his head slightly, then turned and kissed her hands, tears falling from his eyes. "I can't believe you're here," he whispered, his voice choked with emotion.

Reegan could feel her throat constricting as tears fell from her own eyes. For years she had dreamed of meeting her father, never really believing that it was possible. Now, here he was.

"Did they hurt you?" he asked, trying to force his swollen eye open as he searched her face.

Reegan shook her head, touched that he would be concerned about her when he was so badly hurt. "I'm fine."

"I'm so sorry," he began, no longer able to hold back a sob. "I'm sorry I got you into all this."

She looked into his eyes, a flood of recollection overwhelming her. "It's okay," she cried, a warm tear streaking her cheek. "It's okay."

She quickly reached down to untie the rope that held him to the chair. "I'm going to get you out of here."

Reegan pulled the last knot free, letting the rope fall to the floor before helping her father struggle to his feet. Then, for the first time in years, she fell into his arms.

"I've missed you," he whispered, the deep resonance in his voice showing the depth of his emotion.

She nodded as she held him tight. "I've missed you too."

They both jerked around as the door to the damp room swung open with a loud thud.

"How touching," Gionni cooed.

Both Jonathan and Reegan pulled back, their reunion short-lived, as four men entered the room. Reegan's eyes fell on Blaine.

"I hope you two have had a chance to talk," Sabatini said as he separated from the other men and made his way toward them.

"I told you that you could have the negatives," Jonathan said, his voice suddenly desperate. "Let her go and I'll take you to them."

Sabatini began to cluck his tongue and shake his head. "Now you know I can't do that, Jon." He turned and motioned for the three men to join him. "I thought I already made myself clear to you."

Reegan could feel the pounding of her heart clear up in the nape of her neck. She glanced at Blaine, but his eyes were locked on Sabatini.

"Antonio, I can't just tell you where they are. It's been too many years. I'm going to need some time to find them," Jonathan pled.

Sabatini stared at Jonathan long and hard, then motioned toward Mario. "Kill the girl."

Reegan watched in horror as Mario raised his gun.

"No!" Jonathan screamed. "I'll tell you where they are."

Reegan watched breathlessly as Sabatini put his hand across Mario's chest, signaling him to wait. "Where are they?"

"In a safe-deposit box in Philadelphia," Jonathan cried.

Everyone in the room turned to look at Sabatini. "Where's the key?"

Jonathan pointed to Gionni, who had initially taken his keys. Gionni retrieved them from his pocket, fumbled through them until he found one that was much smaller than the others, then held it up.

Jonathan nodded. "Liberty Bank on Kensington Drive. The box number is on the key."

Sabatini's face lit into a menacing grin. "Now was that so hard?"

Jonathan's chest was heaving. "Please let her go. You've got what you want."

Sabatini looked at Jonathan, his face feigning compassion. "I wish I could. But we'll just have to wait and see what's in that safe-deposit box." Then he turned and started up the steps with the other three men following close behind. Blaine glanced back at Reegan, who was clinging to her father, then turned and closed the door.

"What does he want with the negatives?" Reegan asked as soon as they were alone.

Jonathan lifted a finger to his lips to silence his daughter. Reegan looked at him in confusion before slowly lifting her brow in understanding. It was very possible that Sabatini had the room wired and was listening in on their conversations. Reegan nodded, grateful that he had warned her before she said anything about Blaine.

Chapter 22

Blaine stood on the opposite side of the dining room watching Sabatini, who was sitting at a table talking animatedly on his cell phone. From his expression, Blaine could tell that he was fighting to control his temper.

"I told you I'd get them," he snapped, pushing himself back from the table to stand. "In a safe-deposit box in Philly." Sabatini listened for a moment, then shook his head in exasperation. "It's already been taken care of. I sent one of my boys to get them."

Blaine shot a glance toward the kitchen, his hand going instinctively to the bulge under his coat where he had strapped his gun. He needed to get to the warehouse and tell the agents to move in. This might be his only chance. With Sabatini still temporarily distracted, Blaine took a step toward the kitchen. As he did, Sabatini lifted his eyes and impatiently motioned him over to sit. Blaine hesitated, taking one more anxious glance toward the kitchen, then reluctantly walked over to the table.

"I'll call as soon as I know for sure," Sabatini said, then turned off his phone, dropping it into the pocket of his expensive leather jacket. For a minute he just sat there, rubbing at the back of his neck with his hand, clearly agitated.

"What's the matter?" Blaine asked.

Sabatini waved his hand as if to brush it off, though the effect of the conversation still showed on his brow-creased face. "Nothing that won't be cleared up shortly."

"What happens once you get the negatives?" Blaine asked, though he was confident he already knew the answer.

Sabatini's face lit into a grin that made Blaine instantly sick.

"You'll kill them," Blaine stated, fighting to control his voice.

Sabatini shook his head. "No. You will."

Blaine could feel his body tense. For a split second he thought about reaching for the gun that was strapped to his chest and turning it on his father, but he didn't. With Sabatini's men just through the swinging doors of the kitchen, the odds of him, Reegan, and Jonathan getting out in one piece were not in their favor. Just then the swinging doors pushed open, and Mario and Gionni walked through. Gionni had a large slice of garlic bread in his hand and was licking some dripping butter from his fingers. Mario was right behind him with a heaping plateful of fettuccini. Blaine looked at both of them, sizing them up. They were armed. Though Blaine wasn't positive, he also guessed that the two men in the kitchen were also armed, or at least had ready access to weapons. There was no way Blaine could outgun them all. He swallowed hard, knowing he would have to find another way.

"You want me to get you somethin', boss?" Gionni asked, wiping the grease from his mouth with the side of his hand.

"Go find something to do," Sabatini demanded impatiently. "I want to talk to Blaine—*alone*."

Gionni and Mario immediately turned to leave, not once questioning Sabatini's authority.

"Leave your plate," Sabatini said to Mario.

Mario turned back to Sabatini, his mouth almost forming a pout. "But this is the last of the fettuccini. Since we weren't open for business tonight, Franky and Marcel cleaned up the kitchen early."

Sabatini's jaw tightened, while Mario's face immediately registered his mistake.

"That's okay," Mario said, verbally backpedaling. "I'll get something else."

With that Mario placed the food on the table in front of Sabatini and left the room. Sabatini picked up the salt shaker and began to sprinkle it on his food as if nothing had happened. Then, without thinking of getting Blaine something to eat, he took a big bite. Blaine could hear his own stomach growl.

"What happened to Craddick?" Sabatini asked after chewing and swallowing a forkful of noodles.

Blaine fought the nervous reflex to tighten his jaw. "He got careless."

Sabatini jabbed at his food with his fork, though his eyes never left Blaine. "He was one of my best men."

"He got himself killed because of his poor choices," Blaine shot back, trying to look relaxed and under control.

"You were sent to help him."

"I was sent to pick up the girl, which I did," Blaine challenged. "Not to babysit."

Sabatini tried to keep his face impassive, but Blaine could see a hint of pride in his eyes.

"Fair enough." Sabatini took another bite, apparently satisfied with Blaine's explanation.

"So—am I in?" Blaine asked tightly.

"What are you talking about? I already said you were in."

"That's why you patted me down for wires when I got here?"

Sabatini laughed. "You don't get where I'm at without a little caution."

"What's on the negatives?"

Sabatini pushed his plate back and stood. "Maybe nothing. Maybe something."

"There was someone else in the alley wasn't there?"

Sabatini's eyes narrowed, but instead of anger, a slow smile spread across his face. "You catch on quick."

"Who was it?" Blaine asked, praying the fear tingling inside him wasn't as transparent as it felt.

Sabatini drew in a breath as he eyed Blaine thoughtfully. Blaine held his own breath, every muscle in his body taut. Finally, after what seemed an eternity, Sabatini exhaled. "In this kind of business, large amounts of money exchanges hands. How much money and how we come across it could become...*complicated* if it became public knowledge. You understand?"

"So you use legitimate companies to launder the money."

Sabatini nodded.

"But what does that have to do with who was in the alley with you that night?"

"Let's just say those negatives could be bad for business if a certain *legitimate* person was identified."

"And the man you shot that night in the alley?"

"He knew too much," he said, his voice matter-of-fact. Then Sabatini slapped Blaine on the shoulder with a composed smile. "Now make yourself scarce for a couple of minutes, I've got a few matters to take care of."

Blaine thought about pushing the issue, but one look into the man's eyes told him that wouldn't be wise. Instead Blaine slipped into the kitchen where Gionni and Mario were standing at a counter devouring the last of their spaghetti and meatballs. After a quick glance at the two, Blaine edged toward the door.

"Hey, where are *you* going?" Mario asked, wiping a thin trail of sauce from his chin.

Blaine could feel his body tighten as his mind reeled for an answer. "I was just going out for a smoke," he lied.

"I could use one myself," Mario said, placing his dirty plate on the counter and starting toward the door.

 Mario grabbed a coat from a rack next to the door, then followed Blaine out the door. The air was crisp, making Blaine's breath visible as he breathed into his hands for warmth. Mario reached into his coat pocket and pulled out a pack of cigarettes while Blaine's eyes went to the far end of the alley toward the warehouse, knowing the agents would not be able to see his signal from this angle. He would have to get farther down the alley.

"Well?" Mario asked, looking at Blaine curiously. "You gonna just stand out here freezing?"

"I forgot, I left my cigarettes inside."

Mario extended his pack to Blaine, who immediately felt sick; not only would his inexperience give him away, but his mind rushed to the temple recommend stashed in his dresser drawer in Utah. He'd prayed that he wouldn't have to do anything like this on the assignment.

"Thanks," he said, shaking his head. "But I just decided what I really need is some fresh air."

Mario's eyes narrowed, but before he could speak, the back door to the restaurant flew open and Gionni appeared.

"Sabatini just got word—the negatives aren't there."

"I knew Jonathan was lying," Mario sneered.

Blaine could feel his throat constrict so that he could barely breathe. He shot a quick glance down the alley, but Mario already had his hand on his shoulder escorting him back into the kitchen. When Gionni pushed open the swinging kitchen doors, Blaine's eyes immediately went to Sabatini, who was on his cell phone again.

"Don't worry," Sabatini began. "We'll get it out of him this time." After setting the phone down on the table, Sabatini lifted his eyes to Blaine. "You want to know who's on those negatives?"

Blaine's head nodded though the rest of his body felt paralyzed.

"Take out the girl," Sabatini said coldly.

"If I do, Jonathan will die before telling you where the negatives are," Blaine said, knowing it was the truth.

Sabatini's face went flame-red, the veins in his neck bulging grotesquely. "Your job is to do whatever it takes to make him talk. You understand?"

Blaine's mind was racing. He pulled the gun from the strap around his chest and checked the clip, then started for the door to the stairs alone. After pulling the bolt from the lock, he pushed open the door and stepped in, quickly shutting the heavy door behind him.

"What do you want?" Jonathan asked, staggering to his feet, then stepping protectively in front of Reegan.

"Where are the negatives?" Blaine shouted.

Reegan's eyes went to the gun at Blaine's side. "What are you—"

Blaine did a barely discernible shake of his head to silence her, then aimed his gun at the cinder block wall and fired. Reegan let out a shrill scream, then lifted her hands to cup over her ears.

"Where are the negatives?" Blaine shouted, quickly walking over to the wooden chair that Jonathan had just been sitting in and throwing it against the wall.

"I told you where they were," Jonathan shouted in desperation.

"You lied to us," Blaine replied.

Blaine picked up the mangled chair and threw it again. Reegan ducked, protecting her head from the splintering wood with her arms.

"You tell me where they're at or your daughter's dead."

"Okay, okay," Jonathan shouted. "I'll tell you."

Before Jonathan could do anything, Blaine grabbed him by the collar and pulled him to within inches of his face. "I'll leave the door open," he whispered. "Wait for my signal, then come up the stairs."

Jonathan gaped at Blaine. "*What?*" Then he took a step back, shaking his head in confusion. "Who are—"

Before Jonathan could finish his question, Blaine pointed his gun at the wall and pulled the trigger, blasting away a chunk of cinder block. With his chest heaving, he turned to leave. Just before passing through the doorway, he turned back to Reegan, praying that this wouldn't be the last time he saw her alive. She watched him silently, a stream of tears glistening down her cheek. Blaine swallowed hard, then slammed the door shut, clanking the lock as if bolting it, before climbing the stairs.

When Blaine entered the dining room, Sabatini and Gionni were still at the table where he had left them just minutes before, but Mario was nowhere to be seen. Something in Blaine's gut told him that this was it. With or without backup, if he was going to get Reegan and her father out of there alive, he needed to act now.

"Well?" Sabatini asked.

"The negatives are in a safe-deposit box all right, just not in Philadelphia. They're in Trenton. Same key."

"The girl?" Sabatini asked, eyeing Blaine warily.

"She's dead."

Sabatini nodded his head, then turned to Gionni. "Get Jonathan. We're going for a ride."

Blaine could feel his palms begin to sweat as he inched his finger toward the trigger. If Gionni went to the basement, he'd know that Reegan was still alive. As Gionni rose to leave, Blaine raised his gun.

"Sit down" he demanded, purposely keeping his voice low so he wouldn't alert Mario or Antonio's other two henchmen.

"What are you doing?" Gionni retorted, looking from Blaine to Sabatini.

Sabatini smiled menacingly at Blaine, his face lacking the slightest hint of fear.

"Don't move," Blaine demanded, aiming his gun at Sabatini.

"You gonna shoot me? You gonna kill your old man?" Sabatini taunted.

Blaine swallowed. "If I have to."

Sabatini looked at him for several seconds, his eyes as hard and dark as obsidian rock. "I don't think you have it in you."

Blaine veered his gun toward a vase of flowers on an adjacent table and shot, shattering it to pieces, then pointed the gun back at Sabatini.

"Don't try me," he warned.

"Blaine," Reegan cried as she and Jonathan ascended the stairs and raced toward him.

"Get out of here," Blaine said, his eyes going to the men's room left of the dining room where a sliver of light was coming from under the door. "Hurry up. Mario and those other two are here somewhere," he added, still keeping his eyes on Sabatini and Gionni as Reegan and Jonathan quickly turned to leave.

"You'll never get out of here," Gionni snapped.

"Back up," Blaine barked, gesturing at them with his gun.

Sabatini and Gionni hesitantly backed toward the wall.

"Turn around," Blaine commanded.

As Sabatini and Gionni turned toward the wall, Gionni reached for a gun tucked in the waistband of his pants, then whirled around to face Blaine, planting a bullet in the wall next to him. Startled, Blaine returned the fire, shattering the window behind Gionni. Sabatini ducked behind a table, then reached for his own gun while Gionni fired two more shots. Outnumbered, Blaine barreled through the swinging doors leading to the kitchen. Reegan and Jonathan had left the back door wide open. With his heart pumping madly, Blaine flew through the open door into the darkness beyond. Off in the distance ahead of him he could see the dark outlines of Reegan and Jonathan running down the narrow alleyway. As he started after them, running with all he had, his eyes straining the darkness for any hint of the agents he prayed were there, he heard the swinging doors to the kitchen slam against the wall. Seconds later a bullet whizzed just inches over his head. Blaine ducked, then staggered his step, not wanting the next bullet to find its mark. When he glanced back to the dark figures ahead of him, Reegan was slightly ahead of her father, Jonathan's weakened condition slowing him down. As Blaine watched in horror, Jonathan tripped, going down hard on the rough pavement. Blaine was to him in seconds.

"Come on," Blaine urged, grabbing him by the arm.

"Forget about me," Jonathan demanded. "Go after her."

Blaine lifted his eyes to Reegan, who was still running toward the warehouse, unaware that Jonathan had fallen. Just then two dark shapes materialized from behind a metal dumpster and started after her.

"Reegan, there's—"

Before he could finish his warning, another shot rang out from somewhere high above them. Blaine looked up. With the light of the moon overhead, he could see the barrel of an assault rifle protruding from the edge of a nearby roof. He flinched as several more shots echoed down the narrow alleyway.

"Go help her," Jonathan demanded, his tone desperate.

Blaine looked back down at Jonathan, who was clutching his ankle, then across the dark alley to Reegan. In the back of his mind, he knew that Sabatini had a reason to keep Jonathan alive, but the same was not true for Reegan. Giving Jonathan one last helpless glance, Blaine started after her. He had to warn her, but before he had made it ten feet, another shot exploded behind him. This time he felt the sting of the bullet as it grazed his arm. Fear tingled through him, accelerating his speed. He fought the urge to look down at his arm, instead keeping his eyes glued on Reegan as she approached the warehouse. As soon as she disappeared through the door, Blaine's eyes locked on the two dark figures just feet behind her. He raised his gun to fire, but hesitated. What if they were agents? Not willing to take the risk, Blaine lowered his gun, then watched with dread as both men slipped from sight through the open door of the abandoned warehouse.

Chapter 23

Blaine slowly creaked open the heavy door to the old warehouse, an uneasy feeling of warning flooding over him. He had reached the door just in time to hear several shots ring out inside the old building followed by a loud scream. Now everything was eerily silent. Blaine took a step forward, quickly shutting the door behind him, not wanting to make himself an easy target.

"Blaine, look out!" Reegan shouted from somewhere high above him.

As Blaine lifted his head to find her, someone fired at him, the bullet embedding in the door behind him. Not sticking around for them to take another shot, Blaine dove for the floor, then rolled, landing in a crouched position several feet away. With his heart pounding against his chest, he immediately aimed his gun into the darkness, searching the shadows, his training somehow overriding the fear coursing through his body. Off to his left he could hear footsteps start across the floor and then ascend a metal staircase.

"Reegan, hide!" Blaine called out, his voice echoing through the warehouse.

At that second, the door to a room on the second level flew open.

"FBI," a man shouted as two agents burst through the door. "Throw down your weapons."

That declaration sparked a storm of gunfire. Blaine aimed his gun toward the dark forms as he slowly made his way forward, but held his fire because he couldn't see well enough to take a shot. After only a moment, one of the men cried out in pain, his gun falling to the floor with a loud clank. As Blaine watched on in horror, not sure if it was one of Sabatini's men or an agent that had taken the hit, the injured man stumbled forward on the catwalk then fell over the edge, his body hitting the bottom level with a loud thud. As Blaine rushed toward the crumpled form, he heard more shots being exchanged above him, followed by a guttural moan and the clang of a body falling onto the metal walkway.

"Get back," Reegan demanded, her voice choked with fear.

Blaine looked up just as Reegan let out a shrill scream.

"Reegan!" Blaine called out, soliciting several shots from the man on the catwalk.

Blaine dove toward a stack of metal barrels a few feet in front of him that was directly under the catwalk. He could just make out its outline with the moonlight streaming in through the dirty windowpanes. As soon as he had cover, his eyes went back to the body. With his heart beating wildly, he froze. The body was gone. Before he could move, someone gripped his arm. Blaine jerked around, his finger pressing against the trigger of his gun.

"FBI," the man choked out in between moans.

"Larsen? Is that you?" Blaine whispered back, easing his finger from the trigger.

The man nodded, lacking the strength to do anything else.

"Where are you shot?" Blaine asked, then ducked as a bullet pinged off a nearby barrel.

"My shoulder," Larsen groaned, placing his hand over the wound to stop the bleeding. "But I'm pretty sure I broke my leg and a few ribs in the fall. I lost my gun, too." He pointed to something a few feet away from them. "But if you can reach them, those are my night goggles."

Blaine immediately handed his gun to Agent Larsen. "Start shooting, but aim at the wall. I don't want Reegan hurt."

"Just tell me when."

Blaine took a deep breath. "Now!" He said, as he darted toward the goggles, keeping his head low.

Agent Larsen had ripped off several shots by the time Blaine returned. Blaine pulled the goggles over his face and looked up at the catwalk. Reegan was crouched down on the walkway almost directly above them. When he turned his head just slightly to the right, one of the men that had followed Reegan through the alley came into view. Blaine recognized him as one of the chefs that worked in the kitchen at the restaurant. Blaine thought his name was Franky but wasn't certain. The man was slowly making his way across the catwalk in the dark.

"Give me the gun," Blaine whispered.

"It's empty," the agent whispered back.

Blaine felt like he had just been hit. "What am I going to do? Once he finds her, he'll kill her."

Before Larsen could comment, the door to the second-floor room flew open and a third agent appeared. He ripped off several shots, but nothing even marginally close to Franky since Reegan was almost directly behind him. Franky immediately crouched down and began to fire. Blaine didn't waste a second. He grabbed the unloaded gun from Larsen, tucked it into the waist of his pants, and climbed on top of one of the barrels.

"Reegan!" he shouted amid the ricocheting of bullets. "Reegan, jump!"

Reegan scrambled to the edge of the catwalk, then peered over the edge.

"I can't," she cried, her voice tight with fear. "It's too high."

The two of them ducked down as Franky turned his gun in their direction, the agent that he had been exchanging fire with momentarily taking cover behind the door. With Blaine's whole body tingling with fear, he said a quick prayer, pulled the gun from his waistband, then threw it toward a large window behind him, shattering a section of it into tiny pieces. Startled, Franky immediately turned and began firing toward the window.

"Jump!" Blaine yelled.

Reegan took two small steps to the left, closed her eyes, and jumped. Blaine caught her in both arms just as Franky turned and pointed the barrel of his gun directly at them. Blaine could feel his breathing quicken while everything else around him seemed to be moving in slow motion. Out of the corner of his eye, Blaine could see the moonlight now streaming in through the broken glass, illuminating their forms as they balanced awkwardly on top of the barrels.

Franky started toward them, a menacing smile itching across his lips as he cocked the trigger. Knowing that they were both within seconds of death, Blaine dropped his eyes to Reegan, regretting he'd been unable to protect her. A split second later a shot rang out, the sound seemingly amplified in the darkness. Blaine flinched, then braced himself for the inevitable, but nothing happened. Instead he heard a guttural groan, followed by silence. Blaine lifted his eyes just in time to see Franky fall motionless onto the catwalk, the thud resounding through the warehouse. Reegan screamed, then buried her head into Blaine's chest, but Blaine's eyes ran the length of the catwalk until they came to rest on an agent, gun still drawn and aimed at Franky. Blaine gasped with relief, then slowly lowered Reegan to the floor before climbing down beside her.

"Let's get out of here," Reegan said, her voice noticeably shaken.

Blaine shook his head, his arm firm around her arm as he crouched down behind the barrels. "Two men followed you into this warehouse."

Reegan's eyes widened with fear. "Where's the other man?" she asked hesitantly, her eyes slowly scanning the warehouse.

"He's still here—somewhere."

"Maybe he was shot," Reegan said, her voice shaky.

"Maybe," Blaine conceded, though not completely convinced.

Just then several shots rang out from a dark area of the warehouse close to the front door. The agent on the second floor that had killed Franky immediately crouched down and returned the fire.

"Stay here with Agent Larsen," Blaine began. "I'll be right back."

"Where are you going?" Reegan whispered anxiously.

"He's going to make a run for it. Stay here. You'll be safe."

Then, not waiting for her to protest, he slowly made his way across the floor staying low enough that he wasn't readily visible. Once he was safely across the floor, he glanced back at the front door. He had hoped the FBI sharp-shooter that had been on the roof just minutes before would come to their aid, but he figured the agent had probably pursued Sabatini and Gionni instead. Blaine's eyes then went to the room on the second floor where the agent was now taking cover. Slowly expelling a breath of air, Blaine glanced back at the shooter near the front door, immediately recognizing him. As he did, the big man pointed his gun in Blaine's direction. The first shot came so close to Blaine that he could actually hear it slice through the air. Blaine dove to the floor, then rolled behind an empty wooden crate.

"You're not leaving this place alive, Blaine," Mario called out, splintering the wood as he embedded two bullets in the four-by-five wooden crate.

Blaine could feel every muscle in his body tighten. Mario wasn't trying to escape. He was waiting for them. Then an even more disturbing thought sent an icy chill through Blaine. Mario knew where Reegan and Agent Larsen were hiding. Waiting until Mario started firing at the door on the second level, Blaine slowly got to his feet. He was just about to start across the floor when Mario reached for a second gun strapped to his chest, then pointed it toward him. Blaine hit the floor behind the same wooden crate as a shower of bullets poured down around him, the sound making his head throb and his ears ring. Surprisingly, though several of the bullets came close, the first two shots were the only ones that actually hit the box. When the explosion of sound finally ceased, Blaine slowly peeked out from the side of the crate only to find that Mario was gone. As Blaine jerked around to face the stack of barrels, fear pricked his skin. Mario had Reegan in front of him, his gun pointed at her temple.

"I've got your little friend," Mario called out.

"Let her go," Blaine shouted, his heart thumping violently against his chest. "Take me instead."

"I don't need you," Mario sneered, tightening his grip on Reegan. "I'll deal with you later."

Blaine took a step forward. "Let her go, and I'll let you walk out of here."

Mario aimed his gun in Blaine's direction and fired. "It doesn't look like you're in a position to call the shots," he snapped sarcastically. "Now stay where you are."

Blaine held back, watching helplessly as Mario dragged Reegan toward the warehouse entrance. His only hope was that the sharpshooter was still perched on the roof, but since he hadn't made an appearance yet, it wasn't likely. Mario yanked open the door, holding Reegan out in front of him, and stepped through the doorway. Then he turned and fired several more shots into the dark room. Once the shooting stopped, Blaine raced to the door. At the same time, the door to the room on the second level flew open.

"He's got her," Blaine yelled to the FBI agent.

"Don't let him get away," the agent responded as he rushed down the stairs.

Blaine flew through the doorway, bracing himself against the shot that might come. Instead, the only thing he heard was the screeching of tires on pavement. His eyes widened as a silver luxury SUV headed down the alleyway toward the warehouse. It stopped momentarily as Mario shoved Reegan in the backseat and then climbed in beside her.

After gunning the engine and squealing the tires, the driver started down the narrow alley heading straight for him. Blaine was desperate. He couldn't let them take Reegan. If they did, she was as good as dead, and he knew it. Having no gun and seeing no other option, Blaine quickly climbed on top of a metal dumpster that was placed next to the warehouse, then crouched down and waited for the vehicle's approach. When the SUV was almost parallel to him, he took a deep breath and dove for the roof, grabbing onto the luggage rack with both hands.

The driver immediately swerved, causing Blaine's body to go flying to one side. For a second he almost lost his grip, but somehow he managed to hold on and drag himself back to the middle of the roof. At the same time, from behind him, Blaine heard a loud shot echo down the alley. The back tire on the SUV immediately popped, causing the vehicle to swerve recklessly. Blaine's body was flung about like a rag doll, his trembling muscles exerted to the limit as he fought to maintain his grip. The driver had just regained control of the vehicle when they exited the alleyway and flew across a major street into an onslaught of blaring car horns. Several vehicles had to come to a screeching halt to avoid smashing into the side of them.

Blaine tightened his grip and lowered his head, fear and adrenaline pulsing through his entire body with an intensity that he had never before experienced as the SUV skidded, then swerved to join the flow of traffic. Then, within inches of his face, a shot ripped through the roof of the SUV. Blaine yanked his body in the opposite direction, his ears ringing from the near miss. Seconds later Gionni's face rose up from the side window, his beady eyes narrowing as he aimed his gun at Blaine. In desperation Blaine swung one of his legs forward, knocking the gun from Gionni's hands. The gun thumped several times across the pavement behind them before sliding to a stop. Gionni ducked his head back in the vehicle just as the driver took a sharp right turn, causing the SUV to tilt so sharply that Blaine thought it might roll.

Gripping the rack so tightly that his hands ached, Blaine closed his eyes, praying aloud for God's mercy. When the SUV slammed back down on all four wheels, he could hear the flip-flop of rubber from the flat tire and the grinding sound of a metal rim scraping the pavement. Blaine knew they would not be able to go far like this. He held tight to the rack as the SUV swerved down another dark alley until the brakes were slammed. With the force of the stop, Blaine could no longer maintain his grip. He flew over the top of the vehicle, landed on his back with a hard thud, then slid several feet across the black pavement. When he finally came to a stop, he lay there motionless, the wind and his senses forcefully knocked from him.

"He's dead," Gionni said as he climbed from the vehicle.

"Check for sure," Sabatini ordered from the safety of the SUV, "but make it quick. Our inside man can only hold the police off for so long."

Blaine could hear Gionni's heavy footsteps coming toward him, the sound like a rhythmic echo in his foggy head. He fought to control his breathing and hold perfectly still as Gionni stopped within inches of him.

"Well, well, well, look what we got here," Gionni said sarcastically as he examined Blaine.

"Is he alive?" Sabatini called out.

As Gionni turned toward the car, Blaine focused all his strengthened prayers on lifting his leg so that his knee met the back of Gionni's calf, causing the man's knees to buckle. At the same time, Blaine grabbed Gionni's foot and yanked it upward, sending Gionni flying backward. Blaine dragged himself to his feet and grabbed Gionni's gun, while the man lay gasping for air. Blaine's eyes then went instantly to Mario, who had just climbed out of the car. Blaine ignored him, instead pointing his gun at the passenger side of the car where Sabatini sat.

"Tell him to back off," Blaine demanded, feeling the warmth of blood trickling down the back of his head.

Sabatini hesitated.

"*Now!*" Blaine shouted, the effort making him light-headed.

"Do as he says," Sabatini snapped.

With no one in the backseat to stop her, Reegan jumped out of the car and ran to Blaine's side, while somewhere in the distance the sound of sirens rent the air.

"Mario, Gionni," Sabatini said, never taking his eyes from Blaine. "Get in the vehicle."

"You're not going anywhere," Blaine said tightly.

"Then shoot me," Sabatini said as his two men climbed into the SUV.

Blaine stood there, his gun still aimed at Sabatini. His mind was screaming for him to shoot, but his body was unwilling. Sabatini's face lit into a cold smirk as the SUV went into reverse, then fishtailed down the alley.

Blaine let all the air escape from his lungs, then grabbed his bleeding head. He felt nauseated and lightheaded. "We've got to get out of here."

"But the police—they're coming."

"I just heard Sabatini say that someone's on the inside," Blaine began. "We can't take the chance."

"But my father—"

"The agents back at the warehouse will get him. Right now we've got to get out of here and try and find those negatives."

Reegan's eyes opened wide. "*Cities Across America!*"

Blaine lifted his brow in question.

"The pictures my dad took that night for his photo shoot," Reegan quickly clarified.

"Do you know where the negatives are?"

"Maybe."

Blaine grabbed Reegan's arm. "Come on. Let's get out of here."

Chapter 24

With Sabatini's reference to someone on the inside, Blaine decided that touching base with the agency might be just as dangerous as contacting the police. Consequently, the two of them slipped out of Jersey City without telling a soul. Though Reegan was worried sick about her father, she resigned herself to the fact that this was the only way to help him.

After an expensive taxi ride to a truck stop as far out of Jersey as they could afford, Blaine and Reegan caught a ride with a burly trucker heading to Nebraska. Blaine's head ached from the hit he had taken when he was thrown from the top of the SUV, so he stretched out in the back and fell asleep. Reegan, on the other hand, was privy to an onslaught of Ripley's Believe-It-or-Not-type feats that the trucker was proud as punch to perform. After watching him shove his whole fist into his mouth, Reegan leaned her chair back as far as it would go and closed her eyes. Two hours later the trucker pulled over at a truck stop for gas and a late-night snack. Reegan took advantage of the time by borrowing some money from Blaine and going in to buy a few necessities. The cut and large knot on Blaine's head were making him nauseated so he opted to stay in the truck. A few minutes later Reegan returned with three bottles of soda, a packet of white bandages, and a large bandanna.

"What's this for?" Blaine asked, pulling the bandanna from the sack.

"You're going to stick out like a sore thumb if we bandage your head. So," Reegan began proudly, "after I put the bandage on, we'll wrap this around your head and give you a kind of rough, street look."

"Reegan, it's purple," Blaine said flatly.

"It was that or hot pink," Reegan protested. "Now come on, we've got to get it on before the trucker gets back and starts asking questions."

Before Blaine could protest, Reegan jumped in the back to take a quick look at his head. The wound was at least an inch across and definitely deep enough for stitches. His hair was sticky and matted with blood around the cut, but the wound appeared to have clotted well.

"Ouch," Reegan said, tenderly placing one of the bandages over the wound.

"You're telling me," Blaine said, reaching up to hold it in place while she wrapped the purple bandanna around his head. Before she had finished, Blaine lifted his eyes to the front of the truck stop. "He's coming."

Reegan quickly tied a knot in the bandanna, then slipped through the space between the seats just as the trucker climbed into the cab. Within moments his eyes went directly to Blaine.

"Nice fashion statement," he said with a mocking smile. Then he turned to Reegan. "But you might want to put some hydrogen peroxide on his cut if you don't want any infection."

Reegan could feel her mouth drop open. "How did you know?"

The trucker reached through the seat, picked up the crinkled bandage wrapper, and held it up for them to see.

Then he gestured toward the bandanna. "That hides it pretty well, but—" The trucker reached into his glove compartment and pulled out a wadded, navy blue bandanna. "You might want to change colors, especially if you're trying to blend in."

Reegan lifted a brow, but the trucker just raised his hand. "Don't even try to explain. I have a feeling that the less I know, the better."

* * *

"With your bandanna you look like you should be straddling a Harley," Reegan said, admiring him appraisingly.

"With the knot on my head, I feel like I was run over by one," Blaine retorted.

Reegan laughed, then pushed open the door to the truck stop. After driving all night, the two of them were starving. The trucker, whose nickname they had since learned was Bear, insisted on treating. After devouring every bit of their waffles, eggs, and bacon, Bear asked some of the other truckers lining the breakfast bar to see if any of them were heading to North Dakota. After finding one that was going as far as Mobridge, South Dakota, Bear turned back to them with a broad smile.

"Well, at least we'll get you to the Dakotas."

Throwing caution to the wind, Reegan threw her arms around the big man and gave him a quick squeeze. The man's face literally went two different shades of red. Blaine extended his hand to the big man.

"She tends to have that effect on men," he said with a shake of his head.

"Keep out of trouble," Bear said, his eyes suddenly sober.

"We hope to."

Once the two of them got off in Mobridge, they caught a ride with a dairy farmer pulling a trailer of black-and-white heifers from a nearby sale barn. The farmer drove them within ten minutes of Maplecove. After climbing from the back of the king cab, Reegan and Blaine set off the rest of the way to the small town on foot. The two of them were physically and mentally exhausted from everything that had happened in the last few days. Reegan was also beginning to fear that Blaine had a concussion since the nausea he was experiencing didn't seem to be easing.

"We need to get you to a doctor," Reegan said, turning to glance at him.

"I'm fine," he said adamantly, not meeting her gaze.

Reegan continued to stare at him until he finally looked at her. "Okay. I'll go—as soon as we get the negatives."

Reegan relented with a halfhearted smile since she was positive that was the best offer he was going to give. Quickly burying her hands in her pockets for warmth, she turned her eyes back to the snow-covered road.

"How far is this farm?" Blaine asked after they had walked for several minutes in comfortable silence.

Reegan pointed to a clump of trees. "This is it."

Blaine raised a questioning brow, but she just grabbed his hand and led him through the entanglement of brush to the small clearing just beyond.

"*This* used to be a farm?"

Reegan smiled as she looked with relief on the small home. "Don't let the looks of the old place fool you. It's really kind of cozy."

As soon as Reegan opened the door, they both went directly to the jewelry box on the mantel. Reegan quickly reached in and pulled out a small packet of pictures. Then, sliding her fingers into the lining, she pulled out the negatives. Relief flooded through her entire body.

"They're here," she said, stating the obvious as she handed him the packet. "After my dad supposedly died, I found these pictures in a throw-away box. I grabbed a few single shots, and I also snatched this small packet of pictures. I was disappointed when I opened it because they were just scenery shots. In fact, I almost threw them out, but for some reason I just couldn't."

Blaine slowly let the air escape from his lungs in a show of relief. "It's a good thing you didn't. You might have just saved your father's life." He slipped the negatives safely into the inner pocket of his coat.

"Sabatini's going to a lot of trouble to make sure nobody finds out who's on these negatives," Reegan said, her stomach suddenly tightening.

Blaine nodded, then pulled out his cell phone.

"Who are you calling?" she asked, wrinkling her brow.

"The only agent I know for sure I can trust."

Ten minutes later the two of them had a warm fire crackling. Reegan pulled out one of the two worn blankets she'd placed in the trunk and spread it out on the floor in front of the fireplace. As she disappeared into the kitchen for the stash of goodies she kept at the house, Blaine sat down in the rocking chair.

"You're right," he called out to her. "This place isn't so bad."

Reegan came back with a warm smile and a bag of snacks. "I know. It kind of grows on you," she admitted as she sat down on the blanket and began to pull out the contents of the sack.

Blaine's eyes opened wide. "You've got food?" He slowly got up from the rocking chair and sat down on the blanket next to her.

"It's not much—just some raisins, a bag of miniature candy bars, a box of wheat crackers, and—" She pulled the last item out of the bag with a big grin. "Cheese in a can," she said, holding up the spread cheese triumphantly.

Blaine smiled approvingly. "It looks great."

After a blessing over the food, which Blaine both suggested and offered, the two of them dug in. Once they'd had their fill of cheese and crackers, Blaine slowly stood, the grimace on his face indicating that his head was still throbbing. He walked to the mantel, returning with the box of matches.

"Do you know what today is?"

Reegan crinkled her forehead. "I don't know—Tuesday?" she offered, trying to recap the last few days, though they seemed to blur into a solid mass of chaos.

"Tuesday the what?" he asked, picking up one of the miniature candy bars.

Reegan shook her head and shrugged.

"Here's a hint," he offered, sticking one match in the center of the candy bar, then lighting another.

For a second she stared at him blankly, then finally recollection dawned. "My birthday!" she exclaimed, a smile brushing her lips. So much had happened in the last few days that she had completely forgotten. "But how did you know?" she asked in confusion.

"I know quite a bit about you," Blaine admitted frankly as he lit the match that was now serving as a candle, then sat down next to her. "I know that blue is your favorite color; that you've gone to twelve different schools in eight different states; you're allergic to seafood and penicillin; in the sixth grade you broke your arm falling out of a tree, and in the seventh you got braces. You love people, but you've never had a lot of really close friends. You were an honor student all through high school—slipping up a little this year, but not enough to stop your chances for a scholarship. You're five foot eight, a hundred and—" Blaine stopped, smiling sheepishly. "A hundred and *something* pounds. And you're nineteen today. Did I miss anything?" he asked, taking an exaggerated breath of air.

Reegan shook her head, her face showing disbelief. "But how...?"

"Your father helped the agency nail my father, so they helped him by keeping track of you and your mother. It was the one thing he insisted on since it would have been far too dangerous for both of you if he did it himself."

Tears instantly sprang to Reegan's eyes. She wanted to speak, but her emotions wouldn't allow her to.

"I got most of my information from your health and school records," Blaine offered, sorry that he had made her cry. "Well, except for your favorite color. On that I just guessed."

Reegan wiped at her tears and smiled. "It's purple, but we'll let that slide."

"Well, are you going to make a wish and blow out the candle, or am I going to have to put out a small fire?"

Reegan made a quick wish and blew out the makeshift candle. "Thank you," she said, genuinely touched. Then she turned and jabbed her finger into his chest. "And if you ever reveal my weight, I'll hurt you!"

"I'll keep that in mind," he said with a grin.

"Are you sure you can trust the agent you called?" Reegan asked, her expression suddenly serious with the change in topic.

Blaine nodded, his smile immediately gone and his eyes pensive. "There's something I need to tell you."

Reegan could feel that now-familiar unsettling in the pit of her stomach. "*What?*"

"The FBI can't find your father. Agent Woodard thinks that Sabatini has him again."

"But how?" Reegan cried, jumping to her feet. "I left with Mario, so he couldn't have taken him, and Sabatini and Gionni were in the SUV."

"I know," Blaine began slowly. "Agent Woodard said Agent Wesley is also missing."

Reegan's eyes opened wide as she thought back to the agent that had criticized her father back in the motor home. "He's Sabatini's inside guy?"

"It looks that way," Blaine admitted hesitantly.

Reegan shook her head, then walked to the mantel, staring numbly into the flickering flames. "I can't stand the thought of my father in the hands of those monsters," she said, her voice suddenly faltering. "He's never going to make it out of there alive."

Blaine slowly stood and moved to her side, taking her gently by the shoulders. "Reegan, we'll get him back. You have my word."

Reegan searched his eyes, praying that he was right.

"Sabatini wants the negatives, but he's not stupid. He won't do anything until he knows for sure where they are."

Reegan nodded, though she could no longer hold back the flood that was beginning to spill down her cheeks. Blaine wrapped his arms around her, tenderly stroking her hair and holding her until the last of her tears were exhausted. When Reegan finally pulled back, their eyes met. For a minute neither of them moved. Then slowly Blaine reached out and tenderly wiped at her damp cheek, his eyes falling on her lips. Reegan could feel her heart quicken as he slowly moved toward her, the flicker of the firelight playing across the chiseled features of his face. Then, within inches of her lips, he stopped, his eyes suddenly widening in realization.

"I'm sorry," he stammered, stepping back.

Reegan shook her head, praying that her cheeks were not as red as they felt. "It's okay," she admitted awkwardly.

Blaine swallowed hard, the color across his own cheeks deepening.

"We've got to get back to Jersey," Reegan said, turning away.

Blaine nodded, diverting his own eyes. "I'll contact Sabatini to find out about your father, but first Garret wants me to see what's on the negatives."

Reegan wiped at her face, then took a deep breath. "There's a little drugstore with a photomat in Pinewood." She glanced down at her watch. It was quarter to seven, leaving them only fifteen minutes to make it to Pinewood before the drugstore closed. "Come on," she began, starting for the door. "I know someone who can help us get there."

Reegan flung open the door to the little grocery store, her eyes going expectantly to the man behind the counter.

"Reegan!" Mike exclaimed, clearly shocked. "Where have you been? The police have been looking all over for you."

"It's a long story, Mike. I don't have time to explain, but—" They both turned as Blaine entered the store. "Right now, we need your help," Reegan concluded.

* * *

Five minutes later, Mike's car screeched to a stop in front of the small drugstore in Pinewood. A closed sign was already posted in the window. Completely ignoring the sign, Reegan ran up and began pounding on the glass door. Blaine and Mike were right behind her. The shop owner scowled from across the room, then pointed to the sign posted in the window, even as he walked toward them.

Mike stepped forward. "Calvin, we need your help," he called.

"What's going on?" the man asked, the scowl on his face replaced by confusion as he escorted them inside.

"It's an emergency. We need you to enlarge some pictures for us," Blaine said, reaching inside his coat and withdrawing the negatives.

The man took the outstretched negatives, then scratched his head. "Must be some pretty important vacation shots," he said dubiously, lifting a brow.

"How fast can you do it?" Blaine pressed.

"Keep in mind that my wife doesn't hold dinner. If I'm late, I'll be fighting for scraps with the dog."

"If you do this for us," Blaine began, "we'll pay for you to eat at that steak house down the road."

The shop owner's eyes opened wide. "You've got yourself a deal. Half the time I feed my dinner to the dog anyway."

* * *

They all watched as the negatives were fed into the machine, then they waited anxiously for the pictures to come out the other side. After almost five agonizing minutes of watching as Blaine paced back and forth in the room, the first pictures finally appeared. Blaine quickly grabbed them while Reegan leaned in close so that she could see. The first two pictures were of old buildings shot from various angles and with different focal points—nothing that Reegan hadn't already seen in the snapshots. Blaine set the pictures aside, then waited another minute for the next set of pictures to drop. Again, they were much the same as the first.

"Your dad is talented," Blaine said, handing the pictures to Reegan.

She looked down at them, her throat suddenly constricting as she looked at the images before her. "Yes, he is."

Blaine squeezed her shoulder as if reading her thoughts. "You'll see him again."

"I hope you're right," she said, her eyes moist.

They both turned as another set of pictures printed out. Reegan's breath caught. The first picture was of four men in the dark alley behind the Italian restaurant. A man she didn't recognize was pushed up against a brick wall, while another man pointed a gun at him. Reegan recognized the man with the gun immediately. He was an older version of the man standing next to her now. Reegan turned to look at Blaine. She could see the same pain in his eyes that she had seen when Sabatini, Mario, and Gionni had driven away after trying to kill him. Reegan's eyes went back to the tray as Blaine picked up the next picture. It was similar to the first, except that the man that was pushed up against the wall was now crumpled on the ground.

"Can you blow these up bigger or digitally enhance them?" Blaine asked.

"No, we're not equipped for anything like that," Calvin admitted. "There's a photography studio twenty minutes down the road that could, but they won't be open until first thing tomorrow morning."

"How much do I owe you?" Blaine said, gesturing to the pictures.

"Ten dollars—and that steak dinner you promised."

Blaine smiled, then handed the man the money. "Sounds like a bargain to me."

* * *

Though Mike offered to have the two of them spend the night at his house, both Blaine and Reegan refused, not wanting to put his family in danger. They did, however, readily accept his offer to drive them to the photography studio in the morning. After making their way through the brush and into the house, Blaine plopped down on the rocking chair to look at the pictures while Reegan rekindled the fire.

"Do you see anyone else in them?" Reegan asked, motioning her head toward the newly developed photos.

Blaine flipped through the pictures, then shook his head. "Sabatini said that there was someone else, but *I* can't see anyone." He let his breath out hard, his features drawn with fatigue. "Maybe we'll see something when we have them blown up tomorrow."

Reegan sat down on the blanket, then looked at Blaine, who was still studying the pictures. "I guess we better get some sleep," she acknowledged.

Blaine looked at her, then to the blanket in front of the fireplace, his face suddenly showing discomfort. "You sleep there. I'll just curl up in the back room." He stood to leave, then reached over and pulled the remaining quilt from the trunk.

"Tell me about your stepfather," Reegan said, suddenly not wanting him to go.

Blaine glanced down at her, taken off guard by the question. He exhaled slowly, then shrugged.

"I don't know." Then a slow smile spread across his lips. "He's patient, that's for sure. I dished out a lot those first few years."

Reegan tilted her head to the side.

"I was unhappy, and he was an easy target," Blaine explained. "You know, the whole stepparent thing."

Reegan nodded in understanding, though she had never had that experience. "After a while I started testing him to see if he'd stick around." He glanced over at the fire, his eyes focused on the flickering of the flames. "He tried to do father-son things with me. I spoiled most of them. But I remember this one time—" He stopped, his eyes reflective.

"He took me fishing. I was thirteen—you know, the peak age for obnoxious."

Reegan smiled, then scooted over on the blanket as he took a seat next to her.

"I got snag after snag after snag—probably on purpose, just to annoy him."

They both laughed.

"He spent the better part of the day wading through that ice-cold stream to try to save my lures." Blaine turned to look at her. "But he did it. After fishing for a few hours, we climbed up on a big rock to eat lunch. He told me that life was like fishing—there were always going to be snags. I probably rolled my eyes or something like that—but I did listen. He told me I'd had my share of snags in life, but that I had someone who would help me through all of it."

"Him?" Reegan asked, tilting her head to watch him.

"No. My Heavenly Father."

Reegan's interest was unexpectedly piqued by his words.

"He said that God loved me. Then he pulled a book from his tackle box and said if I wanted to know how much God loved me, I should read it."

Reegan raised her brow. "What was the book?"

"The Book of Mormon. It took a few more fishing trips to convince me, but I've read it cover to cover many times since then. It helped me through some pretty rough times."

"That's what changed your life?" Reegan asked, a warmth starting to envelop her.

His dark eyes locked on hers as he nodded. "Yes. That's what saved my life."

"I don't remember too much about going to church," Reegan admitted frankly. "I was so young when we stopped. But I do remember how I felt when my mom read to me from the Book of Mormon. I miss that."

"You don't have to."

For a moment the two of them just looked at each other. Then Blaine smiled and slowly stood. Though his eyes were shining, he looked physically depleted. "We better get some sleep. Good night, Reegan."

"Good night," she whispered.

Reegan lay awake that night watching the fire burn down until it was nothing more than embers, though the warmth inside her continued to burn. She thought about what Blaine had shared with her about his stepfather, as well as what he had said about the Book of Mormon and his Heavenly Father; but the thing that lingered was the way she'd felt when he'd shared it all. It was the same feeling that she could remember as a little girl. As she lay there in the dimly lit room, her heart burning inside her, she prayed that the feeling would never leave.

Chapter 25

Reegan woke the next day shivering from the cold. The fire that she had stoked through the night had burned down to nothing more than ashes, leaving the small house almost as cold on the inside as it was on the outside. Reegan glanced toward the bedroom, surprised that Blaine wasn't up yet. She yanked the blanket up around her shoulders and, using it as a shawl, walked to the fireplace. She poked at the ashes, hoping to see a layer of coals underneath, but there were only thin charcoal flakes that danced up into the flue. Taking a few small sticks that had been piled on the hearth, a rolled up piece of newspaper, and a couple of matches from off the mantel, Reegan started another fire. Once the fire was crackling, she stood and started toward the bedroom.

"Blaine?" she called out softly. "Blaine, are you there?"

Reegan glanced out the window as she passed, thinking that maybe he had gone outside to collect more wood, but there was no sign of him.

"Blaine," she called out a little louder as she knocked on the door.

When there wasn't an answer, she slowly pushed open the door to find Blaine lying on the floor with his back to her. For a minute Reegan just stood there, staring at his back and waiting for movement. Then her eyes went to the bandanna around his head—it was heavily soiled with drainage.

"Blaine?" she whispered, suddenly feeling a tightness in her chest. "Blaine, wake up!" she said again, only this time more forcibly.

As she apprehensively reached to touch him, Blaine began to stir, then slowly turned to face her. At first he almost looked as if he didn't recognize her, then slowly the recollection came.

"I'm sorry," he began weakly, "I must have overslept." He tried to sit up, but didn't have the strength, instead he grabbed at his head with both hands. "Everything is spinning."

Reegan looked into his eyes. One of his pupils was dilated more than the other. "We need to get you to a hospital."

"No. I'm okay."

"You're not okay. You can't even sit up. I'm going for help," Reegan said, her heart beginning to race.

"Reegan," he began, his face imploring. "Don't take me to a hospital. It's too dangerous. They'll find us there." As soon as the sentence was out of his mouth, he passed out.

Reegan ran all the way to Mike's Grocery. When she finally burst through the door, she had to take several breaths before she could even speak.

"What's the matter?" Mike demanded.

"It's Blaine. He's sick."

Mike opened the cash register where he kept his car keys. "Getting an ambulance way out here will take forever. I'll drive him to the hospital myself."

Reegan began to shake her head. "We can't take the risk of being found. We'll have to take a doctor to him."

Mike didn't question her. He simply placed his keys on the counter and instead picked up the phone.

Twenty minutes later, Reegan, Mike, and Dr. Whittle—an old family friend of Mike's—pushed open the door to Blaine's room. He was sitting in a corner, his head resting in his hands. The doctor immediately walked over and bent down beside him. After a quick look at his pupils, he turned back to Reegan and Mike.

"We need to get him to a hospital."

Reegan began to protest, but Blaine raised his hand. "It's okay. I'll go." He lifted his eyes to Mike. "Will you stay with her until I get back?"

"Don't worry. I'll stay right here," Mike said with a reassuring nod.

* * *

The CT scan confirmed that Blaine had a concussion. After stitching up the cut and giving him some acetaminophen and a shot of steroids for any possible swelling, the attending doctor reluctantly sent him home with strict orders to take it easy. The doctor wanted to keep him overnight for observation, but Blaine flatly refused, assuring the doctor that he would follow all of his instructions. Reegan wondered if he crossed his fingers when he said it, but she was surprised that for a good five hours after he got back, he did exactly as the doctor had encouraged—he slept.

Mike had left right after Blaine made it back, though he returned an hour later with a steaming pot of vegetable stew, a couple of homemade rolls, a plate of oatmeal-chocolate-chip cookies, and a warm thermos of extra-rich hot chocolate. He assured her that neither he nor Dr. Whittle would breathe a word about their whereabouts to anyone. Reegan gave him a big hug, then watched him make his way over to where his car was hidden, confident that he would keep his promise.

After that she spent the next few hours tending the fire so that the room would stay comfortable for Blaine. She had insisted that he sleep in front of the fireplace, assuring him that she would be fine in the bedroom when it came time to go to sleep. Though he'd been too proud to like it, he was also too sick to decline. Since then he'd slept like a baby. Reegan sat and watched as the flicker of the firelight played across the handsome features of his face. It was the first time she had seen him this relaxed. Though she could barely admit it to herself, being around him stirred feelings within her that she had never felt before; the attraction was both exciting and terrifying all at the same time. She took another sip of her hot chocolate, reveling in the warmth it provided. When she looked back down at him, his eyes were on her.

"How do you feel?" she asked, slightly flustered imagining he could somehow read her thoughts.

"Rough. But I'll live."

"Are you hungry? You fell asleep before I could get you anything to eat."

"Starving," he admitted.

Reegan pulled a plastic bowl from a sack of things that Mike had brought over with the food. Then she walked to the hearth where the pot of stew was placed close enough to the fire to keep it warm. She ladled a heaping scoop into his bowl, then walked over and handed it to him.

"It's already been blessed," she said with a knowing smile.

He smiled back, then almost instantly the expression faded. "I called Sabatini from my cell phone at the hospital."

Reegan could feel her lungs restrict involuntarily. "*And?*" she breathed.

"He's got your dad. He said he'd contact me tomorrow to tell me where we'll make the switch."

"My dad for the negatives."

Blaine nodded, confirming her assumption. "I called Garret right after that, he'll be here first thing in the morning."

"Sabatini will never allow him to come to the meeting with us," Reegan observed.

"There's no *us* this time, Reegan," Blaine said, his eyes going right through her. "I had Garret make arrangements for you and your mom to go somewhere safe until this is all over."

Reegan nodded reluctantly, not surprised by his declaration. Though she wanted to help her dad, she knew her involvement at this point would only complicate things.

"Where are you sending us?"

Blaine smiled mischievously. "You ever heard of Zion?"

* * *

Reegan was up early the next day, anxious to get to the studio to have the pictures enlarged. After snagging a handful of cookies from the kitchen—justifying that at least they were oatmeal, so she could count them as nutritious—she headed to the living room where Blaine was still curled up on the floor. When she gently nudged him, he immediately opened his eyes. She was instantly relieved to see that both of his pupils were the same size. He grimaced as he sat up, obviously suffering from a severe headache.

"Good morning," she chimed, handing him two cookies, then sitting on the hearth to eat her own.

He looked down at the cookies with a smirk. "Your idea of breakfast?"

Reegan smiled, then held up her partially eaten cookie. "See, some people might view this as a treat, but to me this is just a round granola bar."

"So it's health food?" Blaine mocked.

"Exactly."

"And the big chunks of chocolate—"

"Ahh, the healthiest part. Chocolate comes from the cocoa bean, right? Well, everybody knows how healthy beans are."

Blaine laughed. "How can I dispute logic like that?"

Reegan shrugged with a grin, then looked down at her watch. "We better get going. Mike should be here any minute."

Blaine took another bite of one of his cookies, then slowly stood, swaying a little as he did. Reegan frowned at him, but he just forced a smile and headed to the front door.

"I'll beat you to the road," he baited her.

She shook her head. "You'll be lucky if you *make it* to the road."

Just as they pushed through the last of the overgrowth leading to the dirt road, Mike pulled up. He looked like he hadn't slept all night.

"You two okay?" he asked as soon as they climbed in.

"We're fine," Reegan said, shooting a skeptical look at Blaine, who looked noticeably drawn.

"I worried about you two all night," Mike said before reaching down to grab a basket that was placed between the seats. "My wife packed you a little snack," he continued, handing it to Reegan.

"*Little* snack!" Reegan exclaimed, shaking her head.

There were four or five hard-boiled eggs, two blueberry muffins, two sausage biscuits wrapped in a cloth napkin, and a bunch of red grapes. Placed next to the food were two small bottles of apple juice. Reegan could feel her eyes fill with emotion as she looked back at Mike, but he just smiled and waved her gratitude off.

"This is nothin'. When this is over, my wife will cook you a *real* breakfast—biscuits and gravy, scrambled eggs, and homemade crepes with cream cheese and berries." Mike patted the soft bulge around his waist. "Before I got married, I was skinny as a rail, but once I tasted my wife's cookin', I've never looked back."

"Sounds good to me," Blaine said, reaching through the gap in the seats to snag a blueberry muffin. "Even if it doesn't fit into my new health-food diet."

Reegan shot a glance at Blaine, who was smiling, then she looked back at Mike, her conscience momentarily pricked by his generosity. "Listen, Mike, there's something that I need to tell you about Seth and Wayne—"

"They've been stealing from me."

"You knew?"

Mike nodded. "But thanks for telling me." He smiled, then reached over and squeezed her hand in a fatherly gesture. "I had a feeling you would." Then he turned his attention back to the road. Reegan also looked out the window, then took a deep breath, a portion of her burden instantly lifted.

Twenty minutes later the three of them pulled up in front of a small photography studio. Blaine asked to have each shot of the alley enlarged to eleven-by-fourteen. When it was done, he stood motionless before them, his eyes searching every detail.

"Could you enlarge just the car?" Blaine asked, looking at the shadowed vehicle.

The photographer nodded, then began the process. Once he was done, they all crowded around to see the result. Peeking above the partially opened driver's side window was the profile of a man. The tinted windows still concealed him from the neck down, but where the window was lowered it also revealed the man's hand resting on the steering wheel.

"There's something on his hand," Blaine said, thumping the picture with his finger.

The photographer, who seemed just as interested as the rest of them now, began digitally enlarging just the man's hand. Reegan tapped her fingernails nervously on the counter as she watched the process.

When he was done, the photographer stood back in satisfaction. "It's some kind of ring."

"What's that emblem?" Reegan asked, pointing to the center of the black oval ring.

Blaine shrugged, obviously wondering the same thing. "I don't know."

"That's about as good as we're going to get it," the photographer said, turning off the enlarger.

Blaine nodded, never taking his eyes from the picture. "That's okay. It's enough."

* * *

After Mike dropped them off, Reegan rekindled the fire while Blaine sat down in the rocking chair looking at the copies that he'd had the photographer produce for him. Reegan watched him as he studied the pictures. Several times he rubbed at his head, and from the expression of pain on his face, she could tell it wasn't just out of frustration.

"What now?" Reegan asked, poking at the fire with a long stick.

Blaine let out his breath, then closed and rubbed his eyes. "I'm not sure." He went to the window and stared out for a while, then he turned to Reegan with a relieved sigh. "They're here."

Moments later outside the house, Reegan threw her arms around her mother, both of them sobbing and laughing at the same time.

"Are you okay?" Elizabeth asked, finally pulling back long enough to look at her daughter.

"I'm fine," Reegan assured her.

Elizabeth drew Reegan into her arms again. After their embrace, Elizabeth's eyes fell on Blaine.

"Mrs. Schmitt," he said, extending his hand, "it's a pleasure to meet you."

Reegan looked at her mother. It was strange to hear her being called by a different last name than Richards, but at the same time, it felt good.

Elizabeth clasped Blaine's hand in both of hers. "Thank you for taking care of my daughter."

Blaine glanced over at Reegan. "It was my pleasure."

"Have you heard anything about my husband?" Elizabeth asked anxiously.

"I contacted Sabatini last night," Blaine began, his tone instantly professional. "He said he'd contact me today and make arrangements to exchange your husband for the negatives."

"You have them?" Garret asked expectantly.

Blaine reached into his inside pocket and withdrew the negatives, extending them to Garret, then motioning him toward the house. "Come on. I'll show you what we've found."

As Blaine escorted Garret into the house, Reegan stayed back, turning her attention to her mother. "I missed you," she admitted, her eyes suddenly brimming. "I was so scared that I'd never see you again."

Her mother's eyes filled with compassion as she wrapped Reegan into her embrace.

"Thank you," Reegan choked out.

"For what?" her mother asked, pulling back and searching her daughter's face.

"For loving me when I wasn't easy to love."

Elizabeth tilted her head and took a long, appraising look at her daughter. "Who are you?" she teased.

Reegan laughed, then wiped at her tears. "What are you talking about?"

Elizabeth smiled warmly as she reached out and touched her daughter's cheek. "I don't know. There's just—a change in you," she admitted as she squeezed Reegan's hand. "Now, let's go see what's on those negatives."

As soon as they entered the small house they walked over to the mantel, where Blaine was showing Garret the pictures.

"There was a man in the car," Blaine said. "He was easy to miss because of the tinted windows, but when we enlarged it, there he was."

Garret shook his head in disbelief as he flipped through the pictures. When he came to the close-up of the ring, he lifted his eyes to Blaine. "It looks like some kind of insignia."

Elizabeth glanced over Garret's arm so that she could have a look. "So these pictures are the reason they're still after my—" Elizabeth stopped, her face instantly draining of color. She grabbed the pictures from Garret's hand.

"What is it? What's wrong?" Reegan asked, tilting her head in curiosity as she watched her mother flip through the pictures.

Elizabeth shook her head, her face as white as a ghost. "I know this man."

"You do?" Blaine asked, his shock matching the others in the room. "How do you know him?"

She looked up, though her gaze seemed far away. "I almost married him."

"What?" Reegan exclaimed.

Elizabeth shook her head, the shock of the discovery evident in her expression. Garret immediately took her by the elbow and escorted her over to the rocking chair, worried that if she didn't sit down she might fall down.

"Get her something to drink," he said as he turned to Blaine.

As Blaine started toward the kitchen, Garret knelt down in front of her. Reegan quickly sat down on the hearth, her legs quivering like two boiled spaghetti noodles.

"I don't understand," Elizabeth began, her eyes racing across the pictures. "How he could be a part of this?" Her voice was soft and vulnerable.

Blaine returned with a bottle of water, which he quickly handed to Elizabeth before taking a seat next to Reegan on the hearth.

"Mrs. Schmitt," Garret began slowly, "tell me who the man is."

Elizabeth looked down at the picture, still shaking her head in disbelief.

"Ma'am, please," Garret pressed. "We need to know."

Elizabeth lifted her eyes to the agent. "The man behind the wheel is Charley Madison."

Garret looked like a tractor-trailer rig had just plowed into him. "Charley Madison, as in Charles Madison of Madison and Bentley Consultants."

Blaine looked at Garret with the same astonishment that he had looked at Mrs. Schmitt with. "You know him?"

Garret shook his head impatiently. "No. Not personally. But his company is a Fortune 500 company. The man is head of a multimillion-dollar operation."

"That's how Sabatini is laundering his money," Blaine surmised, remembering his conversation with his father back at the restaurant.

"I used to wonder back then how Charley lived so comfortably on what he made as a police officer," Elizabeth stated.

"He was a cop?" Garret asked in surprise.

Elizabeth nodded.

Garret shot a quick glance at Blaine, then shook his head, his eyes filled with disgust.

"It looks like Charley looked the other way, and in return Sabatini set him up in a very lucrative business," Blaine offered.

Garret turned back to Elizabeth, his expression deadly serious. "Are you *sure* this is him?"

Elizabeth looked down at the picture again, then handed it back to Garret. "I'm positive. The emblem on his ring is a scorpion—the symbol of his college fraternity. He never took it off. But even without the ring..." Her face looked almost mournful, "it's him."

Garret touched her arm, his expression sympathetic. "I'm sorry."

She nodded, though she never lifted her eyes.

"Call Agent Christiansen," Garret said to Blaine. "Have her run a check on Charles Madison."

Blaine pulled out his cell phone, then quickly walked to the door and stepped outside while Garret spoke to Elizabeth. "We've booked you a flight out of Bismark to Salt Lake City, Utah. You and Reegan can pick your tickets up at the ticket counter. When you get to Salt Lake, we'll have two undercover agents there to pick you up."

"What about Jonathan?" Elizabeth asked, suddenly panic-stricken.

Reegan looked at her mother, who seemed as if she were on the verge of tears. Reegan could feel the sting behind her own eyes.

"Jonathan is a survivor," Garret began. "Trust me, I know."

Elizabeth's shoulders lifted, then fell, her expression revealing her feelings of helplessness. "When do we leave?"

Garret looked down at his watch. "As soon as Blaine gets off the phone, I'll have him escort you to the edge of the clearing. An agent wearing a cowboy hat and driving an old, white pickup truck will drive by in about ten minutes and offer the two of you a ride."

"He'll take us to the airport?" Reegan asked.

Garret turned to her with a confirming nod. "From there, you know the rest." Garret reached into his pocket and pulled out a white envelope. "Here's fifteen hundred dollars. If this takes longer than we're anticipating, we'll give you more, but—"

"Let's hope it doesn't," Elizabeth countered.

Garret took her hand and pulled her to her feet, then walked over and placed the photographs and negatives on the mantel. "Come on. Let's get Blaine so he can walk you two to the road."

Reegan walked over and wrapped her arm around her mother's shoulder, then the two of them started toward Garret, who was just opening the front door. As soon as Garret was all the way through the doorway, his body stiffened, his eyes going to something off in the snow-covered brush. Reegan could feel a knot forming in the pit of her stomach even before spotting the man who stepped into the clearing, his gun raised.

"Mario," she breathed, bile instantly rising to the back of her throat.

Before she had time to react, Garret turned and shoved her and Elizabeth back from the door and slammed it shut with him on the other side. They both screamed and stumbled backward as a bullet ripped a fist-size hole through the weather-beaten wood. Reegan could feel a warm trickle of blood make its way down her cheek where a small sliver of wood had sliced her face. Momentarily stunned, she stared numbly at the door.

"Reegan, run!" Elizabeth shouted, snapping her instantly back to her senses.

With the sound of gunfire rending the air, the two of them turned toward their only escape—the back door. As they passed the fireplace, Reegan grabbed the photographs and negatives that Garret had just placed there. Then they raced through the kitchen. Reegan reached the door first. She yanked it open, then grabbed her mother's hand as she started toward the woods behind the house. Reegan could hear someone cry out in pain; she cringed but forced herself not to turn around. Fear pushing them forward, the two of them ran through the snow-covered woods until their lungs ached and the voices behind them were only muffled sounds. Finally, when they were certain no one was following them, they crouched down behind a group of barren shrubs, gasping heavily.

"We've got to get to the road," Reegan said between breaths. "Blaine and Agent Woodard need help."

"The road is the other way," Elizabeth answered, her voice every bit as shaky as Reegan's. "We'll have to double back."

They each took one more deep breath before standing. With their ears tuned to the slightest sound, they made a large semicircle in the woods behind the house, then headed toward the road. The gunfire had stopped, leaving only an eerie silence in its place. Once the road was in view, Reegan and Elizabeth crouched down again.

"I don't see the white truck."

"He'll come," Reegan said confidently.

Elizabeth looked at her daughter, a hint of admiration in her eyes.

"There he is," Reegan whispered, pointing toward a bend in the road a quarter of a mile away.

Reegan shot another apprehensive look behind them before turning her attention back to the approaching truck. She held her breath. He would pass right in front of the house in less than a second, passing them just seconds later. Reegan could feel her blood flow through her veins in enormous surges while adrenaline sent a tingling sensation through her limbs.

"Now!" she whispered, jumping from their hiding spot and darting toward the approaching vehicle.

As they ran into the road, the startled driver swerved, then fishtailed in the snow before stopping. At the same moment, from the corner of her eyes, Reegan saw Gionni emerge from the trees in front of the small farmhouse.

"Get in!" Reegan shouted.

Elizabeth threw open the door and jumped in with Reegan right behind her. Just as the door was slammed shut, a bullet shattered the back window. Both women screamed as shards of glass showered the entire cab of the truck. The agent shifted gears, then stepped on the gas, causing the truck to flip slush and snow into the air before lunging forward.

"*Go!*" Elizabeth screamed.

Reegan held her breath as the agent sped away from the old farmhouse.

"Where are the agents?" the man behind the wheel demanded, his hands gripping the wheel.

"They're back there," Reegan said, turning around just in time to see Gionni lift his arm, his gun aimed at the truck.

"*Watch out!*" Reegan screamed.

Her warning came at the same time that Gionni's bullet hit one of the rear tires. The truck swerved sharply across the snow-covered road, causing the driver to lose control of the vehicle. Reegan's eyes opened wide as the truck veered toward a cluster of trees off the side of the road.

"*No!*" Reegan screamed, the word echoing in her head as everything else around her went black.

* * *

When Reegan awoke she had no idea where she was. Everything was dark and cold. For an awful moment she thought she was dead.

"Reegan, are you awake?"

Reegan slowly turned her head toward the voice. "Mom?" She tried to lift her hands, but they wouldn't separate from each other.

"Are you okay?" Elizabeth asked anxiously, reaching over awkwardly to touch her daughter.

"Where are we?" Reegan asked, bits and pieces of the accident flooding her mind.

"In the back of a truck—maybe a moving van, I'm not sure."

"What happened?" Reegan cried.

"We were in an accident."

"Are you hurt?" Reegan asked, hearing how strained her mother's voice was.

"I'm fine," she answered, though her voice was weak.

"We've got to get out of here," Reegan said, trying to pull her wrists free.

"I've been working on the ropes around my hands, but they won't budge. All I've managed to do is hurt my wrists."

Reegan tried to sit, which made her instantly nauseous. As her eyes went to the sliver of light outlining the back of the truck, she realized that it had to be morning.

"I think we're on a dirt road," Elizabeth offered as they hit another bump.

Reegan felt sick, and it wasn't just from the trauma of the accident. They were witnesses, and it didn't take a genius to realize why Sabatini was taking them somewhere secluded. Reegan dragged herself toward the sliver of light, stopping cold, then recoiling when her hands were placed on something warm and fleshy.

"There's someone here!" she cried, a shiver spanning across her shoulders.

"Are they alive?" Elizabeth asked hesitantly, starting toward Reegan in the dark.

Reegan could feel her breathing quicken, though she somehow controlled it. She reached her hands out aversely to touch the motionless heap.

"They're still warm."

Elizabeth moved in next to the body. As she did, the dark figure lying on the floor groaned and moved. Reegan could hear her own rapid breathing in the dark as the body on the ground slowly began to rise.

"Who are you?" Reegan asked, quickly scooting back.

The shadowy shape froze, then the sound of breath being slowly exhaled filled the van. "Reegan, it's me," he groaned.

"Blaine!" Reegan exclaimed, crawling desperately toward him.

Blaine took her into his arms, then instantly cried out in pain.

"What did they do to you?" Reegan blurted out, instantly pulling back as warm tears stung her bloodshot eyes.

Blaine moaned as he changed positions. "I'm okay," he said, though the effort he had taken just to sit attested otherwise. He reached for her hands, instantly feeling the rope around them. "Let me get this off," he said to her, his breathing labored. "My hands are free."

Before either of them could move, the truck came to an abrupt stop, causing them all to go flying forward. They were still trying to regain their senses when the back of the truck was unlocked and flung open, shooting light into the back of the moving van and temporarily blinding them all.

"It's reckoning time," Gionni called out, his voice sending an eerie chill through Reegan's entire body.

Reegan raised her hand to shield her eyes, then shot a glance at Blaine as Gionni hopped in and dragged him from the truck. Blaine couldn't even stand up straight. His face was swollen, and bright red blood was smeared across his shirt. For a second Reegan's mind flashed to another time when she had seen Blaine's shirt streaked with blood. Then she had looked at him with loathing and disgust, but now she was feeling something altogether different, though just as intense.

Mario climbed into the truck next, grabbing both Reegan and Elizabeth firmly by the wrists and dragging them forward. Once out of the truck, he shoved the two of them toward a large rock positioned at the foot of a steeply sloping hill where Blaine was already sitting. Reegan's attention then went to a man just climbing from the cab of the truck. He reached in and grabbed another man by the collar and dragged him forward. Reegan felt her own heart leap as recognition dawned. Elizabeth immediately let out a scream and lunged toward her husband, but Mario grabbed her and shoved her down. Reegan reached over and took her mother's trembling hand, though her attention stayed with her father as he staggered forward, his hands tied in front of him. Reegan's eyes seared through the man that held him as they neared. Seeing her reaction, the man smiled.

"Remember me?" Agent Wesley taunted, then shoved her father toward them.

As Reegan glanced from her parents, who were locked in a tearful embrace, back to Wesley, she could feel the rage inside her building until her entire frame was trembling. At that moment she was grateful that she was bound, fearing her actions might get herself and those she loved killed. Just then another car pulled up behind the moving van. Reegan's eyes quickly shot in every direction; she was frantic, desperate for an escape. Several flat-topped buttes were in the distance, their bases covered with barren shrubs and timber, while numerous ravines cut across the expanse of flat land between them. To either side of the hill they were sitting on were clumps of leaf-less oak and aspen, as well as sporadic knotted trees growing out of crevices climbing the gravel incline. She tried to imagine a scenario in which they could get to the trees, or hide in the ravines somehow. Reegan's eyes then returned to the vehicle as two men climbed out. She could feel her mother's body stiffen, followed by her quick intake of breath.

"Charley," Elizabeth whispered, the pain of his involve-ment evident in her voice.

The man glanced in their direction, but quickly looked away, obviously choosing to stay next to the car and witness their demise from a safe distance. Reegan's breathing quickened, and her whole body began to tremble as the other man approached, his calculating gaze assuring her that escape was not going to be an option.

"How nice of you all to join us," Sabatini said cordially as if they had been invited there for brunch. Then he turned to Wesley. "Impressive work."

Wesley acknowledged the man's praise with a barely discernible nod of his head, though Reegan could see a supercilious grin tugging at the corners of his mouth. "I'm glad I could help." Then he handed Sabatini the photos and negatives that Reegan had snatched from the mantel back at the farm.

Sabatini thumbed through them methodically, then turned back to the car where Charley was standing and raised the photos.

"Mr. Madison likes the money, but he doesn't like to get his hands dirty," Sabatini said, glancing back at them. Then he turned to Wesley. "The man who developed these?"

"Dead," Wesley said in a matter-of-fact tone.

Reegan felt as though the wind had been knocked out of her. She and Blaine had inadvertently gotten the man killed by asking for his help.

"And Garret?" Sabatini asked, apparently wanting to make sure that all the loose ends were taken care of.

"He's dead," Wesley said, his face slowly lighting into a grin. "I killed him out at that old farmhouse."

"*No!*" Blaine shouted, his cry rending the air.

Sabatini turned to look at Blaine, whose head was now lowered and his shoulders visibly shaking. "You said you wanted in. This is the price you pay to be on the inside," Sabatini mocked, his tone holding no warmth for his own son.

Reegan reached out to touch Blaine just as he lifted his eyes to Sabatini. At first Reegan thought it was ire that filled his gaze, but on closer examination she saw it was sheer anguish, as if he were suffering an actual physical pain.

"And the price *you* paid—what you gave up?" Blaine asked, his voice etched with the same anguish that filled his eyes.

Sabatini's jaw flexed. "I gave up *nothing!*"

Reegan felt sick. She watched helplessly as the last flicker of hope in Blaine's eyes was extinguished. At that moment, with Sabatini's gaze still locked defiantly on Blaine, a loud shot rang out from the rocks.

"FBI. Throw down your weapons!"

Reegan's head whipped around to see several men spring up from behind the trees and rocks behind them. Gionni and Mario drew their guns and fired, then ran toward a scant stand of trees off to the left of the hill. At the same time, Sabatini raced for the car, but it had already been thrown into reverse and was peeling away with Charley Madison safely inside. Instead, Sabatini started toward the moving van.

With pandemonium erupting around them, Blaine reached for Reegan's hands and quickly began to untie the ropes. Reegan's eyes fell on Wesley as he too headed for the cab of the van. A large FBI agent that Reegan immediately recognized ran toward him, grabbing him firmly by the shoulders and pulling him from the door. Wesley jerked around and swung at the agent, but the agent ducked, then came back with a sharp jab to the man's jaw with a powerful left fist. Wesley slammed into the van, momentarily stunned, then reached for the gun strapped to his chest. Agent Hickman, his former partner, pulled out his own gun. Reegan screamed as the shot rang out, echoing off the small mountain behind her. She stared in horror at the two men before her, waiting to see who had been shot. For a moment they both just stared at each other, a look of confusion on Wesley's face. Then, slowly, Wesley buckled to the ground clutching at his chest. Within seconds he was prostrate on the ground, all the life seemingly drained from him.

"Stay here," Blaine demanded, staggering to his feet and starting toward the van.

"Blaine, no!" Reegan screamed.

Reegan's words fell on deaf ears. Blaine was already to the van, yanking open the passenger door at the same time that the van lunged forward. He clutched the door as it swung open. At first he trotted beside the van, but as it accelerated, his feet began to drag. Reegan sprang to her feet and ran toward him. She was barely aware of the figure that passed her, leaping for the back of the moving van. The man's hands caught a handrail, but his legs momentarily dragged across the ground before finding footing on the bumper.

Reegan tried to run faster, watching Blaine in his weakened condition holding desperately to the swinging passenger door, but with her own injuries, she couldn't keep up. Instead she stopped, her heart pounding wildly and her eyes helplessly riveted on the scene before her. The man on the bumper climbed to the roof of the van, then quickly crawled toward Blaine, who was holding onto the door, his legs flinging across the snow-covered road. When the man reached the spot on the roof just to the side of Blaine, he placed his foot on the door, then turned and swung himself into the cab.

The truck swerved, causing Blaine to hit hard into the side of the truck while his legs swung dangerously underneath. Reegan's whole body tightened as she fought the urge to turn away. If Blaine let go now, he would be mangled under the back wheels of the van. Instead the van swerved the other direction, causing the door to swing wildly and drag Blaine's body along with it. Blaine lost his grip and went tumbling away from the truck into the brush that lined the road. Reegan screamed, then ran toward him, praying with everything she had that he was still alive. She could see the van out of the corner of her eyes slowly come to a stop, but her attention remained glued on the man crumpled on the ground.

"Blaine!" she cried out as she fell to her knees before him.

He was lying face-first in the snow, his clothing ripped and dirty and his body still. Reegan could feel the burning behind her eyes quickly turning to warm streaks down her cheeks.

"Blaine," she said again, only this time it was a choked whisper. "Please, don't die. *Please*. I—." Before the words could escape her lips, Blaine began to stir. With an instant rush of hope, she reached down and gently turned him over.

"I'm alive," Blaine whispered, his voice barely audible. "I hurt too bad to be dead."

Reegan's eyes raced across his face as she tenderly reached out and touched his cheek. "You scared me."

He smiled affectionately, then diverted his eyes to the man now standing directly behind her.

Reegan jerked around, her jaw instantly going slack. "*Garret,*" she breathed.

Garret looked down at Blaine, his face instantly flooding with relief as he struggled to catch his breath. "Are you all right?"

Blaine shook his head, his expression one of wonderment, as if he were witnessing an apparition. "I thought you were dead," he said, his voice heavy with emotion.

Garret knelt down beside him. "You didn't think you could get rid of me that easy, did you?" he teased.

"What do you want me to do with him?" a voice rang out.

They all turned toward Agent Hickman, though their eyes went immediately to the man he held handcuffed beside him. Garret stood, his eyes locked on Sabatini.

"I heard what you said back there," Garret began, his eyes fierce. "You were dead wrong though. You gave up more than you'll ever know."

"You know nothing about my life, Garret," Sabatini snapped.

"I know more than you think. I'm the lucky guy who was blessed with everything you threw away."

"What are you talking about?" Sabatini growled.

"Garret's my stepfather," Blaine broke in, causing them all to turn and look at him. Blaine continued, his face resolute. "You might be my flesh and blood, but *Garret* is my dad."

Sabatini's face twisted with an odd mix of emotions as Blaine's words sank in, but before he could speak, Garret waved an impatient hand, signaling for his removal.

Reegan turned to Garret. "That was you on the roof of the moving van?"

Garret smiled and nodded his head, then looked down at his son. "Your mom's right, I *am* too old for this."

"She's going to let you know it too as soon as you get home," Blaine said with a smile, then grimaced at the effort.

"You really are father and son?" Reegan asked, watching the two of them in disbelief.

Blaine nodded. "Garret was the agent assigned to our case once my mom turned state's evidence on Sabatini."

Garret smiled sheepishly. "I have a bad habit of getting too involved in my work."

At that moment Jonathan and Elizabeth came up beside them.

"Yes, you do," Jonathan teased, placing his hand on his friend's shoulder.

Reegan stood, then fell into her mother's arms, relief flooding her whole body. Then she turned to her father. His face still looked like it had been used as a punching bag, but his eyes were shining. He pulled her into his arms and buried his face in her hair.

"I love you, Daddy," she whispered.

"I love you too," he said, his voice choked with emotion.

Garret smiled in satisfaction, then turned toward the sirens in the distance. "Come on," he said, reaching down and helping Blaine to his feet.

With Garret's arm wrapped around Blaine's waist for support, they all started back toward the hill, turning back only when a police car screeched to a stop in front of Sabatini. Blaine turned, his eyes filled with sorrow. Reegan ached for him, but was comforted in knowing that the man beside Blaine loved him enough to be willing to sacrifice his own life for him. They all watched in silence as Sabatini, along with Gionni and Mario, who were also handcuffed and escorted by agents, were secured in the vehicle. With the agents stepping back, the police car made a wide turn through the snow and started back down the road.

"What about Charley?" Elizabeth asked, her eyes going to Garret.

"Agent Wesley," Garret called out to the still form lying where Hickman had shot him just minutes before. "You want to tell Mrs. Schmitt about your little plan?"

Everyone but Garret whirled around to gape at the man sprawled out on the ground. He immediately sat up, his face lighting into a cocky grin. "Mr. Madison met with a nice little roadblock down at the other end of the road," he said, wiping slush and dirt from his shirt.

"You're alive?" Reegan stammered, shaking her head in disbelief.

"Just barely," Wesley blurted out, rubbing at his bruised and tender jaw. "No thanks to Lefty. Next time *you're* the dirty cop."

Hickman laughed, then walked over and helped Agent Wesley to his feet. "But you're perfect for it. You've got that naturally obnoxious personality."

"You're just saying that to make me feel better," Wesley said.

"What about the man at the photo mat?" Reegan asked anxiously.

"He's fine. We put him in protective custody," Garret offered.

They all turned as an ambulance started toward them. Garret raised his hand and motioned it over to them, then turned as an agent tapped his shoulder.

"I'm sorry, sir, but we need you for a minute."

Garret began to shake his head, but before he could speak, Blaine interjected. "Dad, I'm fine," he said, awkwardly stepping back to show Garret that he could stand on his own. "You go do what you need to."

Reegan could almost see Garret's chest swell as he looked at Blaine. He took a deep breath, attempting to control the emotion that clearly showed on his face. "You did real good, son. Real good." Reegan's own heart began to swell. After giving Blaine a quick squeeze across the shoulders, and promising to meet him at the hospital, Garret reluctantly followed the agent over to an approaching police car.

Once he was gone, Elizabeth glanced up at her husband who looked like he had expelled the last of his energy. She wrapped her arm around his waist for support, then slowly began to help him toward two EMTs who were just pulling a stretcher from the back of the ambulance. Reegan watched as one of the EMTs stopped to help her parents. Comforted that they were in good hands, she quickly turned back to Blaine, knowing that they would only have a moment before the other EMT reached them. Blaine's eyes were already glued on her. She took a needed breath in an attempt to control her emotions, but found it next to impossible.

"Thank you for saving my father's life."

Blaine shook his head, obviously not comfortable with the praise. "Hey now, you were right there beside me."

He glanced around at the FBI agents and police officers that were swarming the area. When he looked back at her, her heart began to pound. He reached out and took her hand, his touch sending instant warmth through her body.

"I did mean what I said the other day," he began with a tender smile. "You really are amazing."

"I'm sorry, but we only have room for one more."

They both turned to face the EMT, who had already wrapped his arm around Blaine's waist for support before glancing apologetically at Reegan. "Another ambulance should be here any minute."

Reegan nodded, a hard lump forming in her throat. "Watch out for him," she warned, glancing from the EMT to Blaine. They both looked at her for clarification. "He has a bad habit of borrowing vehicles."

The EMT gave her a confused glance, but her eyes remained on Blaine's weak smile. Even as she looked at him, she knew that no matter what happened in her life, a part of her heart would always belong to him.

"Take care, Reegan."

Reegan forced a brave smile, her eyes suddenly moist. "Good-bye, Blaine."

epilogue

Reegan quickly ran a brush through her hair, then carefully placed her graduation cap on her head, being careful to place the tassel on the left side. After adjusting her cap and reapplying her lipstick, her eyes fell on a snapshot taped to her dresser mirror. It was a picture of her parents at their ward picnic a week ago. She smiled fondly, allowing her eyes to sweep across the features of the two people who had sacrificed so much for her. Having her father around the last few months had been everything that she had ever dreamed it would be, and watching her mother and father together had been even better. The first few months had been admittedly rough, after being separated for so many years, but Reegan had watched them gradually fall in love all over again.

She placed the picture back on the mirror, then dropped her eyes to the wooden box on her dresser that her grandmother had left to her. She lifted the lid to stare down at its only contents—a letter. She pulled the letter from the box and read it, though she already knew what it said.

Dearest Reegan,

This box was given to me when I was a young girl. Now I give it to you with the same advice that was passed

down to me. We come into the world with nothing mate-
rial; we leave the world the same. What determines our
wealth is the love we leave behind. Love is the treasure
you'll find in this box—nothing more, nothing less.

Love,
Grandma Schmitt

Reegan placed the letter back into the box and closed it, grateful for a heritage that she was only now discovering.

"You look beautiful!"

Reegan turned to see her mother poking her head around the door.

"You're going to turn a few heads this fall when you walk across BYU's campus," her mom quipped, beaming.

"You're biased," Reegan said, her mind going instantly to the only man whose attention she was interested in catching.

"Maybe, but I'm not blind," her mother countered. "By the way, your father wants to take a few pictures of you before we leave."

Reegan grabbed her purse, then followed her mom down the hall, passing her father who was heading toward his room.

"Dad, you're going the wrong way."

"I thought I'd better get a few extra rolls of film, just in case."

"Don't forget your zoom lens, video camera, and high-powered binoculars," Reegan teased.

"Already in the car next to my neon congratulations sign and foghorn," he said with a wink.

"Very funny, Dad."

He planted a kiss on her forehead. "Who's kidding?" Then he turned to his wife. "Do you think you could fix my tie? I can't seem to get the knot right."

Reegan shook her head with a smile as she watched her mother fuss with his tie. "Where do you want to take the picture?" she asked over her shoulder as she continued down the hall.

"In the front yard next to the elm tree," her dad called back.

Reegan made her way to the front door, then pulled it open, her eyes going instantly to the man just beyond the threshold who stood ready to knock. For a moment she just stood there staring, then slowly she began to shake her head in disbelief.

"*Blaine?*"

"I just happened to be passing through Maplecove, North Dakota, population 804," Blaine said with a tender smile, "and was hoping maybe we could take that walk now—after you graduate anyway."

Reegan let out a squeal, then jumped into his arms.

"I've missed you," Blaine whispered, his breath warm on her cheek.

"I missed you too," she said, a surge of joy rushing through her.

When he finally released her, Reegan could feel her heart pounding. Blaine smiled, then slowly leaned forward and kissed her, the gentleness of his touch everything that she had dreamed it would be. Then he ran his finger down her cheek.

"So you'll take that walk with me?"

"As long as it doesn't involve jumping barbed-wire fences or fording freezing rivers," she teased.

"And if it does?"

"You know me. I'll be right beside you."